NO PL...

A... ...ume

WITHDRAWN

MILLS & BOON LIMITED
ETON HOUSE 18–24 PARADISE ROAD
RICHMOND SURREY TW9 1SR

*First published in Great Britain 1988
by Mills & Boon Limited*

© Ann Hulme 1988

*Australian copyright 1988
Philippine copyright 1988
This edition 1988*

ISBN 0 263 76017 0

*Set in 11 on 12 pt Linotron Times
04–0388–63,350*

*Photoset by Rowland Phototypesetting Limited
Bury St Edmunds, Suffolk
Made and printed in Great Britain by
Cox & Wyman Limited, Reading*

CHAPTER ONE

IT WAS no rare sight to see a young woman walking alone along a busy London pavement of an evening. But it was no respectable thing, either, as Emma Wainwright knew. She hastened her step, feeling that people stared at her, and fixing her own eyes on the uneven cobbles, well aware that she had got herself into something of a fix and that it was entirely her own fault. She should not have stayed so late at the Wilkes'. Perhaps she should have accepted Mr Wilkes's offer to send out 'one of the kids' to find a cab. Emma had protested that it was only a step to a cab-rank, and resolutely set out alone. But she had not fully realised just how busy the main thoroughfares would be at this time of the evening, nor how dark it had become. By night, everything looked different, and one street corner very like another. Distances were considerably longer on foot than by cab. She was beginning to feel both confused and cross, and not a little nervous.

The house she had quitted had been one of many she visited in poor but decent streets. Steps were scrubbed and windows polished, even though the tenants must have found it hard to find two shillings a week rent. They, and their neighbours, got round this by sub-letting, or taking in a 'lodger'. Over-crowding was a common symptom of poverty, though there were areas where it was far worse, one

house containing three or even four families, some
counting themselves lucky to have a room to themselves. In vain doctors counselled that laundry
should not be done in living-rooms, or meals
cooked where the family slept. The very poor had
no choice.

The families who were on Emma's regular 'visiting list'—the Wilkes family among them—counted
as 'deserving' poor. To help the deserving poor was
an obligation laid on the better-off. The 'undeserving' poor, of whom there were a far greater number, were left to their own devices.

Emma often thought this division into sheep
and goats unfair, and said so to her aunt, Mrs
Somerton. Mrs Somerton did not disagree, but
pointed out the difficulty in helping 'people who
will not help themselves, and frankly, do not seem
to want to be helped!' Emma lived with her Aunt
Rosamond, the widow of an impecunious clergy-
man of Low Church persuasion, and a good woman,
given to good works; the Wilkes family was on her
list of 'deserving' poor, on whom she kept a kindly
eye.

Emma hurried along towards the cab-rank,
wishing that she had not let it get quite so late in the
evening. The sky had grown quite dark, and gas-
lighting now lent a pale shimmer to the scene,
making faces glow luridly and casting sinister
shadows. Those shops which remained open, mainly
grocers', were brightly lit, to attract the last home-
ward-hurrying customers; tired-looking seamstresses and milliners, whose working day lasted
from nine in the morning until nine at night, and
poorly but respectably dressed clerks, who paused

as they scurried home to buy a little tobacco in a twist of paper, a consolation after a long day's toil.

But already London by day had disappeared, and a new, night-time London was emerging from the shadows. The traffic in the streets now bowled along carrying would-be revellers to parties, entertainments and the theatres, and some who were on mysterious errands. Among the pedestrians on the crowded pavements ran the boys shouting that they sold copies of the evening papers, and pallid, rickety children with baskets of posies, who accosted the young couples and wheedled the men into parting with a few pence for violets for their lady-loves. Gentlemen in silk hats rubbed shoulders with garishly-dressed girls who caught at their arms and whispered invitations. Small crowds gathered about the stalls of the hot-potato-sellers. Between them all roamed the pickpockets and thieves of every sort, and the beggars, drifting towards the doss-houses which offered a bed to the homeless for a few pence. Those wretches who lacked even that little money had already settled down in doorways and under arches, shapeless bundles of rags.

Emma hastened through it all, to find, to her great annoyance, that the cab-stand was empty, since this time of night was a busy one for London's hansom cabmen. Now she found herself faced with an invidious choice. She could stand and wait for a cab to return, but there was no sign of one approaching in either direction, and to stand about unescorted at this late hour was not advisable. Some of the ladies of the night affected an outward respectability, so that several men cast speculative glances at the slender young woman with fine fair hair tucked up under her bonnet and a plain but good quality gown and shawl. It would be better by far to walk on through the jostling throng and hope to encounter a free cab, or if not, eventually to reach another rank.

Emma set off again, but she did not know this area well on foot, having always come by cab. She hurried through the evening crowds, noting with disapproval how many very young children were abroad in the busy streets. The dangers they ran were real. Every night, some of those children would fail to return to their slum homes—missing in the hurly-burly of a great city. Many were lured into prostitution. Emma was well aware of this, even though such a subject was not thought fit to be discussed by decent women such as herself. It was the reason she had not wanted the Wilkes to send out a child to hail a cab for her.

Theirs was a mealy-mouthed age where sexual matters were concerned. The eighteen-forties had seen a prudery in word and dress take over from the licence of Regency days gone by. The prudery was only outward, and people went on as they always had done, of course. If Emma had wanted proof of this, she could see it all about her. She glanced round now, and gave a hiss of vexation. In a nearby doorway, two very young girls, perhaps no more than fourteen, were sharing a bottle of gin, passing it from hand to hand and drinking from the neck. Their pale, pinched little faces were garishly painted, and there could be no doubt why they lingered there. Emma wondered whether it was worth approaching them and lecturing them on the risks to their health from imbibing strong liquors, but she knew it would do no good. She had worked among the poor, deserving and otherwise, for long enough to know that an approach of that kind invited violent response. They were likely to throw the offending gin-bottle at her. Besides, the girls had probably been fed gin from the cradle. A teaspoonful of gin kept many a fretful baby quiet in the teeming hovels of the poor.

Nothing could be done for girls like those, thought Emma, as she passed reluctantly by the two in the doorway, unless they could be got away from their environment. But how could such a thing be achieved? There came a burst of shrill giggling, and two very smartly-clad young women clattered noisily out of a dimly-lit entrance and set off up the street, arm in arm. The manner was different—the business was the same. Emma felt not so much shocked, as angry. It seemed to her that a woman reduced to selling her body, repeatedly and without emotion, to any man who had the money to pay had surrendered the only right a woman had, that of dignity. Society did not see fit to grant a woman any other rights, certainly not in law. Married women, especially, were little more than a husband's property, having no right to own anything themselves.

Emma slowed her step and peeped surreptitiously into the doorway the two women had vacated, motivated partly by the maxim, 'Know all you can about your enemy', and partly by human curiosity. It seemed to lead into a foyer, very like that of a small hotel, which just now appeared empty. Glancing over her shoulder to make sure she was not observed, and spurred on by the absence of anyone to stop her, she took a step or two inside and gazed about her. So this was a house of ill repute!

The area in which she found herself was decorated in startling hues of mauve and at great expense. The curtains were damask and all the furniture elaborately gilded, though of poor workmanship. The air was very stuffy, and— Emma sniffed—redolent of perfume. She gazed at it all much as a prophet of old might have looked upon Sodom and Gomorrah.

Suddenly there was a rustle of skirts, and she spun round guiltily to see a stout, motherly-looking woman encased in a remarkable gown which seemed very ill suited to her age and plump figure. It was cut very low to display a bulging bosom, and cascaded to the ground in layers of lace flounces. At various points on the bodice it was ornamented with velvet bows, and the whole gown was complemented by an elaborate head-dress of ruched silk with trailing taffeta ribbons.

Considerably taken aback by this extraordinary vision, Emma asked doubtfully, 'Are you in charge here?'

'Well, dearie,' said the stout lady affably, 'if I ain't, I'd like to know who is! Bessie is my name, and that's what everyone calls me—well, behind me back, they calls me "Old Bessie"—and think I don't know it!' She snorted, but did not seem displeased. She put her head on one side, setting the taffeta ribbons bobbing, and surveyed Emma with eyes which suddenly changed to being very cold and calculating and at variance with the kindly smile and affable tone. 'Now, then, dearie, I'm not

taking on any new girls. Not but what you ain't got
style and the look of a lady. But the fact is, dear,
and you won't take this amiss——' she patted
Emma's arm with a plump, heavily-beringed hand
'—but you ain't as young as I like to hire 'em.
You won't see twenty-one again, I'll be bound.'

'I'm twenty-four,' said Emma indignantly, and
instinctively drawing back from the touch of the
plump, white hand with its garnish of glittering
gems. 'But I can't see what that has to do with you.'

'Oh, it's got everything to do with it, dearie.'
Bessie sighed, heaving her magnificent bosom and
setting all the pink flesh quivering—just like a
blancmange, thought Emma irrelevantly. 'The
gents like them young, you know. I like to take the
girls on about thirteen, before they've started out
on the streets and learnt vulgar ways. I don't like
vulgarity.'

'Indeed?' said Emma, glancing at the mauve
drapery, the gilded chairs and the lace flounces.

'Nor do you, dear, as I see. Very nicely turned
out you are. But, like I say, I takes the girls on
young and see they're broken in proper. Learns the
trade. The trouble with our profession is, there are
far too many amateurs in it, that's what!'

'Now just a minute!' exclaimed Emma forcefully. 'You're making a mistake! I admit I have no
business here, but I just . . .'

Before she had time to explain herself further,
they were interrupted. A figure filled the doorway,
and Bessie turned her head.

A girl had come in from the street. She was
extremely young, to Emma's eye no more than
fifteen, and pretty, though her under-nourished

frame showed the signs of poverty and a hard childhood. She had made some attempt to dress herself with style, in a silk gown, rather grubby and stained, and cut very low, and her brown hair was twisted into a mop of corkscrew ringlets which must have been the work of some labour. But what took Emma's eye more than anything was a disfiguring bruise which swelled and discoloured the flesh on the left side of the girl's face, and must have resulted from a truly savage blow.

The newcomer hugged her bare arms, as if cold, which she probably was without a shawl, and said, ''Ullo, Bessie.'

'Oh, it's you, is it, Kezia Smith,' said Bessie ungraciously. 'I see Sam Leach give you another black eye—or was that one of the punters?'

'It was Sam . . .' The girl sidled in cautiously as if she were unsure of her welcome. 'I come to see if you'd spare a drop of gin for a girl, Bessie. I've been an hour out there and not a customer. Sam will beat me black and blue when I get back, if I ain't got no money. Give us a glass of Mother's Ruin, Bessie.'

'I ain't a charity,' said Bessie. 'You want to give that feller of yours the elbow, that's what. Get yourself a different bully to look after you. You ain't my responsibility.'

'I was once,' the girl said sullenly, but with a touch of spirit. 'It was you taught me the business, Bessie. I worked here till you threw me out.'

'You were a trouble-maker, you were,' said Bessie. 'You had to go. I was mistaken in you, Kezzy. I thought you'd be a natural, but I was wrong. I don't make that many mistakes, but I made one with you. Oh—all right—come into the back and I'll open a bottle.' She turned to Emma. 'You get off with you, dear. Try Mrs Harris in the Strand—she might need a new girl.'

The couple disappeared through an alcove and left Emma in the foyer. She was only too glad of the opportunity to 'get off' and made hastily towards the main door. But as she approached it, she heard, to her dismay, the sound of men's voices, and realised that customers were approaching the brothel. Desperately she threw a wild look about the foyer. To run through the alcove would be to encounter Bessie and Kezia Smith. To stay, however, meant meeting face to face two or more gentlemen who would assume she worked there. The only other route was straight up the staircase, and Emma picked up her skirts and darted up the stairs.

The long corridor above was lit by branched candelabra and papered with an elaborate red silk wall covering. Emma put her ear to the panels of the first door, and caught the sound of giggling. She hastened past, and at the end of the corridor came to a door through which she could hear nothing. She opened it cautiously a crack. The room beyond was in darkness, the curtains drawn. At that moment she heard the sound of men's voices coming nearer and realised that the new customers were climbing the stairs. She had no time to lose, so she pulled open the door, darted through and closed it.

In the darkness, she stood with her head pressed against the door panels and her heart beating so violently she thought it must jump out of her chest. A girl's voice called out, and doors slammed further down the corridor. Silence. Emma heaved a

deep sigh of relief. She was safe. Now to slip out
and back downstairs, to escape to the haven—as it
now seemed—of the streets. She put her hand on
the door-handle, but at the same moment another
hand snaked out of the darkness behind her and slid
in a familiar and possessive manner across her
bosom, tightening uncomfortably on her breast.

'Lily . . .' chided a man's voice huskily in her ear
in a low throaty whisper. 'You little minx, what do
you mean by keeping me waiting?'

Emma gave a low cry of alarm. She tried to
move, but her head was crushed against his chest
and her nostrils were tantalised by a faint aura, not
unpleasant, but strange, of perspiration and something which seemed indefinably but definitely
masculine.

'It's—It's not Lily . . .' Emma managed to
croak through a throat dry with panic. 'L—Let go
of me!'

The hand relaxed its pressure but did not release
its grip. 'Then who are you?' he demanded suspiciously. He was still speaking in a low tone, but it
held undeniable menace. 'I asked for Lily!'

'She—She's coming!' improvised Emma, invent-
ing madly. She tried to recall Kezia Smith's
Cockney tones and to imitate them. 'I swear it,
er . . . guv'nor!' That sounded all right, and she
threw herself into the part with determination.
'Swelp me!' she said fervently. 'She sent me along
to tell you not to fret, she's coming direct.'

'Sent you along to *tell* me?' he repeated incredulously. 'Good God, girl, do you think I mean to sit
about in this whorehouse waiting meekly on some
little jade?'

'She—um . . .' What on earth kept ladies of pleasure from their customers? 'She had, I mean, 'ad, to appear before the magistrates, at Marylebone. She's coming, sir, honest.'

There was a pause. Then, to Emma's surprise and some discomfiture, a chuckle, a low throaty one which sent a strange quiver through her, came from her captor. She wished he would take his hand away from her left breast, since no one, and certainly no man, had ever touched her in so familiar a fashion, and she did not quite know what to do about it.

'And what's your name?' he asked. When she did not reply at once, his grip grew harsher again and she gave a little cry, because he hurt her. His clasp slackened, but he repeated impatiently. 'Your name, girl!'

'Er,' Emma gulped. 'Violet!' she said at random, inspired by the flowery name of the missing Lily.

He burst into laughter. 'Poor shrinking, modest violet!' he said mockingly. 'Well, Violet, as you are here and Lily is not, you will do as well as she for the same purpose. You seem to have a devil of a lot of clothes on.'

Oh, dear heaven, thought Emma desperately, what on earth do I do now? 'I can't stay, guv'nor, honest. Not but what I'd like to, of course . . .' Best to flatter the wretch! 'But I got another— er . . .' What was the word? 'Punter,' she remembered. 'I got another punter waiting for me.'

'Then he'll have to wait. *He* can have Lily. I shall be quite satisfied with you. Come on, I've been here twenty minutes, and although I was more than ready when I came in, I confess that if I sit here twiddling my fingers much longer, I shall be past doing anything at all. I'm starting to think that I would be better off finding a good eating-house and regaling myself on steak and onions.'

'Oh, that's all right,' said Emma hastily. 'You go along, and when you come back, Lily will be here.'

'You're an odd sort of girl,' he said, genuinely puzzled. 'Do you always try and discourage the customers?'

'No.' Any other answer would seem inappropriate.

'Then, dammit, girl, get some of those petticoats off. I don't intend to fumble my way through a load of washing!'

'I don't want to!' gasped Emma in a rising panic.

'Listen to me,' his voice said, suddenly cold and dangerous. 'This is a peculiar house if ever I was in one. One girl doesn't turn up and another decides to live up to her name, and play coy. Now, if you have some idea that I can be made to pay up when I've received nothing, you're wrong, and you can tell the old harridan downstairs so!'

He caught at her shoulders and spun her round roughly. Emma gave a cry of fear and tried to wriggle free, but he gave her a hefty shove and she fell backwards, not on to the floor as she had expected, but, much worse, on to a bed behind them. Before she could roll over and escape, he had thrown himself on top of her, crushing her beneath his considerable weight, for although she could not see him, he was a big, strong fellow, and was grasping at her skirts.

'No, no, you don't understand . . .' Emma cried desperately, trying to push him off her.

'You're damn right I don't! But I know what I came here for and I'm dashed if I'm going to leave without it!' he panted into her ear. His hand clasped her knee beneath her petticoats, and suddenly his mouth, warm and demanding, closed over hers so that she felt she could no longer breathe.

Gurgling incoherently and desperate to escape by any means, she clawed at his back, feeling his tongue pressing against her teeth and his exploring hand sliding along her thigh. She knew then, at that moment and with terrible certitude, that she was just not strong enough. She could struggle and fight, but in the end, by sheer brute force, he would take what he wanted. A shudder ran through her whole body and she stiffened with terror.

To her surprise, he paused in his assault. 'Violet!' he whispered, 'what's the matter?'

She had no need to find an answer. At that very minute the door flew open, and a beam of light flooded into the room from the corridor, but just missing the bed and its occupants. A woman's figure appeared silhouetted in the doorway.

''Ere!' demanded a strange female voice angrily. 'What's goin' on here, and 'oo are you? That's my gent, that is. You get off that bed!'

Emma asked for nothing more. But the customer, it seemed had other ideas.

'If that's Lily,' he said, over his shoulder, 'you can take yourself off. You're late. I don't wait about for drabs. Besides, I've taken a fancy to Violet here.'

'Oh, 'ave you?' said the virago in the doorway belligerently, arms akimbo. 'Well, you ain't having her. Bessie said I was to take number five. That's

the number on the door, and you're the customer.
'Ere, you!' She darted forward, and seizing Emma,
dragged her forcibly from beneath the man on
the bed. 'That gent is one of my regulars. Clear
off!'

'Yes, I will!' gasped Emma. She darted beneath
the arm of the furious Lily and flew out of the door.
Running headlong down the corridor, she was
aware of the man shouting 'Violet!' in stentorian
tones, but fear lent wings. She raced down the
staircase and dashed wildly out into the dark street.
Heaving a deep breath, she set off at a determined
pace. There was some commotion going on behind her. If she judged right, the customer was
attempting pursuit, and Bessie and Lily were hanging on to his arms like grim death and declaring that
he could not leave without paying up.

Serve him right, dissolute wretch! thought
Emma breathlessly. She had reached the corner of
the street and stopped to clasp her hand to a painful
stitch in her ribs, and to take her bearings. Where
now?

'Here, what are you playing at?' asked a curious
voice. 'You one of Bessie's girls, or what?'

Emma gasped and looked up. Kezia Smith
emerged from a doorway and stood staring at her,
arms folded.

'No, I am not!' Emma told her firmly. 'I entered
that place by mistake! I am a perfectly respectable
woman, thank you, and you, Kezia, are much too
young to be drinking gin!'

Kezia unfolded her arms and held up the bottle
grasped in one fist. 'You'd want a drink if you'd
been here all this time and not seen a customer.

You ain't got Sam after you! You're right not to be in this business, you are. It's a stinking business.'

'How did you come to be in it, this—er—business?' asked Emma curiously and with sympathy.

'Bessie come round looking for talent and saw me, didn't she? Thirteen year old, I was. Old cow!'

'How old are you now?' asked Emma.

'Fifteen.' Kezia sighed. 'Where are you going, miss?'

'To tell you the truth, I think I'm lost. I couldn't find a cab, and I started to walk. It was a mistake.'

'I know a cab-rank,' said Kezia. 'You come with me. I'll take you there.'

She hid the gin-bottle carefully behind a pile of rubbish, and they set off up the street, side by side.

'Kezia,' Emma said thoughtfully, 'this man, Sam Leach, who, I understand, gave you that awful black eye. Who is he?'

'My bully,' said Kezia, sounding surprised. 'Every girl has to have a bully looking out for her. Some of the customers, they gets a bit rough.'

'So does Mr Leach, I see!' said Emma sharply. 'Kezia, you say you don't like the life, and are beaten by Mr Leach—surely you can find some other employ?'

'Don't know nothing else,' said Kezia simply.

Emma uttered a little hiss of vexation. 'But you cannot go on in this way. You might, um, you might, you know, find yourself with child.'

'Old Bessie takes care of that for the girls,' said Kezia. 'Anyway, I can't hold no baby. I was damaged when I started out.'

Emma stopped and turned to face her companion. 'You were what?' she exclaimed incredulously.

'Hurt bad. I was only a kid. I said I was thirteen, but fact was, I wasn't quite that.'

'Only twelve!' cried Emma in horror.

''Sright. Got torn bad. Old Bessie, she fetched the doctor—he was a proper one, only he'd got struck off on account of the drink—and he stitched up the tears, hurt something terrible, it did. Only, I suppose, he didn't make too good a job of it. Anyway, best thing—in a way.'

Trotting hoofs sounded on the night air and a cab turned the corner of the street. Kezia darted out into the road and hailed it, and when it stopped, turned to Emma. 'Here you are, miss, you get off home, out of here. This ain't no place for a lady.'

'No,' Emma said slowly. 'And it's no place for any woman. Get in, Kezia.'

Kezia stared and said, 'Beg pardon?'

'Get in!' said Emma impatiently. 'I've no intention of leaving you here. You shall never earn your money in this abominable fashion again! You shall come with me, and I shall teach you something different!'

'Blimey!' exclaimed Kezia, impressed by the young lady's fervour.

'Well, I'm sure I don't know what to say,' said Rosamond Somerton feebly. Automatically her hand strayed out and touched the cover of a small, stout, red morocco-bound book, which held the sermon notes of her late husband. Not a woman of strong intellect, his widow liked to keep his observations by her, and consult them for guidance. She plainly felt in need of guidance now. 'I really don't think we can keep the girl here, dreadful though the case is. You see, I should have to inform Mr Sneadie, the agent for the landlord.'

'Why?' asked Emma bluntly. 'It's none of his business. We pay our rent. Anyway, the landlord himself has never taken the slightest interest in this house. We've never seen him.'

'It is Major Sheldon,' said Mrs Somerton, glad to have the answer to something. 'He also owns a house in Forbes Street. He did own four houses in the neighbourhood, but two of them have recently been sold. Mr Sneadie assures me that Major Sheldon has no plans to sell this one, but the truth is, the rent I pay is very low for such a large house. Of course I couldn't afford any more, but if Major Sheldon were to turn me out, why, he could get a much higher rent from a new tenant. It is my belief that he would dearly like the excuse. Certainly Mr Sneadie hints every quarter that my rent is inadequate, and now I see that the Forbes Street house stands empty. I expect the notice-boards to go up there at any time.' She relented slightly. 'The girl may stay tonight, and tomorrow we'll talk about it again.'

So a bed was made up for Kezia in the attic, she was provided with a bar of carbolic soap, instructed to wash well all over, and to present herself early the next morning to Mrs McGraw, the housekeeper.

Kezia sniffed suspiciously at the carbolic, but was deeply impressed by the tiny attic room. 'What, all to meself? Just fancy! I never 'ad a bed to meself. At home us kids all slept under a blanket on the floor, and then, of course, I had to share me bed with Sam, and he ain't above kicking a girl out on to the floor, neither!'

'Quite,' said Emma firmly, closing off this line of talk.

Though she had explained Kezia's circumstances to Mrs Somerton, she had not told her aunt of her own adventure in what had plainly been a house of ill fame. There were some things about which it was best to keep silent. That did not prevent Emma from turning the events over and over in her mind as she lay in her own bed that night, and the more she thought about it, the greater her disgust. Men were brutes, that was the sum of it. At the thought of that particular male brute who had manhandled her so familiarly in the darkened room, she shivered. She felt sullied, tarnished. The memory of his fingers pressing into the soft flesh of her breast and stroking the bare skin of her thigh sent quivers of horror racing up and down her spine. No man shall ever do that to me again! she promised herself.

It would have been a Christian act, approved by Mrs Somerton, to pray for the reprobate's erring soul—but Emma was not feeling kindly, and vengefully consigned him to hellfire.

CHAPTER TWO

WHEN KEZIA appeared shyly before the ladies the next morning, even Emma was startled. Washed of paint and tidily dressed, the girl looked even younger than she had the previous night.

'Well!' said Mrs Somerton firmly. 'I don't think I had one wink of sleep last night, with thinking it all over, and I have come to a decision. Kezia shall stay. After all, you are right, Emma, and we have a duty to care for her. Nor shall I inform Mr Sneadie. As you say, it's no business of his or of Major Sheldon's if I choose to hire a housemaid.'

For a woman of Mrs Somerton's disposition, this was really raising the rebel standard. Emma suppressed an affectionate smile at the sight of her aunt's flushed defiant face, and leaned forward to kiss her cheek. 'Bless you, Aunt Rosamond, you won't have cause to regret it.'

At first it seemed that Emma might have spoken the truth in these last words. Kezia seemed to settle in well and took a pathetic, childish pleasure in the simple comfort of her surroundings. She touched every item with reverent fingers, and even Mrs McGraw was reluctantly persuaded to allow her to do a little dusting. But, sadly, this proved the lull before the storm.

In the middle of the night, a week later, they were awoken by a terrifying crash and splintering of glass at the front of the house. Emma lit a candle with trembling fingers and ran down the stairs in her nightgown, fearing the worst. In the drawing-room she met the housekeeper grasping a poker, and her aunt who held the stout volume of the sermon notes. Inspection soon showed them that a brick had been thrown through one of the bay windows giving on to the street. Emma fancied she could hear running feet, and carefully avoiding the smashed glass on the floor, peered out. But the gaslit street was empty.

'Oh, Emma, do you think there is an intruder?' whispered Mrs Somerton.

'No, ma'am,' said Kezia in a quiet little voice from the far corner, where she huddled in a plaid shawl. 'It's Sam.'

They all turned towards her. The girl's face looked pinched and drawn and her expression was frightened. 'Sam has found me, you can be sure, ladies. It's his way of saying it, as he wants me back.'

'He shall never get you back!' Emma said vehemently, putting her hands on Kezia's shoulders. 'Oh, come, Kezzy, don't be afraid. No one is going to hurt you.' She put her arm round the girl comfortingly.

'He don't give up, not Sam,' Kezia said. 'Perhaps I'd best go, Miss Emma.'

'I don't think we should give in to a ruffian like that,' said Mrs Somerton unexpectedly. 'I'm more worried about Major Sheldon and what he might do if he finds out. I suppose we can get the window mended quickly ourselves and say nothing to Mr Sneadie.'

Emma heaved a sigh of exasperation and contemplated the broken glass. The unpleasant Sam Leach was a problem that had to be tackled. But no landlord would take kindly to damage of this sort being done to his property, and ultimately Major Sheldon might prove even more difficult to deal with than a Bethnal Green bully.

The next night passed uneventfully. Perhaps Leach waited to see if his attack would produce Kezia. When it did not, they awoke two days later to find that an unseen hand had daubed the outside of the house with crudely-worded and mis-spelled slogans in red paint. To remove them was a job for a professional house-painter, and this time Mr Sneadie had to be told.

The lawyer called on them himself, a little, spare, dried-up, elderly man with gold pince-nez. He was persuaded to take a glass of ratafia, and Kezia was called from the kitchen.

The Kezia who entered the room, with a clean, scrubbed face and neat gown with spotless apron, was a far cry from the painted waif Emma had rescued from the street, but Mr Sneadie was obviously not impressed.

'I shall have to inform Major Sheldon,' he said, rising to take his leave. 'And in the meantime, ma'am, if you mean to keep the girl—count your teaspoons, that's my advice to you, and lock up your valuables. Believe me, you'll wake up one fine morning to find the girl gone with everything she can bundle together of value.'

A week later a letter arrived by the early post. Mrs Somerton broke it open at the breakfast table and spread it out. After a moment, she gave a gasp and exclaimed, 'This is intolerable! Why, Major Sheldon virtually accuses me of keeping a disorderly house!'

'May I see?' Emma asked quickly, holding out her hand. The letter was brief and to the point. It was addressed from Surrey, and written in a bold, sprawling hand. The style was terse and dispensed with the usual compliments, though it did not quite accuse Mrs Somerton in the terms she had claimed.

Sneadie had informed Major Sheldon of the presence of a woman of loose character in the house, and it was not the Major's intention to allow his property to acquire a dubious reputation. Kezia must go, at once. The letter was signed, 'Lucius Sheldon, Major, retd.'

Emma read the last aloud, and her aunt murmured absently, 'Oh, yes, he served in India, I believe.'

Emma threw the letter down among the breakfast things. Kezia was trying so hard, and even Mrs McGraw had thawed towards her. Now everything was to be for nothing. A show of violence on the part of Sam Leach, and they were all to admit defeat.

'No!' Emma said firmly. 'I'll go to the police station, and get them to arrest Leach. Then there will be no need for Kezia to go.'

At the police station, Emma explained their problem to a constable, who referred her to a sergeant, who sent her in to see the inspector.

He was a dapper man in a checked suit, who eyed Emma in a familiar fashion, fingering his trim little moustache. She felt her face burn, but she managed to return his gaze steadily, and eventually he seemed to make up his mind to reply. 'Bless me, ma'am, this is no affair for a lady to deal with. But I can't arrest Leach, not on the word of the girl Smith, nor yet, ma'am, on yours. Only catch Leach red-handed heaving a brick at your windows, or bring me a reliable witness, and I'll have the fellow locked up before you can say knife. But my advice, ma'am, is to turn the girl out. She'll bring you nothing but trouble.'

He was eventually persuaded to order a constable to patrol the street. To Emma's relief, he kept his word. That evening, a stately figure dressed in a blue frock coat buttoned to his chin and a top hat, and armed with stout wooden truncheon, appeared and began to walk majestically down one side of the road and up the other.

The unaccustomed sight of a 'Peeler' in this quiet street aroused some considerable interest. The police force had been created only eighteen years earlier and its number were still relatively small, so the stalwart officer was accompanied the first length of the street by a hopeful band of small boys who enquired if he was on his way to arrest a murderer, and if so, could they please come and watch? The Law ordered them majestically to 'get out of it' and clipped a few heads, after which his admirers left him to his duty.

Whether Sam Leach had also seen him they did not know, but for the following week at least they had no more broken windows or slogans daubed on their walls. However, Sir Robert Peel had not created his force to be private bodyguards, and at the end of the week the Peeler knocked on the door after his evening patrol, touched his hat-brim with his truncheon, and informed them politely that all now seemed quiet and his 'dooties' henceforth called him elsewhere. But two nights later, manure was shovelled over the front step and two more windows were broken. Mr Sneadie was in their drawing-room within hours, and the post brought another letter from Surrey.

This time it was terse to the point of rudeness, aggressive in tone and uncompromising. Were they unable to read? Or had they not received Major Sheldon's previous letter? Did they think he was in the habit of fooling about like this? They should turn the girl out, or get out themselves.

'Lucius Sheldon, Major, retd,' read Emma aloud, and crushed the letter into a ball in her hands. A retired Indian army officer, a white-haired, purple-faced and overweight old codger living in a Surrey country house filled with Benares brass and mementoes of pig-sticking . . . such a man was to send poor Kezia back to Leach, to a life of beatings and prostitution?

'Not if I can help it,' said Emma grimly. She was doubly determined, because she had formed a resolution. Kezia was to be but the first. There must be others like her, very young and not yet hardened in their way of life. In Emma's mind a scheme was taking shape by which suitable girls would be rescued and taught some simple craft or domestic work, so that they could earn their livings by honest means. Even Emma could not imagine that there would be many households like her aunt's, willing to take in the girls and teach them at home. What was needed was a Rescue Home specifically founded to help them. She could imagine it now, not a grim institution, but something small and well run, where the girls could feel themselves to be members of a family. She had some money left her by her father, which had been prudently invested. Mrs Somerton, despite their straightened circumstances, had never allowed Emma to touch the capital, 'since, Emma, you will marry some day and will need a portion.'

Well, Emma did not foresee herself getting married, and anyway that would simply mean giving the money to some man to use as he saw fit. No one at that time—and certainly not the law of England—questioned the right of a husband to his wife's money. Far better, she thought, to stay single and use the money myself to rent a suitable property. Of course, all this would take some time—to get the scheme going, to find suitable premises and interest other benefactors. She knew she could not do it alone. In the meantime, a portly, choleric Indian army officer was to be persuaded somehow to let Kezia stay in the house. She got up, and fetched a stout paper-bound volume from a desk.

'What is that, dear?' asked Mrs Somerton.

'Bradshaw's *Monthly Railway Guide*,' she replied, opening it. 'Yes, as I thought, it's possible to travel down into Surrey by the railway and see Major Sheldon. I shall go tomorrow.'

It was not until Emma was well on her way the following morning that the full import of what she was about struck her, and her courage began to fail. The train rocked gently through the Surrey countryside, but she was oblivious of the changing

view, although normally the contrast of the green
fields with the soot-stained brick of the capital
would have filled her with delight. She shared the
Ladies Only compartment with a stout elderly person in black crape, who had dozed off in a corner.
Not obliged to make any conversation, Emma's
mind became filled with her approaching interview.

Always supposing, of course, that Sheldon
agreed to see her. He had not been forewarned of
her coming, a deliberate omission on Emma's part.
If he knew, he could leave word with the servants
that she was not to be admitted. If he did not, she
had the advantage of surprise. She felt sadly in need
of some advantage, for it was a most peculiar
errand, however it was viewed. Young ladies like
herself were not supposed to know that women like
Kezia existed. They were not even supposed to
have more than the haziest idea of what constituted
physical relations between men and women. Emma
had used her eyes and ears during her work among
the poor, whose one recreation appeared to be just
that—to reproduce the species. Thus, though she
might not be clear as to all the details of the act
involved, she had no doubts about the overwhelm-
ing desires it unleashed. At the same time, she was
aware of the handicap placed on her in the forthcoming interview by her being unmarried, and thus
inadequately informed. She felt much as a badly-
briefed lawyer might do when about to rise to his
feet before a stickler of a judge.

The Major, on the other hand, with long experience of the army both at home and overseas,
probably had a matter-of-fact approach to life on
the streets, gained in garrison towns. The presence

of army barracks in a community always guaranteed a flourishing Foundling Home and a steady stream of young women applying either to the army authorities for justice, or to the local parish for Poor Law Relief for themselves and their infants. The Major would be accustomed to view all this as a matter of discipline, rather than in human terms. He certainly would not normally discuss it with a young lady like Emma. He might, heaven forbid, and Emma's blood ran cold, even have paid for the services of girls like Kezia himself in his younger and more gadabout days. On the other hand, he might turn out to be the respectable father of several daughters and order Emma out of the house before she could corrupt their innocent ears.

By now, her speculations had reduced her to a state of near-panic, and when she climbed down from the train at the quiet country station her knees were like jelly and the warm day seemed unbearably hot. There was hardly anyone about, and no sign of a cab. A porter on the platform told her that the only cab available had gone off half an hour earlier with a fare, and was unlikely to be back before twelve. Yes, he knew of Major Sheldon and Hill House. Yes, it was actually at the top of a hill, and a tidy walk for a lady. Best to wait. They had a decent waiting-room, swept out proper, and he could make her some tea.

Emma thanked him for his kind offer, but said she would walk. The idea of sitting alone in the dreary surroundings of a provincial waiting-room, with nothing to occupy her mind but her forthcoming encounter with Sheldon, had no appeal for her.

She pinned up her skirt and set off briskly for Hill House.

The day was very hot, the gradient steep, and Emma's pace soon flagged. She was not dressed to take much exercise. Her cotton petticoats were both warm and heavy, and the long tight sleeves of her dress, attached to a sloping shoulderline, restricted the movement of her arms. Her shoes were too light for the rough path and stones hurt her feet; her white stockings gradually became grey with dust.

At long last she found herself walking alongside a high, ivy-festooned, brick wall and came to a gate. A very small brass plate, half-covered by the encroaching ivy, told her that this was Hill House, but announced it so discreetly that no one who was not actually searching for the name would have seen it. The wrought-iron gates stood slightly ajar, however, and there was no need to ring for a lodge-keeper. Emma pushed them open with a faint protesting creak of unoiled hinges, and went through.

The house faced her at the end of a long drive. It was surrounded by rhododendrons and azaleas, which were not exactly neglected, but seemed to have been kept tidy without much thought of garden design or improvement. It suggested that the owner was not interested in gardening, and his gardener had given up hope of getting his employer interested. There were no weeds, the grass was cut, the edges trimmed—but even now in midsummer there was not a solitary flower-bed to be seen.

Emma paused to unpin her skirt and shake it out. She took off her bonnet and blew on it to remove the powdering of dust and mopped her face with her handkerchief to remove the shine. Then she walked up to the front door and tugged at the bell-pull.

After a few moments the door was opened by an elderly butler, who regarded her with faint disapproval. In reply to her enquiry whether Major Sheldon was at home, he said, 'It is not yet twelve o'clock, madam. Major Sheldon is at home, but not accustomed to receive morning visits.' His tone implied that ladies did not make calls at this unearthly hour.

'It's half-past eleven,' said Emma, fighting for an assurance she was far from feeling. 'I have come from Town to see Major Sheldon on an urgent matter, and if he is at all able to receive a visitor, please tell him that I should be very grateful for half an hour of his time.'

But she was dealing with an English upper servant, the best defender of his employer's privacy in the world. 'Unfortunately, madam, the Major already has a visitor in Mr Bryant, the veterinary surgeon. He is down at the stables now, with the veterinary, examining a horse the Major has recently purchased. Perhaps, madam, you could return this afternoon?'

Emma sighed. To spend the next three hours wandering about waiting till the afternoon would not only be inconvenient, it would deprive her of the advantage of surprise. The butler obviously already considered her to be eccentric, so there was nothing to lose by shocking him further. She made a decision, for better or worse. 'In which direction are the stables?'

The stables were built like a child's toy fort, a square of mellow brick buildings around an open cobbled yard. It was entered by passing through an arch, topped by a clock-tower and a creaking weathervane of a running dog fox which pointed its metal snout into the wind.

As Emma neared it, she could hear some considerable commotion. It gathered in volume as she passed under the echoing brick-vaulted roof of the entrance, and when she stepped out into the stableyard itself, it was as though into another world—a man's world.

Women never came down here. Something about the atmosphere of the whole yard said it. The smell of horses and tobacco and leather, of neat's-foot oil and saddle soap, manure and sweat, both human and equine. Near to the archway was a stone horse-trough and pump, and by it stood a red-faced boy of about fourteen in cord trousers, gaiters and yellow waistcoat over rolled shirt-sleeves. He was holding a rope halter and shifting from foot to foot in childish excitement, his boots scraping on the cobblestones. A little further away was a stocky, youngish man, likewise in gaiters, but with a broadcloth coat and round hat, who was obviously the veterinary surgeon, though of more gentlemanly manner than the usual dour, practical country horse-doctor. Unlike the boy, he did not display obvious excitement, but pursed his lips and narrowed his eyes as though he had waged on the outcome of a prize-fight and watched its progress.

It was something of the nature of a duel of power and muscle which dominated the centre of the yard. A great red sorrel horse, standing seventeen hands easily, with a Roman nose and feathered hocks, a descendant of the great horse of the middle ages that had carried the doomed knights at Crecy, reared into the air, ears flattened, forelegs thrashing wildly. Nostrils flared and the whites of its eyes rolled, and its mane fluttered in the air as if flames leapt from its arched neck. Steel shoes struck sparks from the cobbles as it plunged furiously to right and left, trying to drag the rope from the hands of the man who held grimly to the other end.

The groom who fought out this epic battle was a tall, strapping fellow of over six feet, stripped to the waist, his sunburned skin and luxuriant jet black hair in striking contrast to the red of the horse, making Emma wonder if he were not of gypsy origin. Man and horse were bathed in sweat. White foam lathered the animal's satin flanks, and the sweat rolled off the man so that his naked skin shone like burnished copper and the muscles beneath swelled and strained, the veins standing out distended and the sinews like cords. In the midst of the struggle the groom was talking to the horse, his opponent, and his voice, quiet, even, but authoritative, could be heard as a dull murmur above the clatter of hoofs and snorting breath. All at once the horse threw up its head and then stood still, eyes still rolling and watching the man. The groom shortened the rope that held the animal, and came a little nearer to it.

'Steady . . .' muttered the veterinary surgeon.

The groom had reached the animal's head, and stretched up a bronzed arm to pat the sweat-stained sorrel neck. The horse snorted and flattened its ears but then submitted, only stamping one hind hoof in a last defiant gesture.

'He has him!' said the surgeon in a satisfied voice. 'There, Tom, you can run and take him now, he'll give no more trouble—quiet as a lamb.'

The stable boy obeyed, and the great beast which had fought so hard for its liberty tossed its head once as the groom handed the rope to the boy, but allowed itself to be led back into the stables, as the surgeon had said, almost lamb-like. The groom, fresh from his mastery of the animal, turned to the surgeon and walked towards him, rubbing his hands over his face to clear it of the sweat. His black hair was grown into sidewhiskers in the dashing fashion called by the French *'favoris'*, and Emma did not doubt that he was a great ladies' man. A tangle of dark hair covered his broad chest, and fine black hairs speckled his brawny forearms and the backs of his large, strong hands. He looked straight past the surgeon to where Emma stood watching in a mixture of horror and fascination, and demanded curtly, 'Who the devil are you?'

She was so astounded at being addressed in this way by a servant, and angered, too, by the way in which he made no attempt to disguise the nakedness of his upper body, that she found her tongue to retort accusingly, 'You are very insolent!'

The surgeon had spun round at the groom's question and spied Emma, apparently for the first time. 'I beg your pardon, ma'am!' he exclaimed. 'I didn't see you there.'

She acknowledged his apology with a nod, but addressed herself to the gypsy groom. 'I am looking for your master, for Major Sheldon.'

The man's dark eyes glittered at her. 'Then you have found him, madam.'

For a moment she could only stare at him uncomprehendingly. Then realisation dawned, and with it, surprise and dismay. 'You, sir, are Major Sheldon?' she stammered.

'At your service, ma'am. I was not expecting a lady, so you'll forgive my appearance.' The tone was plainly sarcastic. 'I take it you've come to beg my support in some worthy cause or other—widows of clergymen, lying-in hospital for wives of the Foot Guards—which is it?'

Quaking though she was in her shoes, his scorn stung her to new courage. 'Neither, Major. I am Emma Wainwright, the niece of Mrs Somerton. I have come to discuss the matter of Kezia Smith.'

'Have you, now?' he said softly. Then, turning aside and ignoring her completely, he spoke to the veterinary surgeon, his manner markedly more amiable. 'Will you come up to the house, Bryant, and take a glass of wine?'

'Thank'ee,' said Mr Bryant, giving the roof of his round hat a blow with the palm of his hand to settle it more firmly on his head. 'But I've two more visits to make, and if I took all the liquor offered to me, I'd not get home unaided. The horse is as sound as a piece of English oak. You'll win your heart's desire with him, if you don't break your neck on him!'

'What desire is that?' asked Emma loudly, forcing her way back into the conversation.

Both men stared at her. 'Miss Wainwright,' Sheldon said politely, 'that beast is going to win races for me, point-to-point.'

So Sheldon was a sporting man. One who rode

hard, careering across country, clearing fences and splattering through the mud, and between times, drank hard and lived hard. Not a man to treat the problems of poor Kezia Smith with anything but coarse levity.

'Major Sheldon is a fine amateur rider,' said Bryant to her. 'But you'll have to get your weight down, Sheldon, not but what that great brute won't carry even your weight easily enough.' He touched his hat to Emma. 'Good day, ma'am.'

They watched him stride briskly over to a bob-tailed roan cob tethered in a corner of the yard, and scramble ably into the saddle. As he clattered out beneath the archway, Sheldon said, 'What Ned Bryant doesn't tell you is that he's no mean horseman himself, and a bruising rider to hounds.'

'Indeed?' said Emma, unimpressed.

But Sheldon seemed to have forgotten about her again. He went to the horse-trough and stooped over it, sluicing water from his cupped hands over his head. The rivulets glistened on the bronzed skin of his broad back and the undulating muscles. It was no sight for a lady to watch, and Emma turned her head away. When she ventured to glance back, he was taking his shirt and jacket from the handle of the pump, which had acted as a peg for them. He pulled on the shirt, but left it unbuttoned, slung the jacket carelessly over his arm, and returned to her.

'Then you had better come up to the house, Miss Wainwright. I suppose I can offer you some tea?'

They walked back to the house, side by side but in silence, their feet crunching on the gravel, and Emma feeling very small and insignificant beside this untidy giant of a man. The first time she had approached the house, from the road, she had paid little attention to it as a building because her mind had been so full of her errand. But as they came upon it from the direction of the stables she saw it at a more unusual angle, and was struck by what a dignified old place it was. Ivy clustered thickly in a dark green blanket over its wall and fringed its stone-framed windows, and the tall stacks of Tudor chimneys rose out of its roof, which was itself uneven and sagged in places with the weight of its years.

Impulsively she exclaimed, 'What a lovely old place!'

Sheldon shrugged his broad shoulders, and muttered, 'It costs a devil of a lot to run, and the confounded ivy is pulling the brickwork apart and needs to be stripped away.'

But she sensed that her observation had pleased him, and it was with a touch more courtesy that he ushered her into a large, untidy but comfortable room, badly lit by inadequate daylight falling through the small windows, but nevertheless obviously used as a study, despite this. Papers of all kinds lay around, as if the maid were forbidden to touch them. They included handbills advertising yearling sales, household and farm accounts, and periodicals of all kinds, in a glorious muddle. A springer spaniel came padding to meet them, wagging his stumpy tail and grinning at them foolishly.

'Take care to mind your petticoats, Miss Wainwright. He will jump up at you if you give him the least encouragement!' Sheldon said sharply. He grabbed the dog's collar and hauled him away.

'You'll excuse me one moment . . .' he muttered, and strode out, the dog at his heels, leaving her alone.

Emma put down her parasol, pulled off her gloves to let the air reach her sticky palms, and looked about her. She had not thought to ask Mrs Somerton whether Major Sheldon were married, but looking around this room, she knew he was not. No wife would have permitted such disorder, not even in a private den. There was a dog basket by the open hearth, a wide, pointed-arched stone fireplace, its empty grate open to the room. There was no woman to embroider a carefully-worked fire-screen. The stone lintel of the ancient hearth was carved with a Latin device. '*O Fortunati, quorum iam muri surgunt*', she murmured, but did not have sufficient Latin to decipher what was obviously a family motto. Sheldons had lived here for gener-ations. On the walls, amid the sporting prints, were their portraits, ruddy, weather-beaten, handsome men, whose appearance suggested that they had been equally addicted to open-air pursuits and the brandy-bottle. But in a corner, away from the fire which would have damaged it, hung the portrait of a young woman, signed by the artist and dated 1810. She was beautiful and a little foreign-looking, with abundant black hair and large brown eyes in an oval sallow-complexioned face.

A noise at the door and a chink of china caused her to spin round guiltily, to see the elderly butler carrying a silver tray.

'Major Sheldon hopes you will take tea, madam,' he said smoothly, setting down his burden. She had outmanoeuvred him in gaining admittance first to his master and then to the house, and his former disapproval had been augmented by wariness.

Emma noticed that the tea-things were for one person only; Major Sheldon did not drink tea. 'Thank you,' she said, and then asked more boldly, 'Who is the lady whose portrait hangs in the corner?'

'That is the late Mrs Sheldon, madam; the Major's mother. She was a Portuguese lady.' Was it her over-sensitive ear, or had the man slightly emphasised the word 'lady'? He bowed and withdrew without offering any further information, but making it quite clear that 'lady' was not a term he would have used of *this* female visitor.

Emma sat down and drank her tea for want of anything better to do, turning over in her mind how best to approach the problem of Kezia. She had prepared a speech in her head during her train journey, tailored to explaining matters tactfully to an elderly gentleman, but the roundabout phrases would not do for a young one, especially this one. Major Sheldon was not a man to mince his own words, and probably appreciated plain speaking in others. Although possibly not in women . . . Emma frowned.

The patter of the spaniel's claws on parquet announced his master's return. Emma set down her saucer in haste, but had no time to re-don her gloves before the door flew open and the dog loped in, Sheldon's burly frame close behind. He looked tidier, and was at least acceptably dressed. His manner was no more gracious, however, and he said brusquely, 'You'll forgive me if I still smell of the stables, ma'am, but I thought you'd hardly fancy waiting while I took a bath.'

He threw himself down in a chair opposite to hers, and stretched out his legs. The spaniel came to rest his muzzle on his master's muscular thigh and beg a caress, ears drooping, stumpy tail quivering. Sheldon absently stretched out a hand to fondle his ears, while staring at Emma in a very direct and critical manner, awaiting her response.

She bridled under that cavalier gaze and felt her cheeks burn. She was being made to feel she had no business here, before she had even explained her case. At the same time, her own sensitivity led her to suspect that defensiveness rather than aggression lay at the root of his discouraging manner. His fingers still scratched slowly at the dog's ears. It was not just that he was fond of the animal, but that contact with the dog helped his own composure. He was good with animals, as his mastery of the horse had illustrated. More at ease with animals, perhaps, than with people?

Plucking up courage, Emma began: 'You'll forgive me, I hope, Major Sheldon, for calling on you unannounced. But, to be quite frank, I thought you might not see me otherwise.'

His thick black eyebrows twitched, but he made no comment, his silence implicitly confirming that what she said was correct.

'My aunt, Mrs Somerton, was very distressed by your letter, and the visits from your agent, Mr Sneadie.'

'Sneadie is an old woman, but in this case I think he had some cause to be shocked,' Sheldon said. 'I understand that Mrs Somerton, whom I'd always considered to be a lady of exemplary character, has taken to filling the house with fallen women.'

'Oh, nonsense!' said Emma vigorously, before she had time to think. 'It's only one girl, and my aunt didn't bring her to the house. I did.'

'Why?' he asked simply, but she could see he was really curious to know.

As briefly as possible, she explained Kezia's circumstances. 'She's terrified of the man, Leach, and it would be criminal not to protect her. Besides, I'm sure she is a girl who can be taught a different way of life.'

'Possibly. In the meantime, my windows are broken, my house daubed with painted obscenities, and the neighbours set their lawyers on to mine. I agree that Leach is no pretty character, but you can be sure he's also a dangerous one. If broken windows don't frighten you into giving up the girl, he'll try something else. You, and your aunt, both run risk of personal attack, Miss Wainwright. All in all, while I applaud your well-meant charity, I recommend you to turn the girl out into the street where she finds her living. In fact, I insist that she leaves my house. You're wasting your time on her, anyway.'

'Oh?' Emma retorted defiantly. 'You think poor Kezia cannot learn a more respectable business?'

'She probably can. It requires no great wit to master the art of black-leading a kitchen stove. But how long do you think she'll stick it before she pines for her old life and the arms of Sam Leach?'

'Why on earth should she pine for that brute?' gasped Emma.

Sheldon sighed. 'Because, dear Miss Wainwright, you're meddling in something about which I strongly suspect you know absolutely nothing. I don't mean the criminal world of the London slums. I mean the physical attraction between men and women, which is not always just as sentimental novels would have it. It is not your fault. It's fashionable to leave young girls abominably ignorant, though from what this is meant to protect them, I don't know. Probably from any hope of being happily married. Even though Sam Leach beats the girl black and blue, it does not mean that she isn't devoted to the wretched fellow. Women of her type accept that sort of circumstance. I'd wager my last sovereign that she'd scratch the eyes out of any other lady of the town who tried to take Leach from her. The girl has simply quarrelled with her bully-boy. In a little while she'll forget and forgive, and go back.'

Pale-faced, Emma said quietly, 'It is you who are ignorant, Major Sheldon, and not I. I may not understand what attraction this man can ever have held for her. But I can understand what it is like to be the recipient of unwelcome advances and to be at the mercy of a man one hates. It destroys a woman's last vestige of self-respect. And self-respect, Major, is all that a woman has—because the law and society take care that she has nothing else.'

Sheldon's hand, caressing the dog's ear, had stilled. He was silent for a while, studying her white face, then he asked bluntly, 'What is it you actually want, Emma?'

She was startled by hearing him address her so

familiarly, and also because he had obviously understood her better than she had supposed. 'I want Sam Leach brought to justice!' she said firmly.

'For blacking the eye of Kezia Smith? A magistrate would not think it worth hearing the case,' he said coolly, almost in a casual way.

'No. For sending a girl of fifteen out on the streets and living off the money she earns there.'

'What offends you? That she is fifteen? It is quite old enough.' Irritably, he added, 'Don't look so horrified! I'm stating a fact. The law requires a girl to be only twelve years of age, and after that any man may bed her, with her consent. He can even marry her if he has a fancy. Why, my own mother was only fourteen when she married my father, and it was as successful a marriage as marriages can hope to be.' He stood up and walked over to the fireplace, and leaned back against it, his hands in his breeches pockets. 'See here, Emma, you must look at this matter as the law would see it.'

'You have not my permission to call me by my Christian name!' she interrupted, angered by this second casual use of it.

'Have I not? Well, you may call me Luke, if you wish. I'm accustomed to old tabbies calling me Major Sheldon, but not pretty girls. Don't sit there seething at me like a pot about to bubble over! Just listen.' There was a note of authority in his voice that made her obey. 'Now, then,' he said crisply. 'You want Sam Leach brought before a magistrate. I dare say I could bring that about if you really want it, but I doubt you really do—because you have not thought about it. You say you want justice, but Justice is usually represented blindfolded, and with good reason. Living upon immoral earnings is a serious offence that carries a penalty of six months' hard labour. But what is our evidence? Why, the testimony of Kezia Smith. Will Kezia testify against her man? Almost certainly not; but let us suppose, for sake of argument, that she is persuaded to do so. Leach is convicted for living on the immoral earnings of Kezia, gets six months at breaking rocks, and emerges at the end of it a worse brute than he is now. But by her own testimony, Kezia is confessing that she works upon the streets of London as a common prostitute. That is also an offence. She is sent to a house of correction, and possibly even to the treadmill. Is that what you want?'

'Then there is no justice,' Emma said quietly, 'at least for that poor girl. She is sent out upon the streets at only thirteen years of age. At fourteen she is in the power of Leach. I am twenty-four, Major Sheldon. What will Kezia be at my age? Raddled, drunken, sunk so low nothing can help her. And the law will send her to the treadmill? Will the magistrate, good, sober, decent man that he is, not consider the suffering of a thirteen-year-old child sold to men for their so-called pleasure?'

Sheldon's swarthy complexion darkened even more. He looked both angry and embarrassed. 'See here, Emma, we are talking of very poor people.' He struck his hand on the shelf of the ancient fireplace. 'Damn it, the horses in my stables are better accommodated and fed than the families in the slums of our great cities. Suppose you have a family of four or five children, some very young. Father is able to get only casual work. Mother or one of the elder girls works at some kind of piece-work, such as making boxes. They have another daughter, twelve or thirteen years of age, who brings in no money but who must be fed and clothed. By some miracle she is pretty. Have you seen slum children, Emma? They are filthy, and their limbs are twisted and deformed. Their skin is blotched with disease and they carry lice in their hair. Yet, in this family, there is that rarest thing in the slums—beauty. It cannot last long. It must be exploited *now*, or it is lost for ever. One day a well-dressed woman comes to the hovel where they live, if such an existence can be called living. She says she can find work for the girl, who will have to leave home, of course, but the parents will receive a few pounds to console them for her loss. Well, they don't ask what kind of work it is or who will care for the child. They take the money, and they give up the child, no questions asked.'

'And is no law broken?' Emma asked bitterly.

He hunched his broad shoulders awkwardly. 'If the parents were genuinely deceived, then yes. Naturally, if you asked them, they would swear on the Bible that they had no idea that she was being taken away for prostitution. But the obliging stranger cannot be found. The parents have spent the money they got for their child and don't want her back on their hands again, and the child herself has been swallowed up in that great morass we call a city. When she surfaces again, it is probably at Bow Street magistrates' court to face a charge of being a common whore. There is nothing you can do about it, Emma, much as you may want to. That is how such people live. And, you know, the girls themselves don't necessarily hold their profession in the abhorrence that you do. It's better than working, say, in the sweet factories, where they are horribly scalded by the boiling sugar, or in some sweat-shop. It is by way of being a necessary evil.'

He saw her pale, delicate face take on an expression of obstinacy, her small, round chin tilted defiantly, and her hands crushed her kid gloves into a ball of crumpled leather. Her blue eyes snapped at him, and she said quietly, 'No, Major Sheldon, it is not.'

There was a long silence, then he replied, equally quietly, 'Don't meddle, Emma. You are not equipped to fight it. Let it alone.'

'Then who will do it? If others will not, then I must.'

'Not from my property!' he said sharply.

She rose to her feet, a small bristling figure whose bonnet-brim came to the middle of his chest. 'I will not turn Kezia out on to the street, and I defy you to turn out my aunt, or myself, either!'

'Your aunt is a little elderly for such a business,' he said crisply. 'And you, madam, are a damn sight too virtuous. I'll give you a week to think it over; after which, either Kezia goes—or you and your aunt do!'

Emma gathered up her gloves and parasol with shaking hands, and exclaimed, 'I see it's useless talking to you. I shan't stay to be insulted! I'm sorry I brought you from your stables. You are so obviously best at home there.'

He flushed with anger. 'Don't lecture me, miss!' he said hoarsely. 'You came here of your own choice on an errand that no lady ought ever to contemplate.'

'On the contrary, sir, I believe it a matter which should concern every decent woman, and gentleman—but you, Major, are not that.'

'How did you come here from the station?' he asked abruptly, putting out his hand towards the bell-rope hanging beside the fireplace.

'On my own two feet.'

'The boy will drive you back in the dog-cart.' He tugged robustly at the rope.

'It is not necessary, Major.'

'It's what I say you will do,' was the calm retort.

She gasped, and sparks flew from her blue eyes. But he was obviously not prepared to brook argument, and a little later she was being borne towards the railway station in the jolting dog-cart.

She was so upset and angered by her encounter that she had difficulty standing still, and was even less able to sit in the ladies' waiting-room, so she paced up and down the platform as she waited for the London train, filled with nervous energy, and attracting not a few curious looks from other travellers. Suddenly she heard her name called through the mists of her rage, and looked up, startled, to see Bryant, the veterinary surgeon.

'I'm waiting for a parcel off the up train,' he explained. He took off his round hat, revealing a crop of curly hair, which made him look not more than thirty. 'You're on your way back to London already, Miss Wainwright?'

'Yes,' said Emma briefly. 'I might as well have stayed there.'

'You must not mind Luke—Major Sheldon,' he

said apologetically, 'His bark is worse than his bite.'

'I find him an extremely offensive fellow!' she said fiercely.

'Oh, no, begging your pardon, ma'am—but he is a very gallant one, with a distinguished army career behind him. He was decorated for gallantry during the campaign of 1838 against the Pathan tribesmen, for the rescue of a fellow officer in quite horrifying circumstances. It's a military family, you know. Old General Sheldon, Luke's father, was in the Peninsula, and retreated to Corunna with Sir John Moore.'

'And is that where he married the Portuguese lady?' Emma asked with new interest.

'Why, yes, he did—Luke's mother. Luke favours her for complexion, and is as tough as any of the old Portuguese irregulars his father used to command. That's how he came by his nickname —Luke, I mean. They call him "the Portuguee".' Bryant grinned. 'And you know the saying, "The devil made the old Portuguee."'

'I didn't know it,' said Emma, 'but I can see how it came about.'

The train puffed into the station in a cloud of white smoke, which enveloped them and sent them both coughing to the rear of the platform. As it cleared, Bryant stepped forward and politely opened the door of a Ladies Only compartment.

'A pleasant journey back to Town, Miss Wainwright.' He touched his hat, and disappeared in the direction of the guard's van to collect his parcel.

*   *   *

Emma travelled back, sunk in thought. Major Sheldon had campaigned in Afghanistan in 'thirty-eight, nine years ago, but seemed well settled in his present circumstances. This indicated he must have resigned his commission soon after the campaign, say, in 1842 or 1843. How old was he? That might be deduced easily enough. The tragic retreat to Corunna had taken place in 1809. Luke's father must have been accompanied on it by his newly-acquired Portuguese bride. The portrait dated 1810 must have been commissioned upon her arrival in England, and completed the following year. The same year had probably seen Luke's birth. The present year was 1847. Luke Sheldon was thirty-seven years old.

Emma permitted herself a faint smile. 'Lucius' was no doubt a family name, inflicted by tradition on elder sons. But thirty-seven tied in very well with what she had observed, and with Bryant's advice when he had chided Sheldon about losing some weight. Bryant was obviously a hunting crony and friend as well as a veterinary surgeon called to the horses. Putting on weight was a common enough affliction for men of sporting persuasion as they approached their forties.

But what had caused the Portuguee to quit so suddenly a promising and distinguished career in the army at the age of little more than thirty? Whatever it had been, old General Sheldon would not have approved.

CHAPTER THREE

To EMMA, the next few days felt as though they were all living in a state of siege. They kept all windows facing on the street closed despite the hot weather, and made sure the street door was securely fastened. It occurred to her that Sam Leach might decide to approach the house from the rear, by climbing over the walls of intervening gardens, so as soon as dusk fell, the kitchen door had also to be bolted and all windows on the ground floor secured. It made the house stuffy and was a tiresome procedure, and they all grew nervous and irritable.

As for Major Sheldon, as represented by Mr Sneadie, he could not be kept out, but for the days following her visit to Surrey, the lawyer did not appear, so presumably the Major had ordered him to wait and see if the ladies would comply with his request (or command), and send Kezia away.

Kezia worked with great energy, if rather unskilfully, but she was a quick learner, and Emma undertook to teach her to read. There was no compulsory education in the 1840s, and little education that was free, so most city children grew up without schooling of any kind. As Emma saw it, this illiteracy kept them in a kind of prison from which they could not escape, barring them from any but the simplest labouring tasks, and if these were not available, leaving them little to do but drift into the underworld of crime. Kezia studied her spelling-book hard, following the words with her finger and muttering them under her breath until she had mastered them. Watching her struggles, Emma was more than ever determined that all this was not going to prove for nothing.

Of course, they had their setbacks. One of their problems was the language used by Kezia herself. 'Profanity in my kitchen,' said Mrs McGraw, 'I will not have.' The trouble was that Kezia could not distinguish between what was acceptable language and what was not, having been accustomed both to hear and to use strong language from childhood. Gradually, however, things were improving.

The weather turned unseasonably warm. Emma walked round to Forbes Street and stood gazing wistfully at the empty house Major Sheldon owned there. It would make an excellent Rescue Home. It was large, roomy, and in a good state of repair. It stood on a corner and was bounded on the other side by a disused Quaker burial-ground, so there were no immediate neighbours to be offended by the close proximity of fallen women, even re-formed ones. Nor was the Quaker cemetery as gloomy a place as it sounded. It contained several trees that survived somehow despite the soot-laden London air, and was overgrown with a riot of weeds, some flowering. Starlings and sparrows twittered and squawked in the boughs and hopped about the mossy, simple headstones. It offered the eye and ear an oasis of leafy greenery in what was otherwise a brick jungle. The house was altogether a splendid location.

The problem, and it was a considerable one, was

how to persuade Major Sheldon to grant her the lease. Asked now, as things were, he could certainly refuse. But, thought Emma optimistically, he might be brought to agree, somehow or other. She could not yet imagine quite how, short of a miracle, but where there was a will there was a way.

She gave the façade of the house a little nod, as if to say: 'Just wait a little, you'll see, I'll have the tenancy of you yet!' and walked away with a brisk step.

Mrs Somerton listened to Emma's plans with a degree of reserve, mixed with some alarm. Her fingers strayed frequently towards the sermon notes, and she made clucking noises indicative of opposition.

'Not because it is not a splendid idea, Emma, but hardly, I fear, practical. You cannot ask Major Sheldon to let you have the house for such a purpose; it would be much too indelicate a request.'

'I already know that Major Sheldon doesn't consider my actions ladylike. And I don't care—not for Major Sheldon's opinions, nor, come to that, for Major Sheldon!'

'I expect he doesn't know what to do about you,' said Mrs Somerton, unexpectedly pinpointing the centre of the conflict. 'Men don't like to have problems sprung upon them, you know. I fear, Emma dear, that perhaps you were not quite tactful.'

'If I was not tactful, then he was extremely rude. He is like all men: they believe the world was created just for them, and women exist only to serve them. If a woman dares to indicate that she can have an opinion of her own, he loses his temper because he has no answer. And if you suggest that there are women whose lives are made absolutely wretched because of the way men behave, he refuses to believe it. He is an obstinate, difficult, even impossible man.'

'How does he look?' asked Mrs Somerton, eyeing her niece shrewdly. 'Is he handsome? You say he is aged only thirty-seven.'

'Oh, he looks fine enough,' said Emma carelessly, adding with warmth, 'But he would lead any woman a dreadful life.'

She leaned back and closed her eyes. The spell of hot weather was proving trying. Her bare-shouldered muslin gown gave a deceptive impression of cool. The laced corset which gave it shape was a prison, and the heavy petticoats beneath it made a nonsense of the light material of the dress.

But there were many women trapped in a worse prison than that of current fashion—that of a bad marriage, for instance. Divorce was possible only by private act of parliament—after proceedings in court to establish grounds. This meant that every wretched detail became public gossip, the racier cases reported in printed broadsheets at a penny a time and snapped up by eager readers. Nor was divorce as easy for a woman to obtain as for a man. The private act of parliament itself required a sympathetic MP to shepherd it through the House. As these were all men, and women had no vote, few women could hope for a kindly interest there. Besides, both the pain and the scandal of divorce

fell more heavily on women than on men. They lost
their children, who were deemed to be as much the
father's property as everything else. Also, there
was an unspoken convention that no respectable
woman would admit publicly to imperfections in
her marriage. The alternative was a legal separ-
ation, if a husband could be persuaded to agree. If
he refused, and his behaviour drove his wife into
leaving him, there was no way he could be forced to
support her financially. The law did not allow
husband and wife to sue one another. Poor Law
authorities were notoriously reluctant to help
married women because of the difficulty they had
reclaiming the money from the husband, as they
were required to do. Husbands were liable for a
wife's debts, but shopkeepers soon heard if the
couple had parted, and like the Poor Law adminis-
trators, feared problems in getting their money
from an unwilling husband, and generally refused
the wife any credit.

Should all this reduce the poor woman to working for a living, then the money she earned was, in
law, her husband's, and he could arrive out of the
blue, pocket her hard-earned savings, and depart.
At any time the husband might apply for restitution
of conjugal rights and force his wife back to him, no
matter how badly he had behaved.

Aloud, Emma said bitterly, 'We are supposed to
live in a civilised society, and there is so much that is
wrong. It's wrong that a child of twelve can be said
to consent to go with a man, because how can such a
young girl understand all that is involved? It is
wrong that marriage can make a wife the helpless
prisoner of a bad husband. It's wrong that magis-

trates will do nothing to help someone like Kezia, who was forced by poverty on to the streets. It is all part and parcel of the same notion, that women are somehow inferior to men, and should be treated accordingly!'

'I dare say it is, dear,' said Mrs Somerton resignedly. 'But that is how it is.'

'Then it must be changed!' exclaimed her niece in a sudden burst of energy. 'The age of consent must be raised. Married women should be given the right to their own property, and how can members of parliament be supposed to understand the situation in one individual household? As if they even cared, with so many seemingly more important matters to concern them!'

Mrs Somerton tapped her fingers on the cover of the sermon notes in some agitation. 'Emma dear, while all you say is no doubt correct, I begin to fear that you grow a little biased. Whatever else, please don't let all this turn you against the idea of being married. My poor Henry and I were very happy together, and I have only the kindest memories.' She smoothed the cover of the sermon notes and smiled down at the stout little red book. 'I still miss dear Henry, and his sensible advice. Whenever I read these notes of his, it is as though I am able to discuss things with him as I used to, hear his point of view and know what he would have advised. They have been a great help. It is almost, you know, as if I heard dear Henry's voice.'

Emma smiled at her affectionately. 'I'm sure of it, Aunt Rosamond. But I'm afraid we need a little more than Mr Somerton's notes now.'

'Well,' said Mrs Somerton more briskly, 'it's

certainly true that Henry had very little to do with fallen women! I must admit that I begin to wish that he had—strictly in a missionary sense, you understand—so that he could have left us some useful memorandum upon the subject!'

There was a tremendous crash from outside the door as Mrs Somerton ceased speaking, and before either of them could jump to her feet, it was followed by a woman's scream and the sound of a rough male voice. The door flew open, and a man appeared framed in it.

He was quite a young fellow, in his middle twenties, and handsome in a flashy, obvious way, though his features were already coarsened by drink, and his eyes held that strange mixture of cunning, ignorance and obstinacy which is the mark of the uneducated bully-boy. His dress was remarkable in that it aspired to a sort of dandyism, from the red kerchief knotted round his thick neck to the shiny brass buttons on his jacket. He was powerfully built, with long arms which hung, swinging slightly, at his sides, and he lowered his head like an animal at bay. Scowling first at one and then at the other of the two women, he demanded in a hoarse voice, 'Where's Kezzy? I want Kezzy. I've come to take her back along of me!'

'Mr Leach, I take it?' said Emma as calmly as she could, though the sight of this ruffian terrified her. 'You have forced your way into this house, and I must ask you to leave it at once!'

'Kezzy,' he repeated obstinately. 'I ain't going without Kezzy.'

'Kezia is not going with you,' Emma said, rising to her feet. 'She is employed here now, and leading a decent life. If you are capable of any kind of affection for her, then you will leave her alone!'

'Fancy talk!' he snarled, lurching towards her. 'I ain't going without Kezzy. You don't have no right to take Kezzy away from me!'

'Mrs McGraw!' called Mrs Somerton, 'Run out and see if you can find a constable!'

'I want Kezzy. I want my woman! Where've you got her hid?' Leach shouted. He swept out a ham-like fist and sent an occasional table loaded with bric-à-brac crashing to the floor, shattered fragments of china flying in all directions. Mrs Somerton scrambled to her feet and took refuge behind a chair, the sermon notes held out in front of her as a shield.

'You shall not have Kezia!' gasped Emma. 'For the last time, I insist you leave this house!'

'Well, ain't you the smart one!' Leach said, swaying slightly, and straddling the smashed china on the carpet in an attempt to keep his balance. Emma could smell the gin now. The man must have been drinking since early morning, and his mood was turning ugly. 'Ain't you the fine lady—taking a poor man's living away from him, taking my Kezzy! She's a good girl, my Kezzy, and knows better than to do me wrong. She wouldn't have done this, wouldn't have run off like she done, if it wasn't for you missie. I ain't leaving here without her, see? Fancy words don't cut no style with me . . .' He lurched towards her again, arms swinging, and suddenly reached out and seized her shoulder. 'So where is she? Speak up now, sharp like — or you'll find out what it is to cross Sam Leach!'

Emma could not help crying out as his fingers

pressed cruelly into the flesh of her shoulder. She tried to pull herself free, and Mrs Somerton ran from behind the chair and raising the sermon notes on high, clouted the astonished Leach a resounding blow on the head. 'Let go of the young lady at once, you brute!'

Leach released Emma and swung round to face Mrs Somerton, but before he could do anything, there was a flurry of movement behind him, and before their astonished eyes, he was suddenly jerked backwards by a pair of strong hands which grasped his shoulders.

'Right!' said a familiar voice grimly. 'That's enough of that, I fancy! Out you go!'

'Oh, Luke,' cried Emma in relief. 'I mean, Major Sheldon! It's Sam Leach, Kezzy's bully, who broke our windows.'

Leach swore luridly and turned, swinging a haymaker of a punch at Luke, who sidestepped it neatly and responded with an unorthodox but effective right-hander to the pit of Leach's stomach. Leach groaned and retched, and doubled up in agony. Luke gasped, 'Excuse me, ladies!' and grasping Leach by the collar, hauled him, purple-faced and still struggling to regain his breath, out of the room.

In the hall they met Mrs McGraw, who had returned, panting, with a constable in tow. There was a brief struggle and Leach was hauled away, still gasping and spitting, finding enough breath only to hurl gurgled obscenities at them all.

Luke returned to the drawing-room, straightening his sleeves. He was dressed to come up to Town, and presented a very different aspect from the wild gypsy who had been revealed to Emma's view when they had first met. Even given some disarray because of his encounter with Leach, he still presented an arresting figure. A handsome man, in a grey frock coat and brocade waistcoat over spotless linen and a black stock, his saturnine looks now appeared distinguished, and Emma found herself thinking, a little ruefully, I dare say he has broken hearts wherever he's gone, and little wonder!

'Poor Mrs McGraw,' exclaimed Mrs Somerton. 'I must just go and see if she's all right. Do excuse me, Major Sheldon, just for a moment. Emma, do offer Major Sheldon a glass of wine—in the little cupboard . . .' She hurried out of the room.

'Well, Emma?' Luke said sternly. 'I hope you're happy, now that you've successfully placed both yourself and your aunt in physical danger.'

Emma turned on her heel and went to the cupboard. 'There is only sherry, Major Sheldon, or ratafia.'

'I don't want either. Turn round, Emma, and look me in the eye! What would have happened if I hadn't come along just then?'

'I'm very grateful,' Emma said, her voice shaking slightly. 'But I wouldn't have given him Kezia.'

'Preferred to see Mrs Somerton in the infirmary, I suppose? What makes you suppose Leach wouldn't black her eye as well as he would black the girl Kezia's? For pity's sake, what on earth has to happen to convince you of the stupidity of taking in that girl?'

He saw her mouth set obstinately in a way he remembered. 'Call it stupidity, if you like. I can't help how you see it. I see it differently.'

'Emma . . .' Unexpectedly, Sheldon reached out and caught her two hands, imprisoning them in his. She drew in her breath, and froze. 'Emma, for the last time, I am telling you to send that girl away.'

'There's no need now. Leach has been arrested.'

To her surprise, Luke shook his head. 'No, only warned. I told the Peeler: no charges.'

'What?' she gasped incredulously.

'My dear girl, can you imagine the reaction at Bow Street court, when the magistrate is informed that Leach committed his assault whilst trying to find some doxy to whom you and your aunt have given a home? Why, your aunt's reputation would lie in ribbons. Not a lady of her acquaintance would either receive her or call on her again! You may not mind running yourself into unpleasantness, Emma, but ask yourself if you have the right to bring all this trouble on your aunt, who is, I need not remind you, hardly a young woman.'

Emma pulled her hands from his with a jerk. 'Aunt Rosamond and I have discussed this all very carefully, and she is as determined as I am to save Kezia!'

'As determined as you are? I wonder!' he said sarcastically. He went to the hearth and turned to lean against it much in the way he had in his own home. 'You are confoundedly obstinate, Emma, and you seem to think it is some sort of virtue. Let me tell you: it is not. That girl goes out of this house—today!'

Angrily, Emma opened her mouth to argue, but before she could speak, a voice from the doorway said quietly, 'It's all right, sir. I'll go. I don't want to make no trouble for Miss Emma, or for the other lady.'

Luke raised his head and stared hard at the girl in the door. Emma walked across and took her by the hand and led her into the room. 'This is Kezia, Major Sheldon. She has worked hard since coming to this house. She is clean, honest and is learning her letters. If we turn her out, perhaps you could suggest where she might go?'

'I know where to go,' said Kezia in the same quiet voice. 'Back where I come from. It always did seem a bit of a dream, like it couldn't be real. I knew Sam would turn up, sooner or later. He's that wild, when he's got the drink in him. It's no good, Miss Emma. He'll be back, will Sam. It's best I go.'

'No!' Emma insisted. 'Kezzy, go back to the kitchen now, and let me talk it over with Major Sheldon. Don't worry, we'll think of something.'

When Kezia had gone, Luke said, 'See here, Emma, you've done that girl no favour, you know. Before you brought her here, she knew no other life. Now she's aware of something better—but she knows she can't have it. Was that a kindness?'

If he had shouted, Emma would have had an answer. But he had not raised his voice, and his quiet words made a deep impression. For the first time, a niggle of doubt entered her heart. He saw the flicker of indecision in her blue eyes.

'I'll come back tomorrow, Emma. When I do, I expect to find that drab gone. Do I make myself quite clear?'

'Quite clear, Major Sheldon,' she said unsteadily.

'Good. Then make my excuses to your aunt

—and I'll see her when I call tomorrow.' Unexpectedly, he took her hand, and raised it briefly, as if to kiss it, but released her without doing so, and walked out quickly, before she could react.

Emma stood alone in the middle of the room, surrounded by the smashed fragments of china and the little table, still lying on its side, and stared down at her fingers which he had held, before uttering a little exclamation and rubbing her hands together vigorously, as if to rub away some stain.

That night Emma slept very badly. The room was warm and stuffy, and the bedclothes twisted themselves uncomfortably about her, like ropes. Her nightgown clung to her body damply, and no matter which way she turned, she couldn't make herself comfortable. She felt tense, restless and unable to relax, under intolerable pressure like an overwound clock-spring. She told herself that it was the upset of Leach's visit, and the worry over Kezia, but she knew, deep in her heart, that the real cause was something else, something she dare not admit, because it raised possibilities more disturbing than any of the other problems which beset her.

I would be a fool, Emma told herself, staring into the blackness of the bedroom, to start a lot of sentimental nonsense like falling in love, at my age —I am twenty-four, after all, very nearly twenty-five, and I ought to have some sense. Goodness, Emma Wainwright, haven't you seen enough misery caused by relationships between men and women? None of this reasoning helped very much, so she became angry with herself, and scolded herself: For heaven's sake, if you must find some man attractive, at least find someone worthy, and one who won't break your heart in two and walk across the pieces!

She twisted and tossed, muttering to herself, and eventually fell into a restless slumber. It was filled with confused dreams, difficult to understand, making no sense, and frightening. At one stage she half-awoke, sure that there was someone in the room with her. She tried to open her eyes, but could not quite manage it. Yet she had a confused impression that the grey light of dawn was creeping through the windows and that a shadowy form stood by her bed. Emma gave a little cry, and pushed herself up on the perspiration-stained pillows, but the room was empty, and in the half-light she could make out the shape of her own dressing-gown hanging on its hook on the back of the door, and thought, amused, so that was the mysterious intruder! Really, Emma, nursery fancies? Goblins and things that go bump in the night, indeed!

When she awoke properly, the sunlight was streaming in. She sat up, aware that her head ached dully and that her eyes were heavy. She pushed back her damp hair with both hands, and her eye fell on a scrap of paper pushed under the edge of her pillow. Emma's heart seemed to miss a beat, and a dreadful foreboding took hold of her. No dream then, but reality. Someone had been there, by her bedside, and she knew who that someone was, even before she smoothed out the crumpled scrap and read, printed in uneven capitals, because Kezia was still very much a beginner in reading and writing: '*I AM SORRY, MIS EMA. I HAVE GONN BACK TO SEM.*'

Emma gave a cry of alarm and jumped out of bed, the note crushed in her fingers. She pulled on her dressing-gown and ran downstairs. Mrs McGraw stood at the foot of the stairs, carrying a tray of breakfast things towards the dining-room. 'Where is Kezzy?' Emma demanded breathlessly, clinging to the banister.

Mrs McGraw pulled a face. 'Upped and gone, that's what, Miss Emma. Not so much as a by-your-leave, and much less any thanks! That's what you get for taking a girl like that in and trying to give her a home. Mind you, she didn't take anything with her that I've noticed. Teaspoons are all there, and the silver.'

'Of course it is!' cried Emma angrily. 'Kezzy isn't a thief! Luke Sheldon, this is all your fault!' She struck her hand on the polished rail. 'We must get her back, at once!'

Mrs McGraw proceeded briskly into the dining-room, Emma on her heels, and began to set out the breakfast dishes. 'How are you going to do that, Miss Emma? She's gone back into the slums where she came from. Could be anywhere. Might just as well have taken herself off to the moon. You can't find her, Miss Emma. You did your best—you tried, you and madam both. And, goodness knows, I tried. Showed her how to wash dishes properly —because she had no idea, you know! Showed her how to set out a table—and had to tell her what half the things were for! I had to stop her eating her own dinner with her fingers, mark you!'

Emma sank down on a chair despondently and sighed. 'I told her it would be all right. Why didn't she listen to me? We could have got rid of Leach eventually. But it isn't Leach who is the cause of all this. I'll never forgive you!' she added fiercely, and Mrs McGraw looked up, startled. 'Not you, Mrs McGraw,' Emma said wearily. 'I mean Major Sheldon.'

'Major Sheldon is a very fine gentleman,' said Mrs McGraw primly. 'One who has had a lot of experience in dealing with folk—soldiers and the like. They get into all sorts of trouble. I remember, when I was a slip of a girl, we had a barracks in our town, and you wouldn't credit what went on. The army used to flog the men in those days, you know, but it didn't do any good. There's a sort of person born to get into trouble. That Kezia, she was one. Born to go to the bad.'

'Rubbish!' said Emma vehemently.

Mrs McGraw looked disapproving, and gathered up her tray. 'You'll see if I'm not right, Miss Emma. You're a young lady, and haven't seen how the world goes. Now, will you have the eggs scrambled or fried?'

'Neither, I don't want anything,' Emma mumbled.

'That won't help. Now then, miss, you're to eat a proper breakfast. I'll scramble them—sits easier on the stomach. And go and get yourself dressed before madam comes down.'

She marched out, and Emma threw Kezia's note down on the tablecloth with a sigh. Had she, then, really failed? She remembered that Luke was coming back later in the day, and her heart sank. She would have to face him, and tell him Kezia had gone, and that he had achieved what he wanted. She would see the satisfaction on his handsome, swarthy face. He would probably make some sort of smug speech about it being all for the best. I couldn't stand it, thought Emma. Aunt Rosamond can see him and tell him—I won't!

She considered this for a moment, and then thought: Indeed, I shan't see him, because I won't be here! I'll go to Bethnal Green and find Kezzy. It can't be impossible, and even if it is, then at least I shall have tried! If I don't try, I'll never forgive myself, much less Luke Sheldon.

Having made up her mind to a course of action, she felt much better. She ran back upstairs and washed and dressed, and after breakfast went down to the kitchen, where Mrs McGraw was weighing out flour carefully into a bowl.

'Mrs McGraw,' Emma said in a brisk tone, 'I want you to think very carefully. Did Kezia talk about her old life at all?'

'Not to me!' said the housekeeper, scandalised. 'Do you think I want to hear about all that wickedness?'

'No, no—I don't mean about the—the men. I mean about where she lived, that sort of thing.'

Mrs McGraw dusted her hands and frowned in thought. 'It was a terrible place, from all she did say. Lived with that Leach in one room. No pump for water or anything.'

'But a street . . . Did she name a street?' asked Emma eagerly.

The housekeeper wiped her hands in her starched apron. 'Not a street, no. It was a court —something Court. Taylor's Court, that was it, I'm almost sure. It wouldn't be a proper yard; it would be just a space in between the houses. I shouldn't think it's a proper name at all, on a plate. Just what folk who live round there call it.'

'Then, if I ask, someone will direct me to it!' exclaimed Emma, jumping to her feet.

'Miss Emma! You come back here!' cried the housekeeper, abandoning her cake-making and running after her. 'You can't go to that place! It's a terrible spot, is Bethnal Green! You'll likely be murdered! Miss Emma, what will your aunt say? Miss Emma, you come back!'

Hansom cab-drivers seemed to have the same opinion of Bethnal Green as Mrs McGraw. They were all unwilling to take a fare there and gave her a variety of excuses, most of them saying that they had never heard of Taylor's Court, and did not believe that such a place existed.

Eventually, however, she found a man who said that he knew of it, but that it was 'a rough neighbourhood' carrying an evil reputation, and certainly 'no place for a lady'. But he agreed reluctantly to take her there, and to wait while she conducted her business and bring her back, once he had been promised half-a-crown over and above his fare. Emma suspected that his real reason for taking her was simple human curiosity, and that he wanted to find out what on earth this young lady could want in such a place. But she had no intention of giving him time to change his mind, so scrambled up into the cab, and they set off towards the insalubrious tenements of Bethnal Green.

CHAPTER FOUR

EMMA WAS not the only person to have spent a sleepless night. Luke had not slept well, and was woken very early by a shaft of bright warm sunlight falling across his face. For a moment he almost believed himself back in India. He could imagine that if he went to the window, he would see the clear bright colours of an Indian hill town, the women with their pitchers walking gracefully to the well, the turbaned *syce*, immaculate from head to toe, standing outside with the horse, waiting for Major Sheldon sahib to arrive for his morning ride.

Luke threw back the sheets and padded across to the windows. It was not India he saw, of course, it was the rolling Surrey countryside, a faint haze signalling the midsummer heat the day would bring later. But it made no difference. He already knew that it was going to be one of those difficult, miserable days, when India would be with him every minute, when he couldn't forget it, couldn't push it out of his mind.

It would not be the whole of his time in India, but just that one episode which dominated all else so completely that he found it difficult to remember anything else: his rescue of young Emerson. He had been given a medal for it. Or, rather, he been presented with it for having rescued what remained of Emerson. Yet that mutilated wreck had had life in it, it was a human being, however unrecognisable. 'It' had been a brother officer, and 'it' was, incredibly, still alive. So he had brought Emerson back, to die two days later, in agony, on a hospital cot. What he should have done, when he first found Emerson, or that wretched thing which Emerson had become, was to take his pistol and put a bullet in the lad's head there and then, and put an end to all that suffering. But he had not been able to do it, not in cold blood. Not out of any moral scruple. 'Just squeamish,' Luke said aloud.

The regiment saw it differently, a heroic episode in its best traditions. They had had a special silver medal struck. The day he had received it, he had walked away from the ceremony, unpinned the trinket and thrust it into his pocket. Riding back to his bungalow, he had passed a wedding procession, colourful, joyful, noisy, a symbol of life. He dismounted and pressed the silver medal into the hand of the bride's father, saying, 'A wedding gift . . .'

As he rode away, the astonished old man hurried after him, crying out, 'Sahib, sahib—this silver coin is of great beauty and worth many rupees!'

He remembered turning in the saddle and gesturing him away angrily, shouting, 'Take it—it is worth nothing to me!'

After dressing, he went down to the stables, where he liked to be and where he always relaxed. Riley, the groom, was there, a wizened, bow-legged little man who had been a successful jockey until a fall and a back injury had ended his career on the turf. Of the boy Tom, there was no sign.

'Will you look at the time?' demanded Riley,

pointing up at the clock in the tower over the stable arch. 'Half an hour since he should have been here. I'll take my belt to him, so I will, when he shows his face!'

'Don't be too hard on the lad,' Luke said tolerantly. 'At his age, didn't you ever oversleep?'

'I did not,' said Riley virtuously. 'And if I'd tried it, wouldn't my fayther have helped me out of bed with the toe of his boot?'

Luke walked down the row of loose-boxes, Riley hobbling along behind him with the peculiar lurching gait his accident had given him. As they passed each box, heads appeared over the doors, ears pricked, as the horses recognised Luke's step. Only at the last box did no head appear. Luke hesitated before it, and then opened the door and went in.

The sorrel stood on the far side. As he entered, it laid back its ears and stamped warningly, showing the whites of its eyes. 'Steady,' Luke murmured, putting a hand on the satin neck.

Riley's shadow fell across the door. 'You'll watch yourself, sir, with that beast. Nearly took a piece out of me, he did. He has a divil in him.'

'People say that of me,' Luke said, but to himself. More loudly, he added, 'He's a fine animal, Riley.' He walked out of the loose-box and closed the door.

'Major!' The groom set off across the yard again in Luke's wake, with his curious crablike shuffle. 'There are good men and bad men. And the same is true of horses. That horse is a bad one. Not in the blood and the bone, I grant you, but bad in the spirit. He'll be the death of you. Get rid of him, sir!'

'I'm going to London today,' Luke said, ignoring his words.

'Railway engines,' muttered Riley. 'Not in nature.'

'Quiet, will you, man, and listen? Turn the sorrel out into the paddock. Do it yourself. The boy doesn't know enough to handle him if he plays up. And don't go thrashing that boy for being late; I won't have it.'

He strode out briskly under the arch of the clock-tower. Glancing up at the weathervane, he saw that the dog fox balanced motionless. Not a breeze. He set off towards the house, but half-way there, he stopped, prompted by some part-memory, and stared, frowning, at the scene it presented. Then he recalled that it was about here, when he had been walking back to the house with Emma, that she had stopped and exclaimed how lovely it was. It was a nice old house, and he was fond of it, glad that she had liked it, too—but he had to admit it had a sadly neglected look. It was not the sort of obvious neglect marked by a lack of paint: it was the neglect resulting from a house having no mistress. Hill House had had no mistress for a great many years, since Luke's mother had died, when he had been only five years old. His father had never remarried, and Luke had brought no wife here. He ought to, of course.

He had not given much thought to it before, but following on his talk with Emma, he had realised how very young his mother had been, only sixteen, when he was born—and dead five years later, not quite twenty-one. She was buried in the elegant mausoleum in the family's corner of the local churchyard, as was his father. Luke never visited it, an omission some people might have condemned as showing lack of filial duty. But he had no happy memories associated with either parent. He could not remember his mother. He remembered his father all right, a martinet of a man, embittered by the loss of his wife, unable to communicate with his young son. Gradually the old warhorse took to the brandy-bottle, and when under the influence of the drink, would give way to terrifying rages. The child Luke had hidden behind the schoolroom door, listening to the dread voice shouting, cursing, railing against humanity.

His childhood friends had always been animals, mostly dogs and horses, with the kitchen cats occasionally admitted to the circle. Later he was sent away to boarding school, and must have been the only pupil there who preferred its austere regime to being at home. After that he had gone to the army—which brought his thoughts full circle back to India again.

Following the Afghan episode, the army had been soured for him as a life. When his father died, in 1842, he had been glad to resign his commission and come home to a civilian life and a neglected inheritance. Gradually he was knocking it into shape, selling off some properties to pay for the restoration of others. He had done it all alone, and knew he needed a wife to help him. But he hesitated, unable to see himself as a family man. Perhaps it would be best if he were the last Sheldon at Hill House, after all. There was a space in the mausoleum, he knew, for him—and, according to Riley, if Luke kept the sorrel horse, he might occupy that spot earlier than he intended! He knew the sorrel was an evil-tempered brute, but he was determined to persevere with it, perhaps inspired by the same kind of obstinacy which made Emma so determined to persevere with Kezia. Kezia and the sorrel were both flawed objects of beauty. Riley had recommended to Luke that he get rid of the horse, and Luke had recommended Emma to get rid of the girl. But he would not be at all surprised to find, when he got to Town today, that Kezia was still in evidence. He suspected that he and Miss Wainwright shared an underlying obstinate streak, which both of them liked to call determination. Emma interested him, because she was unlike the usual run of young ladies. But she was getting out of her depth. The trouble was the obligatory reticence society imposed on even discussing matters of sexual mores. Emma was all set to find herself an object of scandal, the more so because she was unmarried, and unmarried girls were supposed to be so confounded ignorant. What Emma needed was a husband's name and presence to protect her.

Luke realised that he had been standing still, lost in his thoughts, for quite ten minutes. He had to go to London today. Riley might rightly distrust railway engines, but they had revolutionised travel. He could visit London for the day now, when only relatively few years ago he would have had to allow three—one to drive there by carriage, one to conduct his business and recover from the journey, and the third to make his jolting way home. The world was changing. Perhaps that was why his father had hated it so much. Luke pulled himself together and went in to breakfast.

*   *   *

As Emma travelled towards Bethnal Green, shaken from side to side in a hansom cab, she had ample time to consider the advisability of her mission. Bethnal Green enjoyed, if that was the right word, a sinister, even gruesome, reputation, of which even she had heard. It was a by-word for slum living, even in those times, over-crowded, poverty-stricken, disease-ridden, lacking even elementary drainage and water supplies, a haunt of criminals. Peering through the windows of the cab, she was able to observe how the London scene outside was changing, streets growing poorer, passers-by more wretched in appearance. And there were so many people on the streets. Emma was puzzled for a while, and then thought: I suppose if their homes are so very dreadful, they are glad to be outside. A more worrying observation was the great number of young men hanging about on the street corners, outside public houses and gin-shops. She soon recognised them as being of a type of loafer that seemed to be bred in these back streets. Unemployed, dirty, resentful, they represented a real danger to someone like herself. Among them, Sam Leach probably had many friends.

At last the cab halted and the driver came to the door. He looked worried. 'Are you sure about this, ma'am?' He peered at her.

Emma pushed open the door and allowed him to help her down on to the dirty cobbles. She was in a narrow street of neglected houses, crammed together, and each one home, it seemed, to several families. Slatternly women leaned in the doorways, and unkempt children ran about barefoot. Piles of

rubbish were everywhere, and over everything
hung a miasma of decay, disease, filth and despair.
She could not, in all honesty, tell the cabbie that she
was 'sure' of what she was about, so she only asked,
'Which is Taylor's Court?'

He pointed to an opening between some houses.
'Go down through there, miss. I'd come with you, if
I could leave the horse. But I daren't, not here-
abouts. Come back and find the lamps and everything else stripped off the cab. Bless me, around
here they'd take the shoes off the horse's hoofs, if
they could!'

She knew he was trying to encourage her with an
attempt at humour, and smiled at him gratefully
before asking, with an anxiety she could not disguise, 'You won't go off and leave me here, will
you?'

'Bless you, miss, no! Only be quick about what
you want to do. This isn't a place to dawdle. Word
gets round quick. If you have trouble, just run out
of there as fast as you can!'

She promised him fervently that she would, and
gathering up her skirts, set off down the narrow
evil-smelling alley which led to Taylor's Court. The
place proved to be a small yard, surrounded on all
sides by buildings that looked as though they might
once have been warehouses, but had since been
adapted into dwellings of a sort. The ground was
covered with every kind of filth, and rooting about
in it was a pair of spotted pigs, watched by a
slovenly girl, and two half-starved children, with
pinched faces, rickety limbs and matted hair. The
stench was appalling. Emma approached the young
woman and asked after Kezia Smith.

The girl stared at her curiously, her eyes taking in every detail of Emma's gown, bonnet, shawl and shoes. 'What you want her for, then?' she asked.

'On business!' said Emma firmly.

The girl grinned, showing several gaps in her teeth. 'Well, I reckon I know what kind of business that is! You're doing well, ain't you? Fine gown and all, just like a lady!'

She took Emma for a member of the old profession, and one who had managed to do spectacularly well. Emma did not disillusion her—it was safer to be thought that than to be thought an interfering philanthropist of the kind both scorned and resented here. The girl directed her to a doorway on the far side of the yard and she set off towards it, the two children following curiously behind her, watching her with their staring, dark-circled eyes.

It took a great deal of courage to tap on the door, not knowing what she might possibly find behind it. It was opened by Leach, who at first stared at her in blank amazement, and then, to her great surprise, burst into a great roar of laughter.

'Well, got a lady come to visit us, Kezzy! Ain't that nice? Come in, Miss Meddle-in-what-don't-concern-you . . . Come in and see how other folks live!' He aimed a kick at the two children, who scattered out of his way, and held the door open wide for Emma to enter. Filled with foreboding, she went in.

It was a miserable room, though some attempt had been made to keep it clean. It held a bed, a table, one chair, and an open hearth over which a kettle hung on a hook, though there was no fire in it. A scrap of ragged cloth had been nailed over the window in lieu of proper curtains.

Kezia, white-faced, stood in the middle of the room, and whispered, 'You didn't ought to have come here, Miss Emma.' She glanced apprehensively at Leach. 'You let her go, Sam. You got what you wanted.'

'I've come to tell you, Kezia . . .' Emma said unsteadily, terrified by the shambling form of Leach, hovering at her shoulder, but determined to say what she had come to say. She could not just turn and flee ignominiously now. 'To say that you may come home, when you wish. We shall be happy to see you back with us again.'

Kezia bit her lip and looked down, a tear rolling down her cheeks. 'I can't do that, Miss Emma, not now.'

'Of course you can!' cried Emma, seizing her hand. 'You mustn't be afraid to come back just because you ran away once!'

Kezia only shook her head, and Leach chuckled, a sound more sinister than if he had sworn. 'You're too late, Miss Meddle. Show her the bit of paper, Kezzy. She's a lady and can read it, nice and proper. Had all kind of schooling, I don't doubt.'

Kezia went to a cupboard on the wall, and opened it. Emma glimpsed a motley collection of belongings, before Kezia closed it again and turned to hold out a very clean-looking and official-looking paper, which Emma took with a sinking heart. But even she was not prepared for what she saw when she unfolded it.

'Why, Kezzy—these are marriage lines!' She looked up in astonishment and dismay.

'That's right,' Leach said insolently. 'Special licence, got ourselves hitched up an hour ago. You think that because I'm a poor man, I'm a stupid one—but I ain't. That's my legal wife, over there, and neither you nor no one can take her away from me!'

'She is only fifteen! Who gave authority for this marriage?' cried Emma angrily.

'Me uncle,' said Kezia. 'Ma is dead, and our dad, he went off somewhere long ago. So my uncle, he give permission. Sam gave him a sovereign and bought him a bottle of gin.' She gave a muffled sob. 'I'm sorry, Miss Emma, I had to do it.'

'Satisfied now, are you?' asked Leach, still grinning at her. 'Then off you go. And don't come back here no more—or you'll find more than you bargained for!'

Emma made her way out of the building as in a daze, scarcely noticing the misery of Taylor's Court as she passed across it. She had not anticipated Leach outwitting her, thinking of him only as a mindless bully. In underestimating him, she had made a bad and irretrievable mistake.

When she came out at the other end of the alley into the street again, she looked for her cab, and saw with relief that it was still there. But as she went towards it, another cab suddenly turned the corner with a wild clatter of hoofs and careered full tilt towards them. The lathered horse plunged to a halt, the cab door flew open, and Luke Sheldon leapt out on to the cobbles.

'Emma! Emma—what the devil do you think you're playing at? Are you quite mad, coming down here . . .' He grasped her arm roughly, and shook her. 'You must be quite out of your mind! Thank God you are safe! Your aunt is half-distracted with worry!'

'They are married,' said Emma bleakly, and staring at him as if she neither knew nor cared whence he had sprung.

He looked startled, then asked incredulously, 'Do you mean Leach, and that girl?'

'Yes. Leach found some uncle who claimed to be her guardian, and he gave his consent in return for a sovereign and a bottle of gin. I'll never forgive myself for being so stupid as to underestimate Leach.' Her blue eyes grew hostile and seemed to take him in fully for the first time. 'And don't expect me to forgive you for the wretched part you played in this, Major Sheldon. You drove poor Kezzy away from us. Now she's in Leach's power for the rest of her life!'

'I'm sorry you feel that way about it, Emma,' Luke said stiffly, 'but I still believe I had no alternative. Of course you are distressed—and yes, it's a distressing business, so why shouldn't you be? But that girl was always going to return to Leach eventually and, in the meantime, he would have made endless trouble. You are upset and angry now, but I'm sure, in time, you will be more reasonable and see things in a different light.'

'Agree with you, is what you mean!' Emma said with a vehemence which surprised him. 'Well, I don't agree, and I never shall. You are said to be a brave man, from what Bryant told me, and the holder of a medal for your gallantry. What kind of medal do you think you deserve for today's work, Major Sheldon?'

She spoke in anger, but as soon as she saw the expression on his face, she realised that her words had struck deeper than she could have imagined, and had a whole significance for him which was unknown to her. He seemed to struggle, as if she had struck him a blow, and looked so pale that she became seriously alarmed, and whispered, 'I'm sorry, I didn't mean . . .'

But she had no time to finish. A sound of running feet from the direction of the alley caused both to look quickly behind them. Kezia burst out of the entrance in a state of wild agitation, dragging along behind her a terrified little girl of some twelve years of age, with long, unwashed fair hair and bewildered eyes, who stared up at the fine lady and gentleman as if they had been child-devouring ogres.

'It's all right,' said Kezia to the child breathlessly, and shaking the poor little soul roughly by the shoulder. 'Oh, Miss Emma . . .' she turned desperately towards them, 'I can't stay, or Sam will miss me and come after me. He only just stepped out for a minute—only see here, this is our Rosie. You will take her with you, won't you, Miss Emma? Please!' Kezia glanced fearfully over her shoulder. 'Old Bessie has been coming around while I was away, on the look-out for new girls, and she saw Rosie and took a fancy to her, her being yellow-haired and all, what gents like . . . She said she'd be back, and I know she will. Miss Emma, sir . . .' She turned a despairing face towards Luke. 'I don't want our Rosie to end up like me. She's a good girl and won't cause no trouble. Here, Rosie . . .' She pushed the panic-stricken child into Emma's arms, and turning, fled back down the alley towards Taylor's Court.

'Don't be afraid!' said Emma quickly to the child, putting her arms round the trembling little body. She stood up and turned to face Luke, who watched, stony-faced. The little girl cowered against her skirts, obviously already having reason to be afraid of men, whoever they were. Keeping her arms wrapped protectively about the child, Emma demanded, 'Well, Luke Sheldon? You have successfully disposed of Kezzy. Now here is Rose. What do you suggest I do? You heard the future planned for her. Perhaps you think that also a necessary evil?'

Luke glanced briefly at the child in her arms. 'Take her to the workhouse!' he said curtly, but for all its brusqueness, his voice lacked its usual assurance.

'To the workhouse?' cried Emma. 'Is that the best you can suggest? Even if it were a suitable place, which is isn't, how long would the workhouse keep her?'

'Until it found her some employment. Confound it, Emma, the workhouse exists to look after the poor; let it do its job!'

Unexpectedly the child spoke, in a thin, quavering, but surprisingly resolute little voice. 'I ain't going to the work'us. The rats gets you there. You gets sick and spits blood. You has to get up when it's dark and scrub them floors. I ain't going!'

'This is ridiculous!' Luke exclaimed angrily, but Emma sensed that his anger was not directed either at her or at Rose. He saw that the cabman was taking a lively interest in all of this, and added irritably, 'Put the child in the cab and let's get out of here. We can discuss it in peace somewhere civilised. Emma, this does not mean we are taking the child so that you may keep her!' he added threateningly.

'No, Luke,' said Emma, pushing Rose into the cab. 'Of course not.'

He glowered at her suspiciously.

'Not another one!' exclaimed Mrs McGraw at the sight of Rose, and vanished into the kitchen in high dudgeon.

'Explain it all to my aunt, Luke,' Emma begged him, 'and I'll take Rose down to the kitchen and get Mrs McGraw to give her some bread and milk. Come along, Rose.' She took the child's hand and led her downstairs.

The housekeeper accepted Rose's presence reluctantly, but when the child was seated at the kitchen table and devouring the bread and milk like a famished little animal, she thawed and observed, 'Poor little thing. It's a sinful business.'

'Yes, it is,' said Emma. 'Yet every time I talk of doing something about it, or try to do something about it, I am treated as if I am the one to have done something dreadful. Why is it that I should be at fault?'

Mrs McGraw looked embarrassed. 'See here, Miss Emma, you've a good, kind heart. But, well, you're not even a married woman. You shouldn't be getting involved in such things.'

'I wish someone would explain to me why not!' she replied sharply.

Mrs McGraw glanced at the child and lowered

her voice conspiratorially. 'Look, miss, it's not my business to speak of these things, not to a young lady. But there's things as a married women does, has to do in the line of duty, you might say, in order for little ones to come into the world. I'm not saying a decent woman enjoys that sort of thing, of course, but you have to put up with it. It's nature. But, well, men see it different. It's not their fault. It's their natures, they have . . . needs.'

'Mrs McGraw,' interrupted Emma, 'I trust that you, too, are not about to tell me that all this is a necessary evil?'

'No, miss!' exclaimed the housekeeper, affronted. 'I'm trying to tell you as best I can, how it goes—men and women, I mean. You're not a married lady, and you don't understand men. I've been married, and I do!' she concluded with some grimness.

Emma left Rose in her charge, and returned upstairs. When she opened the door of the drawing-room, she came unexpectedly upon Luke and her aunt deep in some discussion. Both looked up startled as she entered, and Mrs Somerton exclaimed, 'Dear me, yes, indeed . . .' and vanished out of the room for no apparent reason.

Emma was past caring what her aunt and Luke Sheldon were plotting. She felt suddenly quite exhausted, utterly drained of all will and energy. She pulled off her bonnet, which she had not yet had time to do, and threw it on a chair. The rough treatment loosened the pins that secured her chignon of fair hair, and it tumbled down in loose locks around her face. She let it remain, and sat down with a dejected bump. She had lost Kezzy. Momentarily occupied with Rose, she had almost forgotten poor Kezia. But Kezzy was out of her reach for ever, condemned to a life with the brutish Leach, selling herself on street corners until her looks were so destroyed that no one would pay for her favours any longer. When that happened, Leach would disappear to find pastures new, and Kezia would be left to gin and the gutter. Before she could stop herself, two large tears rolled down her cheeks. She put her hands over her face and sobbed.

'Emma . . .' Luke exclaimed in some consternation, not prepared for this sign of feminine weakness in his resolute companion. He came and knelt by her chair in an awkward but sympathetic attitude, and urged, 'Don't give way, not now. You did your very best, and if you didn't succeed, it's because you attempted the impossible, not because you didn't try. Don't cry over it, for goodness' sake, because I haven't the slightest notion what to do about it! Female tears are quite outside my ken. Shall I call Mrs Somerton?'

He caught at her hands and tried to pull them gently from her face, but she pushed him away and mumbled furiously, 'Go away, go away! I'm all right!'

Luke seemed relieved at this display of fighting spirit. He stood up and walked away to take up his favourite attitude, leaning against the mantelshelf. Reassured that he did not have a hysterical female on his hands, he had regained his usual assurance. 'Emma, I didn't support you in any of this, because I thought you were behaving rashly and I haven't changed that opinion. But I do admire you for your tenacity, and for fighting for your corner in the way you have, if you'll excuse a very masculine expression!' He smiled at her. 'You're a very courageous woman, and I want you to know that you have my respect.'

'Thank you,' said Emma, thrusting her handkerchief away. 'But I'd rather your admiration and respect were demonstrated more positively. Will you allow me to keep Rose?'

Conflicting emotions fought on Luke's face. Eventually he sighed, and said, 'Yes, you may keep Rose.'

'Thank you!' said Emma again, but with much more warmth.

'That's the first and last time I give my permission!' he said sharply. 'You are not filling this house with deserving cases, no matter how pathetic!'

'I don't want to fill this house. Major Sheldon, Luke . . .' Emma leaned forward eagerly. 'What I want to do is start a proper home for girls like Kezia and Rose. Girls who are very young and either haven't . . . or who are young enough to change their ways. You own a house in Forbes Street, next to this one, which stands empty, and is just what I am looking for. Mr Sneadie says you don't mean to sell it. If you are looking for a new tenant, will you rent it to me? I have money of my own—twenty thousand pounds. I want to found a Rescue Home for girls.'

Incredulity, amazement and horror crossed his handsome face in quick succession. 'Are you quite out of your mind? If I lease that house to you, I shall be associated with the whole lunatic project! Can you imagine what will be said when word gets about among my friends and acquaintances that Luke Sheldon is scouring London, looking for fallen women to rescue?'

'What is more important, your friends' jokes —over what will be a nine-day wonder—or the safety of young girls? As soon as they see the project is a serious one, they will accept it, and forget about your ownership of the property.'

'No, they won't!' he said simply. 'I absolutely refuse.'

She saw that he was adamant, and this was not the time to pursue the subject. 'Well, I am grateful that you have agreed to help Rose, and I'm sure you won't regret your decision.'

'I'm not so sure,' he muttered. 'I'm afraid I may live to regret it very much.'

He was right, but neither of them then realised it.

'Emma,' he said briskly, pushing himself away from the mantelshelf, 'there are a number of things I should like to discuss with you further, but this is hardly the moment. Will you allow me to call again, perhaps at the end of the week?'

She was surprised that he should ask permission, and unnerved by this sudden display of good manners in a man who seemed usually to behave much as he wanted. 'Of course,' she said cautiously. 'I shall have Rose all tidied up by then, and you'll see a great difference.'

'I'm not intending to call and see Rose, but you,' he said crossly.

Mrs Somerton bustled back at that point, and Sheldon took his leave.

*   *   *

Emma was much taken up with Rose for the rest of the week, so much so that she quite forgot Luke's promised visit until he appeared. He caught her unawares, not dressed to receive visits at all, in an old gown of tartan cotton, a pair of white over-sleeves for protection, and an apron.

'There!' she exclaimed hastily, pulling off the apron and oversleeves and stuffing both articles under a cushion. 'I'm so sorry, but I was cutting Rose's hair.'

'I am put in my place,' he said heavily, surveying her flushed face framed by untidy wisps of fair hair. 'I thought you might have remembered that I was coming. Or is Rose more important?'

'No, indeed, but you see . . .' Emma lowered her voice, 'she has head-lice. We've tried carbolic and it helped a little, but I'm afraid the only thing for it is to cut all her hair off and have her wear a little mob-cap till it grows again.'

'Emma!' Luke said with considerable impatience. 'Am I to be allowed to say what I have come to say, or am I to listen to Rose's tribulations all afternoon?'

'I'm so sorry, please do go on,' she told him, and sat down and folded her hands in her lap. 'There, I am all attention.'

'Thank you,' he said sarcastically. He took his place by the mantelshelf, then thought better of it, and began to pace restlessly up and down. 'The other day, I told you how much I have come to admire you—and respect you. You have courage and principle—and you're also dashed pretty!' he added frankly.

Emma flushed, both angered and taken aback.

'Have you been drinking, Major Sheldon?' she asked suspiciously.

'Of course I damn well haven't!' he almost shouted at her. 'Emma, I believe you are the most aggravating female I ever encountered. No!' He held up his hand. 'You are diverting me from my speech, and I had it all rehearsed. Miss Wainwright, I retired from the army in 1842 for reasons which need not detain us now. I had come into my inheritance, and a sadly run down sort of inheritance it was. I have worked very hard these past five years to put matters right, and I have now reached the stage where I believe I can justly feel quite proud of what I've done. I feel I can now look ahead, to the next stage, as it were. So much for me. Now for you.'

Emma raised her eyebrows.

'I believe, Emma, that you need someone to look after you.'

'If you mean by that, that I need a man to do my thinking for me, I assure you I do not!' she told him with some asperity.

'Of course you do not, but you do need a man to protect you from the results of the extraordinary notions you dream up!' was the less than gallant response.' 'In short, you need a husband, Emma, and I need a wife; or perhaps, I should say, Hill House needs a mistress to take it in hand. I haven't time for it. That is why I am making you a proposal of marriage.' He paused, and receiving no reply, added a little awkwardly, 'I dare say it sounds a little odd, our being only slightly acquainted, after all, but it seems to me you might do very well. I suppose I could set about making love to you, if you insist on it, but in the circumstances I expect we should both of us find it a tiresome procedure, and it's better that I just tell you frankly what is on my mind.'

There was a long silence. Then Emma, pale-faced, whispered, 'I see. Is this, by any chance, what you were discussing with my aunt when I came in unexpectedly the other day?'

'I told her of my intention, yes—and asked her if she had any objection. She seems to stand as your guardian.'

Emma got up and smoothed down her skirts. 'If I agree to marry you, will you give me the Forbes Street house to be a Rescue Home for my girls?'

He looked stunned. 'What's that?'

'The Forbes Street house. You are a military man, so let us use military terms. We are about to conclude a truce, you and I. My terms are that you let me found a Rescue Home. What are your terms?' She tilted her chin and stared at him with her clear blue eyes.

'Ah . . .' He scowled at her. 'My terms? Let's see. Very well, you shall have the Forbes Street house for eighteen months. If, at the end of that time, the project has not prospered, you will abandon it. Also, if there are serious scenes of violence at any time during the eighteen months, you will give it up. I don't want to be a widower.'

'And if it prospers, I may continue to run the Home?'

'If you can point to positive success, yes.'

'I shall be successful!' said Emma confidently.

'Mmn . . .' he said drily. 'Other than that, Emma, I have no particular requirements, other than that I should, of course, like to have a son.'

'Yes, of course, I understand that,' Emma said quietly.

'Then am I to assume, Miss Wainwright, that subject to the approval of your aunt, we are engaged?'

He had actually agreed to give her the Forbes Street house! He would let her run the Home! She could hardly believe it, and afraid that he might change his mind, exclaimed, 'Yes!'

It was not until the word left her mouth and could not be recalled that she realised she had just agreed to marry this man, to spend the rest of her life with him, to share his world, his life, his aspirations —and his bed.

CHAPTER FIVE

LUKE WAS prompt in keeping to his word concerning the Forbes Street house. Sneadie arrived the following day with the agreement drawn up and which he had already signed. Emma wrote her name with a flourish, and the Forbes Street house was hers for a period of eighteen months from the date of signing. The Rescue Home existed, even if it was as yet only an empty building. But, in her mind's eye, she saw it already as it would be.

She was touched that Luke had acted so promptly, because she knew that in his heart and mind he was opposed to her whole scheme, and she respected him for not dragging his feet over their agreement. However, she recognised that he would expect her to be equally prompt in fulfilling her part of their bargain—and so he was.

'I have put up the banns, Emma; you have no objection? We can be married at the beginning of next month.'

'I . . . Yes, as you wish . . .' Emma stammered. Three weeks away. Only three weeks! Panic enveloped her.

'And how does your project progress?' he asked affably. 'Is the Forbes Street house about to be taken over by a horde of painted jades, each crying out that she has seen the light?'

They were seated in Mrs Somerton's drawing-room with the tea tray between them. Her aunt had left them with an obscure excuse, but really, thought Emma, she might just as well have stayed. With or without a chaperon, this engaged couple was impeccably behaved. Not a sentimental glance, not a surreptitious squeeze of the fingers, not a term of endearment passed between them. Luke sat opposite her, looking debonair and relaxed. Emma wished she could feel the same ease of mind.

'It progresses well enough,' she said with forced brightness. She overlooked the jibe. He had made several similar remarks, and she suspected that he meant to tease her. 'I am seeking a competent woman to be resident matron, and I believe I have found someone, a woman of strict principles, but neither a fanatic nor a prude. I hope she will agree to come.'

'So long as she is as tough as old boots, I dare say she'll survive,' said Luke with asperity. This time he was rewarded with a warning snap in the blue eyes which hitherto had been watching him with some apprehension.

'I'm not looking for a prison wardress!' Emma said crossly. 'It's a voluntary home. The girls will be free to leave. Will you have another dish of tea?' she added politely.

'No, thank you. I've drunk two, and to be honest, I dislike the stuff. When we are married, you will not be expecting me to appear at four o'clock of an afternoon expressing a preference for Indian or China, I hope?'

'No,' said Emma gloomily. Involuntarily her eyes strayed to the calendar on the wall.

Luke sat down the plate on which lay the crumbs from the slice of Mrs McGraw's special seed cake,

which he had been gallantly masticating for some
five minutes. 'By the way, I believe I can be of some
little help to you. Or rather, Sneadie can.' He
marked her surprised expression and twitched an
eyebrow at her. 'You need some means of finding
suitable girls, don't you? You don't propose to go
out in the streets at night and trawl them up with a
net?'

'Well,' admitted Emma, 'I hadn't exactly
planned how . . .'

'Mmn. I fancied as much. Well, Sneadie has
contacts amongst the magistracy, and in particular
at Bow Street magistrates' court. He has asked that
any unfortunate who appears there and might seem
to offer hope of redemption be referred to you.'

'Oh,' said Emma awkwardly, 'that's very kind of
you, and Mr Sneadie.'

'I must be honest, Emma,' he went on. 'I have a
little request of my own. I have asked Sneadie if he
can trace one particular girl, of whom I know, and
who I think might well be glad of a chance to quit
her present life. She is, I believe, unsuited to it.'

Emma knew her features must have frozen, and
tried not to show her feelings. As Mrs McGraw had
put it, 'men had needs', and Luke, she must suppose, was no different from any other. He was
thirty-seven and a bachelor, so it was to be expected. She wondered how wide an acquaintance
among ladies of easy virtue he had.

'You needn't pull such prim faces at me,' he said
calmly. 'I met this girl very fleetingly, if in rather
compromising circumstances. However, I do
assure you that nothing passed between us of which
any wife, let alone betrothed, need be jealous.'

Emma picked up the teapot and determinedly began to pour out for herself, though it splashed a little.

'The trouble is,' he continued, placing the tips of his fingers together, 'that I don't know much about her, not even having seen her face properly. All I know is that she is called Violet.'

The teapot crashed down, and Luke jumped up and snatched a napkin to swab up the boiling liquid before it tipped into Emma's lap.

'I—I'm so sorry . . .' Emma stuttered. 'I can't think what made me so clumsy.'

Luke! It had been Luke in that stuffy little room at Bessie's! It was a discovery so horrifying that Emma's brain quite refused to function for some moments, and she sat staring at the tea and the wet napkin and Luke, as if none of these had any reality. Then, as the significance of the information flooded over her, she turned first hot and then cold and stared at him with complete dismay.

'I apologise for upsetting you,' Luke said solicitously, 'but I do think that a husband and wife ought to be perfectly frank with one another, don't you, Emma?' His dark eyes rested on her pale face with enquiry, and he waited for her answer.

'I suppose—yes,' she said faintly.

He waited for a moment as if he expected her to add something else, and when she did not, got to his feet and made his farewells.

On Sunday morning he escorted the ladies to Matins to hear the first banns read. At the words, 'spinster of this parish', Aunt Rosamond bent her head to her niece and offered playfully, 'But not for long, Emma dear!'

Emma sat rigid in her pew, but no rescuer leapt forward to offer 'just cause or impediment'.

'One down, two to go,' said Luke calmly, on quitting the church.

'Um,' said his intended in a small, tense voice.

There must have been something wrong with the calendar that year. The days practically flew by with indecent haste. None of the usual delays offered themselves. The dressmaker stitched the wedding gown without a single alteration and at record speed, thanks to the newly-invented patent automatic sewing-machine, which replaced a whole team of seamstresses. It fitted perfectly at the first try. Matching lace was to be had in abundance at the first haberdashers' entered, extra supplies conveyed in a trice from Nottingham by the railway. Even the milliner brought round the perfectly trimmed bonnet a full week before the wedding. Emma felt she was being dragged along by inexorable Fate, and the arrival of the Machine Age.

To combat her growing feelings of panic, and to keep up her spirits, she spent as much time as possible organising the Forbes Street home. The resident matron had agreed to come, and she and Emma set about ordering furniture, curtains and bedding. If the bride showed more enthusiasm for this shopping than for choosing her trousseau, Mrs Somerton tactfully did not remark on it.

In the evenings Emma walked round to Forbes Street, put the key in the lock and made a private tour of the house. It filled her with tremendous

pride and satisfaction to see the rooms gradually fill
with furniture and the Home spring to life, even if it
was, as yet without residents. Looking into each
room with its neat little beds, the kitchen with its
array of brand-new pots and pans, and the chairs
waiting in rows either side of the dining-table, she
could really believe in it all at last.

It would not be easy. She had worked already
among the poor and knew that they were seldom
grateful, usually demanding, and took a perverse
pleasure in finding fault. Yet most were possessed
of indomitable courage, limitless invention and a
cheerful humour which made light of the most
dreadful circumstances. She was looking forward
to having the girls there in Forbes Street, at last.
They would nearly all be very young, little more
than children. They would be noisy, unco-
operative, undisciplined and a problem in every
way. Some would have horrendous personal histor-
ies. In all, their young lives would have been per-
verted and warped. Yet Emma could not wait to
meet each and every one of them.

She pushed open a door to one of the empty
rooms and went to perch on the window-sill. It gave
on to the side of the house and the quiet, green view
of the Quaker cemetery. Those worthy Quakers
slumbering below would have supported her, of
that she was sure. She felt they watched her with a
benevolent, if critical eye. She would not be human
if she were not also a little daunted by her task. It
would be nice to share the responsibility with someone. Aunt Rosamond was there, of course, armed
with the sermon notes. But a stronger personality
would have been useful.

The obvious person would have been Luke. But although he had agreed to the existence of the Home, he continued to express his reservations and could hardly be counted as support. Emma leaned against the window-frame and turned her mind to him. The wedding was only a few days away. Her heart sank within her at the thought. Still, a bargain was a bargain. He had given her the Forbes Street house and, in return, she would preside at his table and bear his child. For her, the prospect was far more daunting than any problems envisaged in the Home.

She forced herself to think about Luke, to concentrate on him, and—as always happened when she did this—panic formed a knot in the pit of her stomach. She tried to picture him in Mrs Somerton's drawing-room—elegant, courteous, a perfect gentleman. But the image that kept returning was that of Luke in the stableyard, wrestling for command of the great red horse, stripped to the waist and sweating. The picture flickered, like that of a magic lantern, to another. Not an image, exactly, but a voice and a touch, and another brief wrestling-match—on a bed at Bessie's.

'I can't do it,' said Emma aloud, leaning her burning forehead on the cool glass of the panes. 'I can't go through with it.'

But you must! replied a stern voice in her head. She gave herself a shake. Yes, she must. Besides, people got married all the time, and survived. Even Aunt Rosamond and her Henry must have had their moments of passion—although it took some imagining. Besides, most women would have counted Major Sheldon a very good catch. Emma's eye ran round the room. He owned this house, and a great deal more. He was wealthy, and handsome, he had a distinguished military record . . . she ought to consider herself fortunate.

'He's a *man*!' she said gloomily to the empty room. And not just a man—but an uncompromisingly, directly, disconcertingly physical embodiment of maleness. She had not the slightest notion what she was going to do about it.

So it was that proceedings went on their relentless way until at last the fatal and, in truth, dreaded moment arrived when Emma found herself all alone with Luke in the shadowy, candlelit bedroom at Hill House on her wedding night.

Her situation was in many ways unusual. She was not entirely ignorant of what would be asked of her, but perhaps, she thought ruefully, it might almost have been better if she had been. Her experience of relationships between men and women had all been of the ignoble kind. Sex, to Emma, was an animal urge which drove men to behave in the most sordid manner. Sometimes it dressed itself up and presented itself with tawdry beauty, like one of Old Bessie's jades. But what it came down to was a sweaty grappling of naked, panting bodies on stained sheets.

Of love, the tender emotion, she knew absolutely nothing, and it was not surprising that, without its gentle flame to inspire her, the sight of Luke in his nightshirt and dressing-gown turned her body to stone and seemed to freeze the very blood in her veins. Suddenly he was not a bridegroom or the husband at whose side she proposed to walk through life, but the embodiment of everything she meant to fight against at Forbes Street. She stood stock still in the middle of the room and watched Luke walk towards hers as Katherine Howard might have watched the approach of the public executioner.

He came to a halt before her, smiled, cupped her face in his hands and stooping, lightly kissed her cold lips, and asked, 'Well, Mrs Sheldon?'

Well, what? What on earth was she supposed to do or say? What did he expect? Hardly that she would fling both arms passionately round his neck, crying out 'My own one!' like the heroine of a romantic melodrama. Theirs was not that sort of coming together. But he surely expected some reaction.

Emma drew a deep breath, and forced herself to speak. 'Luke . . .' The fact that she had managed to say his name emboldened her. 'Luke, please listen . . .' She began to speak faster, the words tumbling out and tripping over each other. 'I dare say you are . . . that is, you have done this sort of thing before, but, you understand, I have not.'

He looked mildly puzzled and amused. 'I assume that, my dear. I was quite prepared to accept that white wedding gown for what it purported to be!'

'Yes, I know, but . . .' Emma hurried on, 'I suppose you expect me to kiss you, and I really don't think I can. I know it must sound quite stupid.'

'No.' He stared down at her thoughtfully. Then he asked in a brisk, practical tone which reassured her immensely, 'Do you want me to leave? I will, if you prefer. I dare say you are tired, so we can postpone all this till another occasion.'

But that would be simply to put off the inevitable, never a sensible course of action. Besides, his kindly-meant offer made her feel ashamed, because she knew it would mean disappointment for him, and to take advantage of it seemed paltry.

'No.' She shook her head. 'I'd much rather you stayed, and—and we got it all over with.'

'I'm not a machine!' he said, suddenly sounding annoyed. 'I never contemplated simply marching in here and just leaping on you. I've been entertaining rather pleasurable daydreams about my wedding night. You seem to view the whole procedure like a visit to the dentist!'

'Oh, Luke, I'm sorry!' Emma cried desperately, thrusting both hands into her long fair hair and clasping her head. She whirled round away from him and stood motionless.

After a moment he said gently, 'Emma?' When he received no reply he came closer, close enough to touch her, and she shivered. He slid one arm round her, pulling her back against his chest, and murmured into her ear, 'Come, Emma, where's that resolute spirit? I never knew you cry off from anything. It won't be such an ordeal, I promise.'

The whispering voice, something in it, a husky note, a vibration of suppressed passion, the possessive touch of his hand on her breast—suddenly she stood again in the darkened room at Bessie's and it was all horribly familiar: the touch, the whisper, and the invitation in both, were the same. This was the same man, and seeking the same thing. Old Adam reigned supreme, after all.

Emma spun round, white-faced, and struck away

his embracing arm as it tightened about her, and shouted vehemently, 'Don't touch me! You are all the same!'

She saw his expression change, the thick black brows meeting threateningly, and the wide mouth narrowing to a thin, hard line. His voice came harshly, 'Stop this nonsense, Emma!'

'It's true!' she shouted at him defiantly.

Luke muttered something beneath his breath, turned and walked quickly away across the room, and threw himself down in an armchair.

Emma hardly knew what she was doing. Her brain was in turmoil and her nerves alive with jangling awareness. She felt a great anger surge in her, because by his attitude and expression he seemed to suggest that her feelings were nothing but hysterical foolishness, and that he made no effort to understand what inspired them. Yet, she told herself, she knew him for what he really was —which was a regular at Bessie's, who now, beneath a civilised veneer and with the sanction of a wedding ring, came to her for the same reason as he had previously turned to Lily.

'Don't treat me as though I had done something wrong and you were without fault!' she accused him. 'You told me that you believed husband and wife should be honest with one another, but perhaps you have not been quite honest with me, Lucius Sheldon. Are there no corners of your past behaviour of which you are not a little ashamed?'

Very quietly he said, 'Of many things, and of one in particular.'

Something in the way he said it silenced her. After a moment during which he seemed sunk in thought and almost to have forgotten her, he stirred and shook himself and said more briskly, 'What is it you want? A salacious description of my amorous career? I'm afraid I haven't led a life of hedonistic debauchery, if that's what you suspect. You will perhaps be disappointed, but I've never even kept a mistress. My encounters with women have always been temporary, and as required.'

'Women like Kezia, you mean!' Emma threw at him.

'Not literally off the streets, good Lord, no! That sort of thing invites a dose of the pox. No, I always went to reputable establishments where the girls were clean. Nor has my taste ever run to thirteen-year-old children. I have always paid for the services of grown women.' Suddenly there was a taunting look in his dark eyes. 'But you already know that, don't you?'

She gasped, and flushed crimson. He knew!

'It was you that night, wasn't it, at Bessie's?' he asked.

'Did you know all along?' she whispered.

He shook his dark head. 'No. I only saw the girl running away. I would have gone after her—you —but I had Lily and Bessie hanging on to me like gaolers. I hadn't forgotten the incident, because it was so odd. But I didn't connect you with "Violet" until that morning in Bethnal Green when Kezia mentioned Old Bessie. A bell rang, very muffled and faint, it's true, in my mind. After that, something nagged away in the back of my brain. It took me a little while to make the connection—but eventually I did.' He paused, but receiving no comment from her, added, 'I suppose it's no use my asking for a sensible explanation of how you came to be there?'

'The explanation is very simple,' said Emma tersely. 'I looked in at the door and there was no one about and I was curious . . . so I just stepped in, only meaning to look round very quickly. But first Bessie came in, and then, when I wanted to leave, I heard people coming—some men—and I had to hide.'

She waited for his response, and to her surprise he put both hands over his face and muttered through his fingers, 'I don't believe it!'

'But it's true!' she protested. 'I know it was foolish and wrong, but that's what I did.'

Luke took his hands away from his face. 'Yes, I know it's true, Emma, but only you . . . Violet!' The name exploded from his lips with such force that Emma nearly jumped out of her skin. 'Why "Violet", for heaven's sake? It's such a confounded awful name!'

'It was all I could think of,' she confessed miserably.

Luke slapped both hands down on the arms of his chair and pushed himself to his feet. 'Emma, come over here to me. Yes, yes, come on, walk over here, towards me.'

Nervously she obeyed. He gave a little nod and took both her damp palms in his. 'Now listen to me. I am an ordinary man, which means that I am neither a saint nor a monster, but an odd sort of mixed-up creature like a gypsy's cur. A fellow like me has aspirations and ambitions which he hopes he may fulfil and knows he may not—and he has all kinds of failings which he wished he hadn't, and knows that he has. Do you follow me?'

She nodded. 'Yes, Luke, I think so.'

'So, Emma, we shall not spend our wedding night trading our unhappier secrets, but go straight away to bed as bride and groom are supposed to do—and you are to stop looking at me as if I were Attila the Hun!'

He saw her mouth quiver and almost, if not quite, turn up at the corners. 'Yes, Luke.'

His own swarthy cheeks creased into a grin. He twitched the bow securing the neck of her long-sleeved nightgown, and said, 'This is a very pretty piece of linen, but superfluous. I really wish you would take it off.'

You seem to be wearing a devil of a lot of clothes . . . echoed the voice in her memory. Whether she was Emma or Violet, perhaps it made little difference to him, after all. Yet she had to trust him, if the future was not to be marred by a wretched fear of each encounter.

'If you want,' she said uncertainly. 'Only, I wish you would put out the candle first.'

He turned without a word and went to the candle, stretching out his hand and pinching out the flame.

Emma pulled her nightgown over her head and scrambled into bed in a great rush, thankful for the enveloping blackness, and with her heart beating like a drum. She burrowed into the feather mattress like a crab trying to dig itself frantically out of sight of a predator on the sandy sea floor. She could hear Luke moving about, and then the sheets were jerked, the bedstead creaked and he slid into the bed beside her.

He turned towards her and pulled her gently into his embrace, and as their bodies touched she re-alised with shock that he, too, was naked, and she recoiled automatically with a gasp. But he held her fast and whispered into her ear, 'No, Emma, there's nothing to be afraid of . . .'

She felt herself relax in his arms and half-curious, half-fearful, at first submitted and then slowly and hesitantly began to respond to his advances, so that they travelled together on the journey of mutual discovery to its goal of union of body and desire.

When, at long last, she fell asleep, it was in Luke's arms, and when she awoke the next morn-ing, she turned her head to see his on the pillow beside her. Asleep, he looked oddly vulnerable. He had pushed the pillow into a heap and wrapped his arms round it. His black hair was tousled and he was unshaven and untidy, and she noticed for the first time that he had long black eyelashes that lay lightly on the skin. Emma took her hand from beneath the warm bedclothes and touched his black curls, and he wriggled, turning his face into the crumpled pillow like a child which does not want to be woken, and she could not suppress a wave of tenderness towards him.

Emma lay back, staring up at the ceiling, and thought: Well, then, I am a married woman. A beam of sunlight pierced the curtains and she lay and watched it travel across the room, and waited for Luke to wake.

Thanks in large part to the enquiries of Mr Sneadie, the first half-dozen girls were installed at Forbes Street, and the whole project really was truly under way at last. Emma allowed herself the luxury of a small glow of pride, even though the way ahead was obviously going to be pitted with obstacles. Almost at once they lost two of their protégées, who took themselves off, declaring that they preferred 'a bit of fun' to being 'cooped up here in this mausoleum'. But two more were quickly found to replace them, and the Home flourished.

The problems that beset them were both foreseeable and unforeseeable. They ranged from the delicate matter of medical inspection of new arrivals—upon which Luke insisted, and Emma had to admit he was right—to the difficulty of persuading the girls to sleep at night in single rooms. All of them came from large families living in overcrowded accommodation, and had never in their entire lives spent a whole night all alone. They were terrified of the dark, and migrated like swallows to nestle together all in one or two beds, leaving half the rooms untenanted. Their language was colourful and, at times, hair-raising. One was discovered to be pregnant, and special arrangements had to be made for her lying-in, and a charity found to take the infant when it should arrive. Originally, Emma had set her face against taking any girl found to be in the family way, as they simply had no means of coping with infants. But, in this case, she could not bring herself to send the girl, only fourteen, to the workhouse to give birth. After that, they were more careful in selecting their guests.

Both setting up the Home and buying all that was needed, and maintaining it afterwards, to say nothing of feeding healthy young women, took a great deal of money. Emma, as so many other charitable workers before her, found that much of her time was now spent making calls on wealthy and influential citizens and begging their support, both moral and financial. There was no doubt that her married name was invaluable in this context, for it was doubtful, had she been single, that any of these people would have agreed even to receive her, much less discuss with her such a delicate subject.

She kept Luke informed of their progress, or occasionally of their lack of it, and he listened and made occasional comment, but did not otherwise interfere. He still did not approve, that she knew, but at least he did not object.

Emma had not only removed herself and her possessions to Hill House, her new home, but she had taken Rose along as well. She had grown very fond of the child, and was reluctant to leave her. Besides, it hardly seemed fair on Mrs Somerton. Luke's agreement had been necessary to the transfer, of course, and she had asked him with some timidity if he would mind having Rose under his roof.

At first, he said crossly, 'She will get in the way—tease the dogs and frighten the horses, swing on the trees and break the branches.'

'She's a little girl,' objected Emma, bridling. 'She won't swing on trees.'

'All children swing on trees,' said Luke. 'I did. I was beaten for it regularly.'

Emma cast him a thoughtful look. He had never spoken to her of his childhood, but instinctively she sensed that it had not been happy.

But as she sought about for some argument in Rose's favour, he unexpectedly said, 'Well, it is better for a child to grow up in the country than in city soot and fog.'

Emma interpreted that as giving his permission, and Rose arrived in their midst at Hill House. The child was amazed at the sight of so much open space and 'things growing', to say nothing of 'real cows and sheep, and that'. She immediately took a great fancy to Samson, Luke's springer spaniel, and child and dog set up one of those special relationships that only a child and a dog can have.

So Emma divided her time between Hill House and Forbes Street, and bewailed the fact that the days were just not long enough for all she had to do in them. Luke ran his estate and saw to his horses, and conducted his financial affairs. Rose, with Samson, pottered about the house and grounds, falling out of the hayloft and into the horse-trough, and tearing and muddying her gown and shoes.

From this it can be seen that Rose was not a well-behaved child: Luke's instincts had been right. Frail in appearance, once she got over her fears, she proved a real street-Arab. She had roamed freely about pavements from infancy, and knew no discipline other than if people swore at her or struck her. Since it quickly became apparent that Luke would no more permit anyone to strike a child than he would have flown to the moon, Rose was not slow to exploit the situation and consider herself given *carte blanche* to do as she wished without fear of punishment. Eventually, it was Emma who took Rose aside and scolded her severely. Rose sniffed and looked pathetic. Emma nursed a bad conscience all day, and late that night could not retire to bed herself without going to peep at Rose and see if she was all right. Opening the door of the child's little room, she found that the incorrigible girl had smuggled Samson in there. Child and dog were curled up together, Rose's thin arms wrapped firmly round her canine friend's neck.

Samson waggled his stumpy tail, but gave Emma a somewhat old-fashioned look, as if to say, 'Now this little one is in my special care, and you are not to interfere or come scolding again!'

Luke, who understood better than Emma the bond between a lonely child and a dog, received Emma's complaint about this with equanimity.

'It can't do any harm. Old Samson won't bite her. He's the silliest dog I ever owned, and the worst gun-dog.'

Emma began to feel that what with being newly married and needing to think about a husband, and having to be mistress of Hill House, to cope with the many problems of Forbes Street, and to keep an eye on Rose, she needed as many arms as an Indian deity, and a supernatural ability to be in two places at once.

It still seemed very odd to share her life with a husband. His behaviour veered between the autocratic and the careless. He had an uncompromising masculine viewpoint on life, and was as obstinate as a mule. He got up with the sun and went out, and came back at breakfast-time having ridden miles or done half a day's work. This, he explained, dated from his Indian days, 'when early morning was the best time'. He was incorrigibly untidy, and walked in muddy top-boots over newly-polished parquet. He ate, to Emma's eye, an enormous quantity of beef and mutton. He had a fondness for nursery puddings, like bread-and-butter and jam roly-poly. Served up meringues, Emma's attempt to enliven Hill House's stodgy menus, he demolished the delicate dessert with a fork, demanding suspiciously, 'What the devil is this?'

Unused himself to having a lady in the house, his language often caused Emma to stop her ears. They argued freely and frequently, but though energetically out-spoken, Luke only rarely lost his temper outright, and—as his tolerance of Rose's naughtiness showed—could be unexpectedly kind. Yet he had what Emma soon began to call his 'dark days'. For no reason that she could understand, he would wake up in a black humour and stride about all day in moody silence, as if he brooded over some insoluble problem and could not get it out of his system. It was useless, when he was in this frame of mind, to try and discuss anything with him, as he was surly and monosyllabic. These episodes usually ended with his shutting himself up in the study with the brandy-bottle, and spending the night asleep in the chair there, dead drunk. This was all the more strange, because at other times he was not a heavy drinker.

She puzzled over it, and got alternatively cross and alarmed, without coming any nearer to solving the riddle. She began to think that if she had begun this marriage knowing less about men than she thought she did, then she knew less about Luke than most—and the longer she knew him, the less she understood him.

Emma had forgotten the old Greek adage: To admit you know nothing is the beginning of wisdom.

CHAPTER SIX

EVEN WITH so much to occupy her mind and her days, Emma could not forget Kezia. Kezzy occupied an especially sorrowful corner in her heart, because the girl had been the first she had taken from the streets, marking in some ways her first success as well as her most spectacular failure. It was hard not to feel responsible for Kezia's sad return to her old ways. To underestimate Leach, Emma thought in bitter self-reproach, had been a case of bad negligence on her part, and she ached to be able to remedy it.

Accordingly, one day Emma took a cab and went to Taylor's Court. She had steeled herself to discover almost any horror there, but when the door was opened, it was by a complete stranger, a brawny woman with straggling greasy hair.

In reply to Emma's enquiries, she said that she had never heard of anyone called Leach or a girl named Kezia. She and her family had moved to Bethnal Green only three weeks earlier from Whitechapel, and she had no idea who had lived in the place 'afore us'.

Emma was able to see into the room, which now presented an even more miserable appearance than when Kezzy had lived there with Leach. At least Kezia had kept it clean, but now it was utterly filthy, and stank of rancid air and unwashed bodies. To Emma's distress, on a heap of sacking in the corner and covered only by a tattered blanket lay a little boy, whose emaciated body was in the grip of a hectic fever, marking the last stages of consumption. All she could do was to beg the woman to take the child to the infirmary, though it was obviously too late to save him, and give her some money to buy food, which she knew would probably be spent on gin. She left Taylor's Court with a heavy heart and stood looking about the street outside as if, in some way, a clue to Kezia's whereabouts might offer itself.

'Are you finished here, ma'am?' asked the cabbie, who was growing restive and looking nervously about him at the sordid surroundings.

The words touched a nerve. 'No,' Emma told him. 'I'm not finished. I mean to enquire in that public house at the corner. Please follow me with the cab and wait outside.'

In the mean tavern with a dirty, sawdust-decked floor, Emma's entrance caused a stir of attention, and several pairs of eyes, all unfriendly, watched her make her way to the man she took to be the tapster. He was an unprepossessing fellow, with a barrel chest and a set of cauliflower ears, who looked as though he might once have earned his living in the prize ring. His response to her questions was, predictably, the same as the woman's. He'd never heard of a Sam Leach or a Kezia Smith.

'You must know of Leach,' exclaimed Emma, growing exasperated. 'I'm sure he drank here often enough!' She turned to face the company, and demanded loudly, 'Does no one here know of Sam Leach, or of Kezia Smith?' She then made a bad mistake. 'I am willing to pay for the information.'

She saw the faces about her change, from curious to rapacious. In her ear, the pugilistic tapster muttered, 'What do you mean, letting on you got money about you?' Suddenly he grasped her arm and declared loudly, 'I know your sort, and I don't want 'em in my house—you go on out of here, missie, and don't you show your face in here no more!' He hustled her at speed across the floor, past the furtive, cruel faces, and sent her sprawling out of the door and into the arms of the cabman.

The cabbie summed up the situation in an instant, thrust Emma unceremoniously into his cab, scrambled up on his perch and, whipping up his mare, took them away at a gallop. Emma threw herself back on the shabby squabs in despair. So Kezzy had gone, no one knew where, and it was with real pain in her heart that she was borne away from the squalid hovels of Bethnal Green.

She had no time to brood on it, however, for on her return to Forbes Street from this melancholy visit, she found the Home in an uproar. Two of the girls, newly-arrived, had fallen out over ownership of piece of tawdry finery, a comb set with glass 'rubies', and had set about battle royal, screaming abuse, scratching each other's faces and pulling out lumps of each another's hair. All attempts to separate the combatants failed, and they were beginning to do considerable damage, not only to each other, but to the furniture and fittings, when Emma parted them at last by the drastic expedient of throwing a bowl of cold water over them.

As she supervised clearing up the wreckage, she uttered silent thanks, and not for the first time, that the Home had no immediate neighbours to complain of noise or disorder.

But Emma was wrong in thinking that no one observed the Home. The little Quaker cemetery which lay next to it had an occupant—a live one, assisting at the ghostly meeting of departed Friends. It was not a companion whom those sober Quakers would have appreciated. Sam Leach, whom she had sought in vain, had established himself in a 'den' among the overgrown greenery, and there, safe as a fowler in his hide, he sat on an old tea-chest and watched the comings and goings at the Home. He had heard the rumpus over the comb, and grinned happily.

'Bitten off more than she can chew!' he said to himself with deep satisfaction. He took an apple and a penknife from his pocket and began to cut off segments of fruit and stuff them into his mouth. 'And that's only the beginning, Miss Meddle. You still got Sam Leach to reckon with!'

Sam and Kezia had left Taylor's Court for the reason that lay behind most departures in that part of the world—they owed a month's rent, and Sam had spent the money. They had transferred themselves to Wapping, where, as Sam pointed out, there was plenty of trade for Kezia among the seamen visiting the docks and wharves. What was more, sinister though the district was when dusk fell, and rough enough, goodness knew, by day, Wapping was definitely more salubrious than Bethnal Green. 'Goin' up in the world!' said Sam in jocular manner.

Sam spent his own days, when not in public houses, in his green hideaway in the cemetery. He was that peculiar product of the slums: a survivor, cunning, ruthless, amoral, brutal. He had a long memory, and carried with him a reputation for settling wrongs done him, no matter by whom or how long ago. Sam had not forgotten that Emma and Luke 'owed' him, as he put it. To be sure, he had outwitted Emma, but she still went about interfering in other folk's business, and taking away poor men's living. 'Taking away their women,' said Sam disapprovingly. 'It's a disgrace, that's what—and she ain't going to get away with it.'

As for Luke, he had worsted Sam in their brief scuffle, and that was an act Sam could not let go unrevenged. If word ever got round that a fancy swell had floored Sam Leach in an exchange of fisticuffs, Sam would be laughed out of every public bar within the sound of Bow bells.

So Sam sat and watched and waited and plotted. Now, as the clamour died down from the Home, he threw away his apple-core, folded his penknife, and slipped silently out of the cemetery on his way back to Wapping.

Wapping had a smell all of its own, compounded of tar, grease and exotic spices unloaded from the ships. Its streets were crammed with eating-houses and gin-shops, catering to a motley throng of customers, both permanent and transitory, of every race and creed under the sun. Seamen's lodging-houses, chandlers' stores, office buildings of the shipping firms, all jostled together in picturesque and sometimes squalid proximity. Respectable clerks of shipping houses worked in Wapping, and men whose word was their bond. Yet brothels and opium dens spread like a rash through the area, and all manner of vice was displayed on all sides.

When a ship paid off, there were more drunken seamen lying in the gutters of Wapping than there were stray cats pillaging its rubbish heaps—which was saying something, for the feline population, some of which, like the seamen, had jumped ship, roamed Wapping in hungry throngs. In Bethnal Green one seldom saw a cat—since any unfortunate animal foolish enough to stray into that locality was instantly dismembered by the first group of small boys it encountered. Cruelty bred cruelty; each group, itself at the mercy of some predator, gaining revenge by preying on a weaker.

Sam walked briskly among the coils of rope and stacks of tea-chests until he reached a street corner on which stood a public house of dingy exterior, and dingier reputation. He rubbed a clean-ish patch on one grimy window with his hand and peered through. Yes, there he was, the old boozer, and three parts drunk already by the looks of it. Sam nodded to himself and went in.

The man he was so interested to find was a balding, shabbily-dressed individual with a purple nose and unshaven jowls, who crouched gloomily in a corner, hugging an emptied tankard to his chest and muttering fitfully to himself in the manner of those whose brains, never strong, are beginning to succumb to the ravages of alcoholism. As Sam approached and put a friendly hand on his shoulder, he started and glanced up fearfully.

Seeing Leach, he looked only partly reassured and croaked, 'Oh, it's you, then, Sammy. What you want o' me?'

'Why, Micah,' said Sam affably, taking a seat at the same stained, delapidated table, 'I just looked in and saw you, a-sitting here all alone. I thought I'd just come in and have a drink with you, you being my wife's uncle. A man can have a drink with his family, can't he?'

'Right enough,' said Micah Smith, staring meaningfully down into his empty tankard.

Sam took the hint and signalled to the potman to bring more ale. 'I'm a great believer in family,' said Sam, when the ale arrived. He raised his tankard. 'Here's mud in your eye, Micah. Families ought to stand together, I reckon.'

Mr Smith was not so far gone as to miss the implication of this last statement. 'I don't know what you want done, Sam, but it ain't no use asking me to do it. I got the Law breathing down my neck, I 'ave. I can't be doing with no more trouble.'

'No, no, Micah . . .' Sam soothed him, resisting a natural desire to punch his companion's unlovely head. 'I was only making an observation. Knowing that you're a family man, yourself . . . in a manner of speaking.'

This touched a chord in his listener. 'Right enough,' said Micah gloomily. 'I brung up them two girls, didn't I? Your Kezzy and little Rosie. I brought them up like they'd been my own flesh and blood, and not my brother's. He got himself hung, you know.'

Sam, touched by superstitious dread, spat on the sawdust-covered floor and glanced nervously over his shoulder, as if he feared to see the gallows set up in the corner of the taproom, and Jack Ketch himself quaffing ale at the next table.

'You looked after them girls fine, Micah.'

'They was ungrateful,' said Mr Smith, noisily imbibing his ale. 'Never a word of thanks.'

'You molly-coddled them,' said Sam severely to him. 'That was your mistake. You spoiled them. It don't pay to go molly-coddling women. They don't appreciate it. Best way to treat a woman is to black her eye now and then. Why, they likes that kind of treatment.'

Mr Smith looked interested, and Sam warmed to his theory. 'As I see it, if you black a man's eye, he tries to black yours, don't he? Because that's the way men is by nature.'

'Right enough,' agreed his companion.

'Now, a woman, if a fellow blacks her eye, she respects him for it. And why? Because it lets her know where she stands, that's why. She knows what's expected. She knows where she is. Women like that. It makes 'em feel safe.'

Micah considered this argument in silence for some five minutes, and eventually gave it as his opinion that it was 'right enough'. He added, by way of illustration, that he himself had frequently blacked his late wife's eye, and she had never been heard to complain.

'Mind you, I'd 'ave blacked the other one, if she 'ad,' he felt obliged to add. The look of a man ill-used crossed his unprepossessing countenance. 'She went and fell down the stairs, in the end, the silly bitch. Broke her neck. She done it a-purpose, if you ask me. I only give her a bit of a clout, affectionate like, and down the stairs she went, stupid biddy!'

Sam was sufficiently distracted from his own

plans to ask with genuine curiosity, 'How did you get away with it, Micah?'

Smith gave a snort of derision. 'Easy. I got half a bottle of booze and I poured it over her. When the Law come, all they done was sniff the air. "Ow dear!" they says. "This unfortunate woman has fallen down the stairs while in a drunken stupor", and they wrote it down on a bit o' paper. Coroner agreed.'

'You're a sharp'un, Micah,' said Sam admiringly.

'Right enough,' said Mr Smith.

Sam leaned forward confidentially. 'You was smart, Micah, because you used the Law to work for you, see? That's what you got to do. Old Bessie, she was ready to pay up ten pounds for your Rosie, wasn't she?'

'Guineas!' corrected Micah. 'I made her make it guineas—only in the end I got nuffink. Kezzy, she sneaked Rose away.'

'Well, she wouldn't do that again!' said Sam with cold satisfaction. 'I took care of that! I made her sorry she done it. But them as took Rose away, and tried to take Kezzy from me, and is still busy taking other men's women away from them, they're nobs. Fine folk. They got to be stopped, Micah. And you and me is going to do it, with the help of the Law.'

Micah became agitated. 'Us—the Law!' he exclaimed, taking his face out of the tankard. 'The Law don't help no honest working men, like me and you, Sam. It deprives us of our living, that's what it does. You know what the Law done to me, twelve months since? It took away the donkey.

How's a costermonger to make a living without his moke, I ask you? Took that donkey off of me and banned me from keeping another for two years. Two whole years! Why, a man could starve in that time. And why? Because that donkey kept lying down in the road. Magistrate said that donkey was skin and bone, and it was a dirty lie!' Smith began to gesticulate wildly, splashing ale, so that Leach swore at him. 'I fed that moke better than I fed meself! It weren't my fault it kept falling down. It was lazy, that donkey, that's why it kept lying down. Why, I've stood in the street many a time and kicked that donkey in the ribs for ten minutes, and it wouldn't get up. Just shows you how lazy that donkey was!'

'Yes, yes, Micah,' Leach soothed him again. 'But you'd like, wouldn't you, to get your own back on them as wronged you? Them as took your living away?'

'Right enough,' said Micah morosely. 'But you got to 'ave a weapon, Sammy, if you wants to take on them as fancies themselves better than a poor working man. I don't mean no fists nor broken bottles. They ain't a-feared of that, because they don't come out and fight fair. They hides behind the Law.'

'But we got a weapon, Micah,' Sam said, and leaning forward, whispered in Smith's ear.

Smith looked startled and uncomprehending, 'Rosie?' he croaked.

'Rosie,' said Sam. He saluted Micah with his tankard. 'Drink up, Micah, and just you leave it to me. I'll set it up. You just do like I say.'

*   *   *

Rose, the unwitting tool of Sam Leach's revenge, sat on the paddock fence, swinging her legs, and watching the sorrel horse graze a few feet away from her. It was getting cool of an evening. Summer was over. But Rose did not feel the cold because she was accustomed to it, previously running about the streets in her ragged garments in all weathers. She was tidily dressed now in a clean gown and white stockings, both of which had suffered a little from their wearer's having tramped through the orchard with Tom, the stable boy, in search of the last hard green apples that were too small and damaged by the birds and no one bothered to pick. Tom was very good at climbing the trees, while Rose stood guard at the bottom in case the gardener approached.

Tom was only two years older than Rose, and they had struck up a great friendship. Privately, Rose was determined to marry Tom when she was a little older, but with feminine prudence she had not yet informed him of the fact. In law, of course, Rose at twelve and Tom at fourteen were old enough to marry already. But even Rose did not think that Tom's mother would take kindly to the idea, much less Major and Mrs Sheldon.

Now Rose sat alone on the fence and watched the sorrel, holding in her hand one of the stolen apples. Rose loved all animals. Unlike most slum children, she had never teased or hurt one. Whenever she had seen street urchins torment a puppy, or hide behind pillars with a cache of stones to throw at dray-horses' legs, she had leapt upon the offenders, scratching and kicking, until they ran away. She had wept as much to see her Uncle Micah beat his donkey as she had when he beat her. But the sorrel was the most beautiful animal Rose had ever seen. She had never set eyes on a horse of this wonderful red colour. The Major had pictures on his walls of racehorses, but none of them was as fine as the sorrel.

Rose knew that she was absolutely forbidden to go anywhere near the great red horse the Major rode. The Major had forbidden it, and Riley, and Tom. But Rose longed to be the sorrel's friend. She had taken to sneaking down here of an evening and sitting on the fence and talking to the sorrel. At first she had not been able to get anywhere near, but tonight the horse grazed peacefully enough, only ten feet away. She stopped swinging her legs and called him by name, which was Sultan. She thought Sultan a very romantic name, though not quite sure what it meant. She vaguely thought it had something to do with fruit cake. As fruit cake was a rare delicacy in her world, it seemed quite suitable.

Rose slid down from the fence on to the forbidden turf of the paddock and began to walk slowly towards the grazing horse, holding out the apple as a token of friendship. The sorrel seemed to take no notice, though he swished his tail a little more and his ears twitched. As she got nearer, Rose realised how very large the sorrel was. She felt very small alongside it. She could see now that his eyes seemed very white, and he had flattened his ears in a way which made his beautiful head suddenly full of menace.

'Don't be frightened, Sultan,' she said timidly, holding out her tribute of the apple. 'I've brought you this.'

Sultan swung up his head, and for a brief moment she thought he meant to come and take the apple. Then everything happened all at once. Rose realised that she had made a mistake, that the sorrel saw her not as a friend but as an enemy, and that she was in great danger. At the same moment she heard the Major shout her name, and from the corner of her eye saw him put one hand on the paddock fence and vault over it, and begin to race towards her. At that very instant, the great red horse reared up, front hoofs flailing, and Rose stumbled back, throwing up her arm to shield her face, and that was the arm the iron-shod forehoof struck with a sickening crack.

It was Riley who brought the news to Emma, hobbling towards the house in his crooked way, and calling out, 'Mrs Sheldon, ma'am, will you not come quick? To be sure, that black-hearted divil of a horse has moidered the darlin' child!'

Emma ran down the path in the direction he pointed and met Luke coming, with Rose in his arms. Terrified that Riley had spoken the truth and that the child really was dead, Emma did no more than glance at Luke's face, and notice that it was deathly pale, before turning her attention to Rose. Fortunately Rose was not dead, but had suffered a broken arm, and the local surgeon had to be called to set it. It was a painful business, and Rose screeched, Emma wept, and Tom lurked outside the window and cried in sympathy, even though he was fourteen, because no one could see him. Riley went down to the paddock and leaned on the fence and swore at the sorrel in English and in the Irish, until he ran out of invective and breath.

When at last the surgeon had departed and Rose was tucked up in bed, Emma and Luke were discussing the matter in the study.

'That horrible horse!' cried Emma, quite beside herself. 'I don't know why you don't sell him. He has already bitten poor Tom and kicked Riley, and he might have killed Rose!'

'He would have done nothing to Rose if the child had done as she was bid and stayed away from Sultan!' Luke shouted. 'I knew bringing that child here would mean trouble. She's a wild little street-Arab who hasn't the slightest idea how to behave in the country!'

'Why,' cried Emma, incensed, 'you are the one who would never scold her! That horse is dangerous; Riley says so!'

'Riley finds fault with everything—that is Riley's way!' Luke returned hoarsely. 'The sorrel stays, and Rose goes!'

'Goes?' cried Emma, aghast. 'Goes where?'

'How the devil should I know? Send her back to your aunt.'

'I will not send Rose away,' said Emma in a quiet but determined voice.

'This is my house,' Luke snarled, 'and I say what happens under this roof. Damn it, I will be master in my own home!'

'It is my home, too, and if I am your wife and not just a housekeeper, then I, too, should have some say in what happens here!' shouted Emma.

Luke swore and whirled on his heel, marching over to the window and standing with his arms folded, staring out. Beneath his swarthy skin he still looked very pale, and beads of perspiration gleamed on his forehead. Emma's anger was beginning to die down, and now it occurred to her that he looked not merely angry, but distressed.

Trying to sound calm, she said, 'Rose was very naughty, but has certainly learned the hard way that she must do as she's told. She will never do anything so foolish again.'

Luke unfolded his arms and spoke over his shoulder, sounding more in control of himself, but still very tense. 'Emma, in taking these girls, whether Kezia or Rose or any other, away from their own world, you run endless risks. I was wrong to allow you to keep Rose, wrong to allow you to bring her here. It is wrong, because it is unfair to Rose. She is not a country child, she is a child of city streets, and that is where she ought to be.'

'Running on the streets, in every kind of moral danger?' Emma demanded sharply.

He uttered an exclamation of vexation. 'No, of course not, Emma!' Suddenly he turned towards her and held out his hand. 'Come over here and sit down with me.' A little uncertainly, she followed him to the sofa, and sat beside him. 'Now, Emma,' he said firmly, 'I have let you have your way in almost everything, and you know that it has been against my better inclinations. Perhaps you should consider what has happened here today to be a warning. In meddling with people's lives, you act at your peril. You may mean well, but who knows what odd tricks Fate has up her sleeve?'

'You promised me Forbes Street for eighteen months, and it is not yet a year,' Emma said in a cold voice. 'Are you now asking me to give it up?'

FREE BOOKS CERTIFICATE

Dear Susan,

Your Special Introductory offer of 14 free books is too good to miss. I understand they are mine to keep when the clock and Surprise Mystery Gift. Please also reserve a Reader Service Subscription for me. If I decide to subscribe, I shall, from the beginning of the month following my free parcel of books, receive 14 new books each month for £16.80, post and packing free. If I decide not to subscribe, I shall write to you within 10 days. The free books, clock and Surprise Mystery Gift will be mine to keep, in any case.

I understand that I may cancel my subscription at any time simply by writing to you. I am over 18 years of age.

_____   Signature _____

Name _____

Address _____

_____   Postcode _____

3A8RA

To Susan Welland
Mills & Boon
Reader Service
FREEPOST
P.O. Box 236
CROYDON
Surrey CR9 9EL.

'I know I promised you the house for that period, and I even put my name to a written agreement —but I think you have taken on too much. You run real risks, and moreover you are getting tired and worried. I am your husband, and you cannot expect me to sit here and watch that happen without even making some comment!' He was beginning to sound exasperated.

'You are angry with Rose and taking out your anger on me!' Emma said, getting agitated again. 'I won't give up Forbes Street, I won't send Rose to my aunt—and I won't have you tell me how much I can do, when I know myself very well how much I can manage!'

'I refuse to get into a stupid argument!' Luke said sharply, 'We'll discuss this when you're in a mind to talk sense!' He got to his feet, and strode out.

That night, for the first time, they went to bed with a quarrel unresolved. They had argued before, but always managed not to let the sun go down on their anger. Tonight was different. The accident had shaken Luke badly, as Emma—now calmer —was able to realise. He felt in some measure responsible because the sorrel was his horse, and Sultan's bad temperament was well known. Above all, he hated to see a child hurt.

Emma lay unable to sleep and turning it all over in her mind, thinking not so much of Rose now, as of Luke. When they had made their agreement, he giving her the house in Forbes Street and she accepting his proposal of marriage, Luke had said that he would like a son. She had agreed—but she had not realised then, or indeed until this moment, how much he wanted children. The realisation was

so new and so sudden that it quite shocked her. She
had already realised that her husband was not a
man to speak much of his innermost feelings, but
now she remembered his white, strained features as
he carried the injured Rose towards the house. She
also remembered the stable boy, Tom, who, good
lad though he was, was the despair of his widowed
mother when it came to getting out of bed in the
morning, and was often late—and yet, Riley complained vociferously, the Major would never permit him to so much as box the miscreant's ears.

Emma tossed on the pillows, and eventually got
out of bed and lit a candle. Throwing a shawl round
her shoulders, she let herself out of the door and
made her way to Rose's room, to see if the child
slept, or was in pain and restless.

Samson had been barred from the room, lest he
knock the newly-set arm, but he was curled up on
the mat outside Rose's door, and raised his head to
peer up at Emma like a crusty old sentry. Recognis-
ing her, he stretched out his head to sniff at the hem
of her nightgown, and then wagged his stumpy tail.
Rose was asleep, her cheeks tear-stained. Emma
stood above her, holding up the candle and watching for a little, but Rose did not stir.

Emma made her way back through the silent,
sleeping house. Her path led her past Luke's door,
and before it she stopped. She had never entered
his room at night of her own volition. He had
always come to her. That was the expected thing.
Respectable women were not supposed to make
the first advances; that was a husband's preroga-
tive. But for the first time in their marriage, Emma
wanted to open that door and go in and wake Luke

in order to tell him she was sorry about their quarrel. But perhaps he would misunderstand the reason for her visit. He might be shocked. No, Luke would not be shocked—but he would be startled. A rueful expression crossed Emma's face in the shadowy corridor, the candle-flame leaping about in the draught, casting fanciful images about the walls.

By day, when not actively arguing, they got along tolerably well. In a perverse sort of way, they had both of them come even to enjoy the arguments. By night, on those nights when he did come to her room, he had always been a considerate lover. There was something basically lacking in their relationship, however, and whenever Emma tried to pinpoint it in her own mind, she grew confused and fearful—as if she knew the reason, but did not want to recognise it.

But she recognised it now. He was strong and passionate. He liked arguing with her, because he liked her best when she forgot herself and her blue eyes blazed at him, and her fair hair tumbled out of its restraining pins. He had made her a sober and practical offer of marriage. But in sexual matters he was not by nature a sober or practical man but a highly-motivated one, capable both of giving and receiving a high degree of sexual satisfaction and finding himself denied it with her. In bed, she bored him.

Try as she might, Emma was rarely able to respond to his lovemaking with anything like ardour: a barrier remained between them, even at their most intimate moments. She was still horribly shy about dressing or undressing in front of him.

Getting up in the mornings, after those nights spent together, she felt foolishly awkward, and generally managed to scurry into a corner and roll on her stockings while he was busy shaving. He was obligingly good at the husbandly duty of lacing up her corset, but even that embarrassed her, and even worse, so good at it was he that she was left gloomily wondering where he had gained so much practice.

As for touching him anywhere other than on the face or shoulder or arms, she could not bring herself to do it. The worst of it was that she knew he wanted her to, but on the only occasion her fingers had accidentally encountered his aroused manhood in the dark seclusion of the sheets, she had snatched her hand away as if it had been burnt, and almost leapt out of bed with embarrassment. Their physical unions were already, after such a short married life, developing into a sort of ritual, in which she allowed him to take possession of her whenever he wanted, but herself remained inert and unresponsive in his arms—and neither of them was satisfied.

Emma felt dimly that she was a prisoner of that fashionable dictate, that ladies did not behave like whores in the bedroom—but did not know how to break free. Luke, on his side, was growing frustrated and irritable, and although he tried to disguise it, she sensed it, and that made her even more perplexed and awkward.

But he, too, was a victim, for he had been brought up to treat 'respectable' women with deference, so he never insisted, and when she drew back from his more intimate caresses, he sighed and resigned himself to kissing her lips and keeping his hands at shoulder level.

Yet both of them knew it could be different. In the sleazy and abandoned ambience of Bessie's establishment, when he had thought her 'Violet', his approach had been altogether different. Since that one occasion, he had never again seized her roughly and thrown her down on a bed. On the one hand, the idea that he might once again make his demands so uncompromisingly filled Emma with alarm, yet quite paradoxically, and for no reason she could explain, she sometimes found herself wishing that he would. Their whole physical relationship was disintegrating into a vicious circle of disappointment.

But today, for the first time, their daytime relationship had failed, too. They had squabbled and gone off to their separate beds, the pair of them, thought Emma, in a fit of the sulks. It was childish, and unnecessary. One of them had to make a move to put things right.

'And it might as well be me,' she said to herself, and putting out her hand, turned the handle of his door.

He was sprawled out, lying face down in the pillows, as he usually slept, and scowling to himself in his slumbers. Emma stooped over him with the candle held high, as she had done over Rose, and studied his recumbent form. She saw the long eyelashes flicker, the muscles around his mouth twitch, and he opened his eyes, twisted his head, and squinting into the glare of the candle-flame, stared up at her.

'Emma?' He pushed himself up on one elbow

and thrust back his untidy black curls from his forehead. 'What's wrong? Is Rose in pain?'

Yes, he was startled to see her, his wife, standing at his bedside—and he immediately assumed it must be for some reason other than a need of him.

'Rose is sleeping,' Emma said, her voice sounding flat. 'I've just been to look. I thought . . . I wanted to come and say I'm sorry for the silly squabble.'

She saw Luke smile, his swarthy cheeks creasing. He hauled himself up in the bed and rested his arms on his knees. 'Are you, now? Well, I suppose I'm sorry, too, for what I said. I was—upset. I wouldn't really pack Rose off back to London, if you didn't wish it.'

'I know that,' Emma said. 'I knew you wouldn't do it.'

And she had known it, even when shouting at him angrily. She might not know him well, but she knew him well enough for that. She set down her candle and said awkwardly, 'I'm sorry to have woken you, only as I came past the door . . .'

'You don't have to apologise for that,' he said, sounding slightly amused. 'I don't mind being woken up—by you.'

There was a new note in his voice, a slight huskiness, which she recognised. The old nervousness took hold of her, and she reached out to take up the candle again, but he caught at her wrist and whispered, 'No, stay . . . Why run away now?'

He was pulling her gently but firmly towards him, down into the bed. Her shawl slipped from her shoulders, rustling to the floor with a seductive little sound. Emma sank into the feather mattress. It smelled faintly of perspiration, and of that odour of sleeping bodies which warm beds emit. Luke leaned over and slid his arm about her and his mouth closed over hers, warm, inviting, asking for a response and promising pleasure. Her hands slid across his ribs and her fingers pressed into his back, feeling the lean hard muscles of the shoulders, dipping down into the long, curving recess of the spine. His mouth nuzzled at her neck, his fingers running lightly over the gently swelling mound of her breasts, and playing with the nipples that hardened beneath his touch.

Emma felt a curious trembling run over her, and for a moment her body rose to meet his, and then, as his thigh slid across hers, that old instinctive, deep-rooted panic took hold and she stiffened, gasped, and grew unyielding in his grasp.

Luke paused, raised his head and asked sharply, 'What's the matter now?'

'I . . . Nothing . . .' It was no good, she was beginning to stammer, her face flushing, her eye unable to meet his in the flickering candlelight.

He muttered an oath, and pushed himself away from her. 'Damn it, Emma, if you didn't want this, why the hell did you come?'

'To tell you . . . I was sorry about the quarrel . . .' she confessed miserably.

'Confound it! That, at least, could have waited till morning!' he snarled. He threw himself back on the crumpled pillow, one forearm thrown across his brow, his eyes staring up into the velvet shadows of the ceiling. 'You had better go back to your own room, then,' his voice said, cold and uninviting.

'It's all right, Luke,' she faltered, wishing desperately that she knew how to put matters right. 'I don't mind . . .'

'Don't mind?' He threw himself over on to his side, facing her, his face twisted in anger. 'Well, dammit, I mind! It's like trying to make love to one of the eleven thousand virgins of Cologne! You make me feel like a confounded rapist! I don't want a martyr, Emma, lying flat under me like a log, and just about as responsive! I want a partner!'

'It's not my fault!' Emma cried out, humiliation spilling out into anger.

'Well, madam, it certainly isn't mine!' he said icily.

'Why not?' she snapped furiously, and then realised, but too late, that she had done the unforgivable. Whatever she had meant by her question—and she was not sure herself what she had meant, the words had sprung from her lips impulsively, thoughtless, foolish—to him it had seemed to cast an aspersion on his virility, to suggest that in failing to arouse her he had failed in his manhood. It was a criticism no man forgave.

'Go on back to your room, Emma!' he said hoarsely.

Humiliated, angry, miserable and desperate, Emma scrambled out of the bed, snatched up her shawl and her candle, and stumbled through the door. She had buried her pride and gone to him, and the result was worse than anything she could have envisaged. He had rejected her.

CHAPTER SEVEN

NOVEMBER CAME, and with it the onset of wet and windy weather. Winter storms had set in at sea, and the trading vessels began to overrun their expected dates of arrival. Luke, who although he never drank tea had interests in imports of this commodity, ran a finger down the list of latest arrivals, and then tossed the gazette aside.

'Is it of the tea-clipper that you hope to have news?' asked Emma, over the breakfast table.

'The *Star of Bengal*, yes. Two weeks overdue, and one begins to wonder if she hasn't gone down!' Luke glared at the window and the grey skies outside. 'I'm going up to London,' he announced suddenly, pushing back his chair. 'I need to see the shipping agent on other matters, anyway, and I can find out if he has news of *Star of Bengal* at the same time.' He paused. 'What do you have planned for today?'

Emma sighed. 'I've a list of local calls to make, hoping to persuade new subscribers to support the Home. Riley can drive me, if you are to be away and won't need him. I'll tell Cook that we'll have dinner late tonight.'

It was a poor day to have chosen to visit the metropolis, as Luke soon found. Low cloud trapped the moisture rising from the river, and the smoke belching from an untold number of chimneys had combined with it to create a thick, evil-smelling, choking fog.

There was nothing like the London fog. It seemed less a trick of the weather and the season than a malignant life-form all its own. It wrapped the city in an oozing, dirty yellowish-grey blanket, blinding the inhabitants, who stumbled about like lost souls, groping their way helplessly. At mid-day, it might have been night. Lamps were lit, but did little to help, shrouded in the impenetrable gloom. The pedestrians continued to fall over one another on the pavements, coughing as the foul mixture lay clammy fingers on their throats and lungs, and narrowly to miss being run down by invisible vehicles on the roads.

Luke, finding his way with difficulty towards the offices of the shipping agents in Wapping, cursed the fog freely. It hung above the greasy, refuse-strewn waters of the river, and crept ashore to drift across deserted wharves, alongside which the barges were lifeless, ghost vessels, abandoned by their crews. It insinuated itself among the maze of dockland alleys and warehouses, so that he became disorientated and began to think he was wandering in circles, and all the while the fog slithered snake-like round his legs and seemed to chuckle triumph-antly in his ears.

Pulling out a handkerchief, he clamped it to his nose and mouth, cursing that he had chosen today of all days to come here. He might have been alone in the world, but then his ears caught the disem-bodied patter of footsteps ahead of him and a woman's figure materialised out of the swirling, cotton-wool mass and cannoned into him. They rebounded off one another, and the girl, as he could now distinguish the figure to be, peered up at him.

She could not see his face because of the hand-kerchief, but his clothes clearly marked him as a gentleman, and she pushed back the shawl she had wrapped about her head, and exclaimed with professional cheeriness, 'Well, it's a bit of luck you bumped into me, sir, for it's a nasty sort of day, and I know a better place to be than this!' She caught at his sleeve invitingly.

Luke took the handkerchief from his face and said, 'Yes, it is a piece of luck, Kezzy.'

Panic flooded her face as she recognised him. She let out a squeal, and turning, dashed into the fog. He knew that, if he lost her now, he would never find her in this filthy murk, and launched himself forward and managed to grasp at her fluttering skirts. She stumbled, and he flung both arms round her, refusing to let go, though she wriggled and kicked and finally begged, 'Let me go, sir! Let me go, please!'

'Not if you mean to run off, Kezia. I want to talk to you,' he panted.

'I won't run,' she said, sounding dejected, and growing limp in his grip. He thought she meant it, and released her cautiously. 'I got a room nearby,' she said reluctantly. 'Place where I live. We can go and talk there. Sam won't be there . . . me being about me business, bad day for it though it is.'

Luke understood her. When Kezia was 'about her business', the bed was needed, and Leach obligingly absented himself. He followed her

through a series of winding alleys, reflecting ruefully that he was putting great faith in the girl, and
trusting that no bully lurked nearby to crack open
his skull and relieve him of his valuables. But at last
he found himself in a small, dark room. Kezia lit a
lamp, and its dull glow illuminated the poverty-
stricken surroundings. By its light he could see that
she had a partly-healed split lower lip.

'Always dark in here,' she said apologetically,
'even when it ain't a day like this. If you want to sit
on that there chair, sir, it won't give under you,' she
added with quaint courtesy.

Luke took off his hat and set it on the table, and
seated himself on the rickety chair, hoping she was
right. It rocked on uneven legs, but seemed secure.
Kezia perched on a stool and leaned her arms on
the table.

'I ain't got nothing, only gin.'

'No, thank you,' Luke said, hastily refusing this
offer. Lord knew what sort of concoction was dis-
tilled around here and sold as gin. Somewhere in
the house a baby was crying, wailing dismally on a
thin, feeble note. The damp and the fog seemed to
have followed him into the room and to seep out of
its miserable walls.

'Did you know that Miss Emma and I are
married?' he asked.

Kezia brightened. 'Are you? I'm glad o' that, for
I know she always did fancy you, even when she
was that set against you—if you follow my meaning.'

'Did she?' asked Luke, startled. He frowned.
'Emma—Mrs Sheldon—has tried to find you, and
has been very worried about you, Kezia.'

'You won't tell her, will you, that you seen me?' Kezia begged. She looked up at him, shamefaced. 'Me being back at my old trade, and that.'

Luke's gaze fell on her injured mouth. 'I gather Leach is still about, and up to his old tricks.'

'Oh, him,' said Kezia bitterly. 'Sam's about, all right.'

'Kezia!' he said urgently, leaning forward. 'I was mistaken in driving you away before, and sorry for it. Come back with me now. We'll keep you safe from Leach!'

'You can't,' said Kezia simply. 'He's my husband, and he's got his rights. Knows 'em, too.' Her tone grew earnest. 'Sam ain't forgot you, sir. He means to be revenged. He's spiteful, is Sam, and don't forget no wrong done him. He's been drinking with my Uncle Micah, and hatching up some devilment. Take care.'

'Leach doesn't worry me,' Luke said, 'but you do.' He fished in his pocket and put some money on the table. 'Here, Kezzy, hide it away. It's for you, and not for Leach to spend on drink.'

Kezia fidgeted. 'Don't seem right, taking money off you, when you ain't had nothing for it.' She glanced at the bed. 'We can, if you want.'

'No, no.' Luke shook his head and got to his feet. 'Listen, Kezzy, if you should ever find yourself free of Leach, then you know you may come back. Go either to Mrs Somerton, or to Forbes Street.'

'Everyone's heard about that home Miss Emma runs in Forbes Street,' said Kezia. 'Some folk is mortal upset about it. Sam, he's been hanging about the place and watching it.'

'Has he?' growled Luke. 'Then I'll have a word

with the local constabulary. "Loitering with intent" should cover that. You're sure, Kezia, that you won't come with me?'

Before Kezia could answer, there was the stamp of a heavy footstep outside and an ominous creak from the door. Kezia gasped, 'Sam!' as the door swung open, and Leach's powerful and ungainly form appeared framed in it.

For a moment he stood staring at Luke, bemused. Then a twisted grin crossed his face, and he chuckled, 'Well, look who's here. Drifted in with the fog, I reckon. How did you find us out, then? She tell you?' His voice and glance sharpened, and he pointed threateningly at Kezia.

'No, she did not!' Luke said vigorously. 'I'm in Wapping on business, and chanced to stumble into her. Leave the girl alone, Leach, for God's sake!'

Leach came further into the room and his glance fell on the money Luke had put on the table. 'Well, so the fine gentleman ain't above fancying my Kezzy! I understands that. Reckon my Kezzy is better in bed than that meddling, strait-laced piece you're wed to.'

Luke hit him, so suddenly and with such force that Leach, who had not been expecting the blow so soon, or realised his opponent could move so quickly, flew backwards and struck his head against the doorjamb. Swearing luridly, he lurched upright and stumbled towards Luke, sending the table crashing aside out of his path.

Sam was a street-brawler of considerable power and ferocity, and long experience. But young as he still was, alcohol had already begun to slow his reflexes, and fury and a desire for revenge further clouded his brain. He flung himself at Luke in a red mist of rage, throwing punches one after the other in a hail of blows.

Not surprisingly, half of them missed. Some found their mark and Luke winced, but he kept his head, and motivated on his side by an icy anger which cleared his head instead of muddling it, he timed his punches with deadly accuracy, and by the time Sam had realised that his opponent knew a thing or two about fist-fights and had no gentlemanly objection to landing low blows, the tide of battle was already turning against him. Leach swung aside, blood pouring from his mouth, and seized the chair, raising it on high. Kezia screamed. Luke leapt aside fractionally in time, and the chair crashed down, fragmenting into kindling. Momentum carried Leach forward, and Luke helped him on his way by his coat collar. Sam crashed into the wall and slid senseless to the ground. Silence fell, and Luke wiped his hand across his mouth, staring down at his defeated foe.

Kezia ran forward and pushed his hat at him. 'Go on, sir, you get going! Folk will have heard the rumpus and know it's a mill, and will come to see who's won. Sam's got his friends . . .'

Luke grasped her wrist. 'Come on, Kezzy, I can't leave you here with that brute! When he comes to, he'll be thirsting for vengeance, and wreak it on you!'

'I can't, I can't!' sobbed Kezia, tugging her wrist free. 'Look, sir, you left me money, and I'll run and buy a bottle. Sam will like that, make him happy, see?'

She peered up at him, her eyes begging him to believe this pathetic lie.

'God forgive me!' muttered Luke. He took his hat from her outstretched hand and stumbled out into the street, leaving her with the unconscious Sam Leach.

In no mood now to seek out the shipping agents, Luke went to his club, where his appearance gained him some startled and curious looks, but politely no questions, and cleaned himself up before setting off home. He certainly looked as though he had been in a brawl. One eye was puffed and swelling, and bruises were appearing on his cheekbone and jaw. Fellow passengers in the railway carriage regarded him with awe and alarm.

He would have to give Emma some explanation for his appearance. What he could not tell her was that he had seen Kezia. Luke knew Emma well enough to realise that the information would send her immediately to Wapping, and he could not allow her to run the danger of encountering Leach.

She was still out visiting when he got to Hill House. Glad that he had not to face her straight away, Luke gave orders that he was not to be disturbed, and would not require dinner, and went to the study, where he flung himself into a chair.

The room had remained much as it had been when Emma first saw it. It was marginally tidier, but he refused to allow her or anyone to touch his papers, because however untidy they looked to others, he knew where everything was. Otherwise, the study was that of a sporting gentleman.

Emma had often remarked that, unlike most

homes of people who had served their time in India, Hill House boasted no array of native curios. He had always replied carelessly that he had never been a man to weigh down his luggage unnecessarily with useless objects, which became meaningless once torn from their original setting. But he had once owned a Pathan dagger. He had not told her about that. A beautiful thing, the hilt inlaid with silver, he had been rather proud of it. But during the long sea voyage home, he had unwrapped it one day in his cabin, and looked down at it as it lay winking in the sunlight on the scrap of velvet. Then he had remembered Emerson's mutilated body and what such a knife could do, especially in the hands of a woman. For, after battle, the tribesmen warriors withdrew to celebrate their victory. The wounded enemy, helpless on the ground, was left to the women to finish off. The pitiless savagery with which they accomplished this task was a cruelty the more sickening because it was inflicted by women.

He had taken the dagger up on deck and hurled it over the rail, far out into the blue waters. It spun into the air, describing a great arc, and fell, gleaming and glittering in the sun, down into the translucent sea with a faint splash. He had leaned on the rail and been able to see it through the clear, transparent waves, turning and gleaming, sinking down, down to be lost for ever in the misty and mysterious depths. He could imagine it now, lying on the sea-bed, its steel dulled, its silver blackened, and tiny barnacles fastening on to its ornate hilt and once shining blade.

Luke stirred, and fetched the brandy and a glass.

He wondered, not for the first time, where humanity lay, and what made men and women turn into brutes. He asked himself why he, Lucius Sheldon, must always seem to misjudge his duty. The memory of that lone, dangerous sortie to find the mortally-wounded Emerson, and his failure, once he had found him, to deliver the merciful *coup de grâce*, was now augmented by that of his refusal to allow Kezia to remain in Mrs Somerton's home, thus driving the girl back to her wretched life with Leach, from which he could not now rescue her.

He could hear voices through the study door, Ned Bryant's among them. But he had given orders he was not to be disturbed, and he did not intend to make an exception, even for Ned. Luke unstoppered the decanter, and splashed brandy into the glass. He could vanquish Leach, but not his memories. If he drank enough, however, they became dulled, and oblivion rescued him from their tormenting grip.

When Emma arrived home after an exhausting round of visits, all made in the name of the Rescue Home, it was to be greeted with the news that the master had come back unexpectedly early, but had shut himself up in the study and refused to see anyone, even the veterinary surgeon, and wanted no dinner.

That Luke had refused to see amiable, good-natured Ned Bryant was significant, and could only mean that he had succumbed to one of his 'black moods'.

Oh no, thought Emma. Here am I, quite worn

out, and now I find Luke is sulking, and probably drinking—and whatever is wrong, he won't tell me. It really is too bad!

The drinking bouts disturbed her deeply, not because she had ever witnessed them—he always shut himself away—or because he became in any way noisy or violent, but because she recognised that they were an outward sign of some deep inner despair. It frightened her that Luke could feel this way. She did not understand it, and resented that he would not explain. So these rare, but recurring, bouts of silent, morose drinking remained like a canker in an apple. Somehow or other the cause had to be discovered and cured.

Emma took off her bonnet and marched briskly to the study, and threw open the door. The light had failed and the room was gloomy. Luke was slumped in a chair, with his back to the door, facing the window. She could see the top of his head above the chair-back and his long legs stretched out in front of him. He must have thought her a servant come with candles, for he said angrily, 'Go away! If I want any damn light, I'll ring for it!'

'It's Emma,' she said. She walked across the room to stand by his chair and glare disapprovingly at the decanter.

He glanced up. 'Oh, you're back, are you? Are all your noble deeds accomplished for today?'

Disliking the churlish tone, she said, 'Nothing noble at all, only practical. They tell me you have said you want no dinner. Well, I certainly want mine, and I'd rather not sit and eat it alone.'

'Don't nag at me, Emma,' he said quietly, and meant it.

Emma bit her lip. 'Will you at least have a candle? What is the virtue of sitting in the dark?'

'Oh, very well,' he growled.

But when the candle came and its flickering light fell on his face, she gave a cry of alarm, and forgetting her anger, gasped, 'But you're hurt! Whatever has happened? Was there a railway accident?'

'Good Lord, Emma, no! Don't fuss!' he told her irritably. 'I met in the fog with a fellow who thought to relieve me of my fob-watch and money. He failed.'

Luke did not know if she would accept this explanation, but to his relief she seemed to do so. She stood looking down at him with concern in her blue eyes, and he avoided her gaze, ashamed of his lie, and of the reason for it.

Emma thought his face looked tired and lined, and he seemed older than his thirty-seven years. 'What is wrong, Luke?' she asked gently. 'I know it isn't only having a scrap with a thief. It's more. What is it that brings on these moods?' When he only shrugged and muttered, she added, 'Is it something I have said or done?'

'No.' The monosyllable was bleak and discouraging.

Emma sighed. 'Then if you won't tell me, and I suppose you won't, will you at least put away the brandy? It frightens me, when you sit alone and drink.'

That got more of a reaction than she had expected. His features grew animated, and he looked truly contrite. 'Does it? You've never said so.' He pushed the glass and decanter away with a rough gesture.

Emma's brows puckered in a frown. He looked quite startled, almost alarmed, as if she had brought something to his notice of which he had been unaware.

In a way, she had. Luke, glancing at the brandy, asked himself: Am I going the way of the old man? God forbid! Aloud, he said, 'I'm sorry about the drinking bouts. Take it away, the brandy. Go on, take it away!'

He sounded so agitated that she quickly removed the decanter to a cupboard out of sight. As she turned back, her eye fell on the portraits on the wall, including that of Luke's mother. In a burst of intuition, she asked, 'Your father, did he drink—a lot, I mean?'

'As he got older.' Luke paused. 'I dare say he drank when he was a young man, but rode it off with days in the saddle. They damn nearly starved during the Peninsular campaigns, and kept going on local wine. He told me that once. When he got older, here at Hill House, he didn't burn the alcohol off with activity— it made it more noticeable.'

Emma perched on the arm of his chair. 'Did he . . . shout, or anything?'

'Lord, yes. You could hear him all over the house.'

'And—was he violent?'

Luke was silent. Perhaps he did not wish to be disloyal to his dead parent.

'Towards you?' persisted Emma. 'When you were a child?'

'Occasionally. I dare say he didn't mean . . .

Perhaps he didn't realise his own strength.'

Determined to get to the bottom of the problem, now that he seemed prepared to talk for once, Emma asked, 'And is that what brings on these "dark days" of yours? Memory of your father?'

'No!' Luke shouted so loudly that she looked alarmed, and he repeated more quietly, shaking his head. 'No, it's something else. Another memory. It has to do with India.'

'And you can't tell me?' Half-resentfully, she added, 'I am your wife.'

For a moment, Luke almost retorted, 'If you are my wife, then why the devil don't you stay at home and look after me, instead of running around God knows what infected slum all day, worrying about other people?' He did not say it, and was surprised at himself for even thinking it. Angry, too. The anger that had been brewing inside him all day found its outlet now in a desire to upset her, to exact a sort of petty revenge. She wanted to know what troubled him. Very well, he would tell her. He would tell her about Emerson, and how he had 'won' that confounded medal.

So he told her. He withheld none of the gruesome descriptions: let her hear it, every last grisly detail. As he spoke, narrating it all, it became a sort of catharis, as if telling it at last lifted a weight off him. He was scarcely aware, by the time he had finished, that it was Emma to whom he spoke. He was telling it for himself, not for her. When he finished and looked up, he saw that her face looked drawn and pale in the candlelight, a bit green about the gills. He hoped she was not going to faint.

'Forgive me,' he said contritely. 'I should have spared you that.'

'No,' she said quickly. 'I'm glad you told me.' After a moment she added, 'That poor young man! But you could not have shot him in cold blood, Luke, no matter how much he suffered.'

'Why not? Such things have been done before on a field of battle, when men have been forced to leave a wounded comrade.'

'But you didn't leave him; you brought him back.'

'All I did,' Luke said harshly, 'was to let him go on suffering.' He glanced up at her, and stretching out his hand, took hold of her fingers. They felt cold, and he squeezed them comfortingly. 'There, I am over my fit of the sulks. I'll tell them to come and make up the fire.'

Her fingers closed on his and she smiled at him hesitantly. He got up and went to the fireplace, and kicked at a smouldering log, which spat sparks out on the rug.

'See that?' He tapped the carved inscription over the hearth. 'It's by way of a family motto. It's a piece of Virgil, from the *Aeneid*. Aeneas contemplating his task of building Troy, and exclaiming: How fortunate are those whose city walls are already built. I feel about this house and the estate, sometimes, as though I shall never be finished with it. I dare say you feel that way about Forbes Street.'

'I must admit,' she confessed, 'that sometimes my courage fails me.'

'Our courage always fails us,' Luke said, 'and often when we need it most.'

Hesitantly, Emma suggested, 'You know, I am

not very hungry, either. We don't have to eat dinner. If you like, I can tell them to serve us some soup in here, and it will do well enough.'

So they sat and ate their soup in the candlelit study, the firelight playing about the walls. Luke talked about his childhood, a jumble of memories —from a tree-house he had built, to a notable cricketing victory at school—till the candles burned quite low, and the logs crackled and fell in upon one another.

Emma afterwards thought that she had learned a great deal that evening. A great deal about Luke, who was not quite the person she had thought him, but someone much more complex. Yet not only about Luke. She had also learned something about herself. That she had been too quick to assume that, because he appeared so assured and had been a soldier, and had criticised her wish to help the women, he was without sensitivity, or doubts and fears of his own. She had looked upon him first and foremost as 'a man'—an insensitive brute—even if he was her husband, and she had recognised that he had had also his good qualities. She had been too apt to make facile judgments.

'But I shall not do so again,' she said to herself.

CHAPTER EIGHT

AFTER THEIR conversation in the study, Emma felt
that there was a new understanding between herself and Luke, and she hoped it would mark a new
beginning for them. But events were about to
overtake them. On Luke's side, the drama that
burst upon them was not entirely unexpected, because he had been warned by Kezia that Leach
meditated some mischief. He had not, of course,
any idea what form it would take, but at least he
knew it was brewing. Emma, on the other hand,
was blissfully ignorant of the impending storm until
it broke about their heads.

The first she knew of it was, in fact, when the
butler came to her one morning to inform her that
Major Sheldon would be obliged if she could spare
him a moment. As she approached the study,
Emma could hear the murmur of male voices.
When she opened the door, she saw, to her surprise, that one voice belonged to the lawyer,
Sneadie, and the other to a sturdy, red-faced constable, who stood stiffly by the hearth, as if he were
on parade, with his top hat tucked under his arm.

'Ah, Emma . . .' said Luke, rising to his feet, 'I
am sorry to have disturbed you, my dear, but here
is Sneadie with some rather disturbing news.' As he
spoke, he took her hand and squeezed it hard.

Emma rightly interpreted the gesture as a warning that the affair was serious, and that Luke

wished her to leave him to deal with it. She saw that he looked angry and ruffled, as if he had been thwarted in some way, and her heart sank, because she felt sure that it must be to do with the Rescue Home. But what brought the constable? Had someone, after all, complained of rowdiness from the Home, or objected to the presence of 'loose women' in the neighbourhood of Forbes Street?

It was a dreary day, wet and windy, grey overhead and lowering to the eye and to the spirits. Sneadie's expression wore more than its usual gloom. He avoided her questioning gaze, and began polishing his gold pince-nez. The constable shuffled his feet, and barked the word 'Ma'am!' either as a greeting, or perhaps with the intention of beginning some speech.

Luke cast him a quelling look, and the Peeler's florid face grew redder. 'It concerns Rose,' Luke said briskly. 'It seems that a complaint has been made.'

'It's about time someone complained,' said Emma, misunderstanding. 'No one seems to care about these children.'

'No, no!' Luke interrupted hastily. 'The complaint has been made about us.'

'About *us*?' cried Emma incredulously.

''Fraid so, ma'am,' said the constable, introducing himself firmly into the conversation. 'On behalf, ma'am, of one Micah Smith, what has declared himself uncle and guardian of the said Rose Smith. The child is, as I understand, at present in this house?'

'If that is the man who wished to sell Rose to Old

Bessie,' said Emma energetically, 'then I would suggest that he is in no situation to complain about anything!' She could see Luke glaring at her, but ignored him.

Sneadie looked alarmed and clipped his pince-nez on to his thin, aquiline nose. 'Mrs Sheldon, ma'am, I am afraid I must point out that you only had the word of the girl, Smith, that there was such a plan. A court might well doubt her word, given that she is scarcely of good character.'

Emma rounded on him. 'I have always found Kezia utterly truthful!'

Luke signalled to her to be quiet, though he had little hope she would obey. 'Sneadie is right, Emma. We only had Kezia's word that he meant to sell Rose to Bessie. We failed, or rather, I failed, to take any steps to verify the tale.'

'Exactly so,' said Sneadie. 'As I was just saying to Major Sheldon, I wish you had informed me of the circumstances which led to your, ah, offering shelter to the child, Rose Smith. I should have warned you. Rash, ma'am, very rash.'

'But what have we done that is wrong?' cried Emma, baffled.

The constable cleared his throat. 'Depriving the lawful guardian of the child, ma'am. It's a serious matter. Taking away said Rose Smith without the consent of said Micah Smith.'

'Despite what he meant to do? And don't tell me Kezia isn't to be believed. I believe her story completely!'

'You may have believed it, ma'am,' said the constable. 'You and your husband both. But fact is, Micah Smith has been and laid complaint against you both. Seems he has grounds, ma'am. The charge is serious.'

'What charge?' cried Emma, incensed.

'Abduction,' said the constable. 'Smith claims you have abducted his niece. Major Sheldon has already admitted to me that the child is here.'

'Why—yes . . .' Emma faltered, the true horror of what was happening slowly dawning on her.

'And that you brought her away without authority.'

'But Kezzy—I mean, Rose's sister, Kezia Smith —told us that the uncle, the Micah Smith you mentioned, had agreed to let some woman called Old Bessie have Rose—for immoral purposes.'

'Well, then,' said the constable, 'no doubt we can find this Kezia Smith, and she'll testify as such.'

'But we don't know where she is . . .' Emma exclaimed.

Luke touched her arm. 'Constable, the girl Kezia is married to a lout named Leach, who certainly ill-treats her, and who, I strongly suspect, is behind all this. We cannot expect Kezia to testify in court. Leach would never permit it. To ask Kezia to disobey Leach would be to put her in great personal danger.'

The constable clucked his tongue disapprovingly. 'Well, sir, that ain't my province, as you might say. That's one for the courts, that is. My job, sir, is to take charge of the girl, Rose Smith. Perhaps, sir, you'd be so good as to have someone fetch her.'

Emma felt the colour drain from her cheeks. She put out a hand to grasp a chair-back for support. 'What do you mean, take charge of Rose? You can't mean, surely not, to take Rose away?'

Luke took her arm. 'Emma, I'm afraid the constable means precisely that.'

Emma gasped, and snatched her arm from his restraining grip. 'And you'll let him take Rose? You'd let Rose go? Well, I most certainly will not!' She turned on the constable, eyes blazing. 'Before Rose came to us she was half-starved, clothed in rags and wretchedly treated. She lived in an appalling slum with an uncle who, no matter what he may choose to say now, cared little enough for her then! Do you—or those who sent you—really think I will agree to return her to the miserable surroundings in which we found her? And for such a purpose? Constable, the child's elder sister begged us to take Rose away from that terrible place, and told us of the awful danger she was in!'

'I'm sorry, ma'am,' he said awkwardly. 'I don't make the decisions. The law is the law, and I'm its agent, that's all.'

Emma contemplated him. 'Are you a married man, Constable?' she asked him more quietly. 'With children of your own, perhaps?'

He looked even more awkward and miserable and muttered, 'Indeed I am, ma'am, and believe me, this job don't bring me no pleasure. But it has to be done.'

'Mrs Sheldon, ma'am,' said Sneadie, in his dry, precise way, 'we have no choice in this matter. Now the child will have to be given over to the constable, and sent into a safe place until this unfortunate affair has been sorted out.'

'But Rose is safe here!' cried Emma vehemently.

Sneadie turned to the constable. 'In view of the serious allegation—that Micah Smith intended, ah, to dispose of his niece in a quite reprehensible fashion—I take it that there is no question of the child being returned to him without enquiry being made?'

'I'm sorry, sir, that ain't my province,' repeated the constable heavily. 'I was sent to fetch Rose Smith, and without Rose Smith I can't leave these here premises.'

'What do you advise, Sneadie?' Luke asked tersely.

'Hm,' Sneadie pondered. 'That we go before a magistrate and make clear our doubts about Micah Smith's true intentions towards his niece. We'll ask for an order that the child be put in some suitable place, an orphanage or some such, until the courts decide whether Smith can have her back. I believe we can make a strong enough case.'

Emma sat down on the nearest chair with a bump. 'But this is awful! Surely, surely the magistrate will at least let us keep Rose here while everything is—is clarified.'

The constable shuffled his feet and looked embarrassed, but obstinate. Luke caught his eye.

'Emma, we must do as the constable asks. You heard Sneadie. Don't worry, Rose will be quite safe, and we'll get all this put right in no time.' He was far from convinced this was so, and his doubt echoed in his voice.

She heard it, and cast him a look of supreme scorn. 'Is that all you can say? Just—let Mr Sneadie sort it out?'

'Yes, Emma!' Luke said curtly, and with such authority that she was silenced for the moment. He drew a deep breath and strode to the bell-pull. At the appearance of the butler, he ordered, 'Fetch down Rose—and get one of the maids to put her things together.' To the constable, he added, 'The child has not long recovered from a broken arm, and is to be treated gently!'

Emma could not trust herself to speak. She turned her back on the assembled company and walked jerkily to the window, to stare out at the wet, soggy, dismal gardens. The scene that followed was worse than anything she could have conjured up in the most desperate nightmare. Rose, as soon as she realised she was to be taken away, fell into hysterics, and clung screaming to Emma's skirts.

'Oh, Rose, dear, please—it is only for a little while!' Emma begged, trying to calm her and to sound reassuring.

But Rose burst into floods of tears, screaming wildly, 'I won't, I won't! I want to stay here with you and Samson and Tom and Riley and everyone else! I won't go!' Her hands closed on the material with the strength of desperation.

Eventually, after all attempts at persuasion had failed, and an attempt by the constable to assert his authority and order the child gruffly to 'Let go at once and stop that yowling!' had been angrily repulsed by Emma, it fell to Emma herself, with tears running freely down her own cheeks, to prise Rose's white fingers loose as gently as possible. The poor little soul was half-led and half-hauled away by the guardian of the law, in a state of near collapse.

'For God's sake, Sneadie!' Luke ordered in a shaken voice. 'Go with the fellow, and make sure that child is put into safe hands. I don't want her locked up overnight in the local gaol!' He turned away, his back to them all, and rubbed a hand over his face and hair.

'Quite so, quite so . . .' Sneadie hurried out in the wake of the constable and his small prisoner.

As he quitted the room, Emma turned on Luke, in a turmoil of rage and despair. 'How could you allow it? You could have done something to help Rose! But you never wished to have her here, and now you are quite satisfied to see her taken away!'

'Stop that, Emma!' he said coldly. 'You don't seriously think I cared for that appalling scene and to have it take place under my roof?'

'I won't!' she cried. 'What do you care about Rose or any of the others? You let poor Kezzy go, and goodness only knows where she is now! Now it is poor little Rose's turn! You object to my work, and you want me to give it up. You will do anything in your power to see I'm not successful. Oh!'

The cry was caused as Luke strode forward and seizing her shoulders, shook her sharply, cutting off the words in her throat. She was so horrified and taken aback that she fell silent and stared at him, lips parted and eyes wide, but unable to speak a word.

'It was necessary,' he said briefly. 'You were hysterical.' He released her and turned away.

Emma swallowed, and made an effort to gain control of herself. 'Yes. I—I'm all right now.'

Luke began to turn up and down the room, his hands clasped behind his back. 'I have something to tell you, Emma. It's by nature of a confession. Perhaps I should have told you before.' As briefly as possible, he told her of his encounter with Kezia, and subsequently with Leach. 'I was afraid you would want to be dashing off to Wapping, and I couldn't have that. So I said nothing of it,' he concluded.

'You should have told me,' Emma said in a quiet voice.

'Possibly. Although I did not think so at the time, nor do I think now that I was wrong to conceal it from you. However, right or wrong, it can't be helped now.'

'So you think Leach has plotted this?' she asked.

'Put my last guinea on it. The fellow is a rogue, but a clever rogue in his way. I doubt that Micah Smith will turn out to have enough brain to fill a thimble. It makes no difference. Emma, we are in a devil of a scrape—or rather, I am.'

'Why you?' she asked simply. 'It was my idea.'

'You are my wife. The law will assume that you took your instructions from me.' He glanced at her and pulled a wry face. 'The law does not know you, you see.'

'But this is ridiculous!' she gasped. 'It was all my doing! Why should you be blamed? You wanted to send Rose to the workhouse, and I wouldn't allow it. Oh!' She threw up both hands in despair. 'I do believe the world is quite mad! Everything is topsy-turvy. We took Rose from a wretched life and a worse fate, and that is called abducting her. Rose is dragged by force from where she is safe and happy, to be locked up in a cell or in an orphanage. You are responsible for none of it, and you are to be held to blame! For goodness' sake, tell them it was my doing and mine alone!'

'Will you listen for once, Emma?' he shouted at
her. 'I am your husband and this is my house, in
which Rose has been living. I was there when the
child was taken from Bethnal Green. I am responsible!' As she fell silent, he added, breathing
heavily and struggling for self-control, 'What's
more, I don't intend to offer lame excuses
and certainly not to run and hide behind a
woman's petticoats! The blame is mine because I
went against my own better judgment! I was a
fool to do so, and now, it seems, I must pay for
it!'

After a silence, during which the echo of his
voice faded slowly in the room, Emma asked more
steadily, 'But there must be some defence we can
offer.'

'Yes, we must show, somehow, that we truly
believed Rose to be in moral danger. But without
Kezia . . .'

'We cannot call on Kezzy.' Emma shook her
head. She frowned, racking her brains for a sol-
ution. 'Luke, do you remember the cabbie? The
man who drove me to Bethnal Green that day? He
must have overheard what Kezia said to us. He was
a witness. I'm sure I could find him again. He might
well remember me, though it was some time ago,
because I had such difficulty to persuade him to
drive me to Taylor's Court.'

Luke shrugged. 'We can try and dig him out.
But, you know, I doubt he'll remember much, not
enough to impress a judge, anyway.' He glanced at
her. 'You do realise, Emma, that if I am put in the
dock and it goes against me, there is more to be lost
than Rose?'

'I shall lose the Home!' Emma wailed in despair. 'Everyone will withdraw their support.' She gave a start, and added guiltily, 'Of course you will lose much more; you will lose your reputation.'

'I was thinking of my liberty,' he said sarcastically. 'But perhaps the idea that I might be locked up as a common malefactor doesn't seem important to you.'

Emma's cheeks drained of colour and she sat down again, her knees turning to jelly, and stared at him ashen-faced.

'Well, well,' he muttered, 'we must do as William of Orange, I suppose: hope for the best, and prepare for the worst.' He gave a snort of derision. 'The popular press will make much of this!

At first Emma clung desperately to the hope that somehow Sneadie would sort out the whole horrible muddle. Gradually, however, it became clear that matters had gone too far for that, and that Luke was indeed to be charged with the abduction of Rose. Sneadie, visibly outraged and wretched, strode about his tiny office, waving his arms like an agitated stick-insect, in a manner no one could recall ever having seen him do.

'If we could but shake Smith, but he sticks to his story. In fact, the wretched fellow sticks to it too well, repeating it word for word, time after time. He has been well rehearsed.'

'Leach,' Luke muttered.

'Someone, certainly,' the lawyer agreed. 'The plaintiff is a very low type of person, illiterate, drunken and of bad character. But he is the lawful guardian of the child, being her nearest relative

other than her sister, and having brought up both
girls from infancy.'

Against all the odds, they were successful,
however, in tracing the cabman who had first taken
Emma to Taylor's Place. He said that he did remember the occasion, only his mind was somewhat
hazy, as it was a while ago. He remembered there
being a little girl, but could not recall exactly what
had been said. He thought he remembered Luke
saying to the lady, 'This does not mean you can
keep the child', or words to that effect.

'It is something,' said Sneadie. 'It shows there
was no premeditated plan to take the child away.'
He shook his head dolefully. 'But unless we can
come up with something a little more substantial
than our cabman friend—who may well, on the
stand, remember more than we should like—then I
fear, Major Sheldon, that our defence is very
shaky. The fact is that you took the child away, and
even removed her from London completely. That
might be argued to show an attempt to hide her. We
already have a trial date, early in February. It gives
us very little time.'

Luke swore softly. Then he gathered up his hat
and cane and got to his feet, his solid form filling
what little spare space there was in Sneadie's clut-
tered office. 'Well, you will do your best, Sneadie, I
don't doubt.'

'You may rely on me, Major. I have engaged Mr
Kennedy, who is a capable barrister, to speak on
our behalf. He was more than willing to take the
brief, since he has expressed admiration for the
work done by Mrs Sheldon.'

Luke gave a muffled snort.

                    *   *   *

Not everyone viewed the approach of the trial with gloom and despondency. Sam Leach was in fine fettle. Not, as he told himself, that it had been easy to set up. It was a full-time job, all on its own, trying to keep old Micah sober, and making sure he said all the right things.

'What was you when you found the kid gone, Micah?'

'Fair out of me wits with worry,' said Mr Smith promptly. 'Her being the apple of my eye.'

'And what did you do?'

'Hunted high and low for her!' repeated his pupil.

'And Old Bessie?'

'Never set eyes on her!' declared Micah triumphantly.

'That's very good, Micah,' said Sam approvingly.

'It's worth a drink, anyway, Sammy. It taxes a man's brain, all this worrying with what to say, 'Ave I got to say all this to the beak, Sammy?'

'You have,' said his mentor. 'And if you turns up drunk, Micah, so help me, I'll wring your neck for you. You might practise spilling a few tears.'

'Whaffor?' asked Mr Smith.

'You bone-headed old soak, for when you're speaking of how terrible upset you was, to find Rosie gone.'

'Oh, that . . .' said Micah.

Sam sighed, and wondered if he could keep himself from doing serious damage to the stupid old ruffian until the trial was over.

Old Bessie had presented a slightly more difficult problem to Sam, for whereas Micah was afraid of him, he, in turn, was wary of the procuress. She was a woman to be reckoned with, and Sam had approached her with some caution, well aware that the prospect of being put in the dock on account of Rose Smith was not one likely to appeal to her.

But he was in luck. Bessie was smarting from having been obliged to 'shut up shop for a bit', as she explained to Sam, over a convivial glass of gin. 'The Law's bin coming around and poking their noses in. Well, I got convictions, Sam, and I can't run no risks. So I put up the shutters for a month or so. Out of business, temporary, as you might say.'

'Looks like you and me might do each other a favour then, Bess,' said Sam.

She eyed him thoughtfully, and he shifted uneasily in his chair. 'That's right, my dear,' she said at last. She smiled and patted his arm. 'I'd like to see that so-called Rescue Home,' and Bessie snorted scornfully, 'shut down once and for all! As if it ain't enough having the Law come round, ruining my business. I can do without interfering ladies, with time on their hands and nothing else to do, taking girls out of the business altogether. Mrs Harris has lost two promising youngsters, and magistrates is sending girls off to that place in Forbes Street as fast as they appears in court.'

No wonder Sam was in a good mood as he made his way home to Wapping late that evening. It was bitterly cold, and a few flakes of snow drifted down on the chill wind. It was city snow, not white and crisp, but dull grey and damp. Sam turned up his coat collar and paused to buy a hot potato from a vendor. He tossed it in his hands for a while before eating it, to warm his fingers, and then munched at it as he went along. There were few people about, and it occurred to him that Kezzy would not be having much luck, not on a night like this. A pity, because he was mortal short of money. That she might easily catch pneumonia did not worry him.

His good humour was dispelled a little when he got to their wretched lodgings and found Kezia there and not shivering on a street corner as he had supposed.

'What are you doin' here, then?' he asked her in a surly voice.

'It's mortal cold, Sam,' Kezzy said, coughing a little. 'I don't feel so good.'

'Well you'll feel a lot worse, my girl, in a minute, if you don't get out and about your business!' he promised her.

'You looks pretty pleased with yourself,' she observed, peering at him suspiciously.

He chuckled. 'Well, I got good reason. I got your precious Miss Meddle and her dandy of a husband right where I wants 'em. We'll see how fine they look when old Micah stands up in court and tells 'em how they took Rosie away from him.'

'It's a bad thing you're doing there, Sam,' Kezzy said. 'If Micah gets Rose back, it will only be to put her out on the street, like he done with me. She's only a kid, Sam; why don't you let her go? Let the Major and Miss Emma keep her? It ain't no loss to you.'

Sam got to his feet and opened the one cupboard and took out a bottle. 'You fetch me a glass, and keep your mouth shut. It don't concern you.'

'If the judge was to hear what I had to say, things might not go so well for you and Micah!' she said sullenly.

Leach's thick-set brows drew together in a
threatening frown. 'You ain't threatening of me,
are you, Kezzy? Because I don't like that. You
know me, Kezzy, and what I can do.'

'I know it, well enough,' she said with a flash of
spirit. 'You took me away from Miss Emma, when I
had a chance to have a better life than this . . .' She
flung her hand out at their sordid surroundings.
'Now you means to ruin things for Rosie. Maybe I
ain't going to stand for it, Sam!'

For a moment he looked at her in real surprise,
not accustomed to have a revolt on his hands. But
he had his own way of dealing with that, and setting
down the bottle, took a quick step towards her,
and before she could dodge out of the way, struck
her a vicious blow which sent her spinning across
the room. 'You ain't doing nothing, Kezzy, you
hear me?' When she did not reply, he seized hold of
her and struck her again. 'You hear me, Kez?'

'I hear you, Sam,' she whispered.

Sam chuckled again. And then, because he was
not the only man on whom violence acted as an
aphrodisiac, he said, 'Well, maybe it ain't worth the
while you going out on a night like this. You can
stay here and keep me happy.'

'No, Sam, please . . .' she begged, because she
feared his violent and repeated sexual demands
more than his blows.

But he dragged her across to the bed and threw
her down on it, sprawling across her and tearing at
her petticoats, thrusting himself into her while she
twisted her face and buried it in the dingy pillows to
stifle her sobs. When he had satisfied himself for the
time being, he stumbled back to the table and the

abandoned bottle of gin, and sat drinking from it, while she huddled on the pillows and waited, knowing that, when the drink was finished, the urge would come on him again, and so it did. Eventually he fell asleep, satiated and snoring drunkenly, one leg still thrown across her and imprisoning her.

She did not dare to stir until morning, when she slid cautiously from beneath his prostrate form, and crept out into the yard. The pump was frozen, but eventually she and another woman from a nearby lodging managed to coax enough water out of it to fill a couple of buckets. Kezia took hers back and washed herself and put on a different skirt to replace the one Sam had torn the evening before. He was still asleep. She peeped at him, holding her breath, and then tiptoed out again. Outside, she threw her shawl over her head, glanced up at the sky which threatened more snow, and set off hurriedly through the cold, grey streets.

CHAPTER NINE

THE COBBLED pavements beneath Kezzy's hurrying
feet were slippery with early frost and ice, and her
breath hung in the air in clouds of moisture. From
time to time, as she hastened along, she glanced
over her shoulder, afraid that Leach might have
woken, and guessing where she had gone, set off in
pursuit. But she need not have worried, for Sam
was slumbering on, little aware that his brutish
attempts to prevent his wife from telling her tale
had decided her on just that intention.

'Ain't no one can help me,' Kezia muttered to
herself as she dodged between the lumbering teams
of dray-horses and avoided the creaking wheels.
'But you won't have Rose, not if I can help
it!'

A milk-cart was just setting off, and rattled past
her, the contents of its churns emitting a sickly,
tepid odour. The milk that was sold in the great
cities came in large part from cows kept tethered in
byres and fed on all manner of scraps, never seeing
a field. The resulting milk was thin, unwholesome
and curious in colour, ranging from greyish blue to
a dirty white. The man who led the pony paused in
his cry of 'Milk-o!' to ask Kezia, 'How about
you, my dear? A cup of warm milk on a cold
morning?'

She shook her head and scurried on, stumbling
over the uneven surface and thinking, In the

country, where Miss Emma took our Rosie, there's cows in fields. Somehow or other I'll get Rose back there again, though I don't know how.

At last she reached the scrubbed steps of the lawyer's offices, and after a moment's hesitation, entered the polished hall, and deciphering, with puckered brow, the nameplate on the first door she reached, opened it and went in.

Sneadie's chief clerk was busy directing his most junior underling in how exactly to make up the fire in the outer office, using the least number of lumps of coal. A feeble flame had just been persuaded to flicker in the meagre hearth, when the sudden cold draught from the outer door extinguished it. Not best pleased, he turned majestically, a man who had been twenty-five years employed as clerk to the same legal practice, and saw Kezia standing by the door. He noted with disapproval that she was dressed in a red skirt of cheap quality but garish hue, and had a shawl wrapped round her head and shoulders against the cold weather.

'What do you want?' he demanded sourly. 'We don't need beggars here. Take yourself off!'

The girl by the door stood her ground and announced, 'I want to see the lawyer, the old fellow, name of Sneadie.'

The most junior clerk, on his knees before the smoking fireplace, raised his head and permitted a grin to cross his fifteen-year-old features. He was quelled by a look from his senior.

'Mr Sneadie don't see the likes of you.'

'He's acting for the Major, ain't he?' she retorted. 'You go and tell him that Kezzy Smith is out here and wants a word.' She pushed back the shawl and stared at him defiantly. Her face was badly bruised, but that was no rare thing in a woman of her background.

He clicked his tongue disapprovingly. 'You just wait there, young woman. And you, Wilkes, you keep an eye on her, and make sure she doesn't touch anything!' He straightened his coat and tapped deferentially on a further door.

When he had gone to explain the visitor, young Wilkes stood up and offered, 'Best come over here and warm your hands. Not that the fire is up to much, Mr Sneadie being on the mean side with the coal.' When she approached and held out reddened fingertips to the feeble flame, he added, 'Think you can help the Major, do you?'

'I might,' Kezia said cautiously.

'Hope you can,' he said. 'Mrs Sheldon, before she was married, used to come visiting to our house, Ma being an invalid and times being hard. We all thought a lot of Miss Emma—a real lady, not like some as is all airs and graces and nothing else.'

Kezia smiled at him, and young Wilkes thought she really was very pretty. He was sorry about the bruises, and longed gallantly to punch the head of whoever gave them to her. The sound of the door of Sneadie's sanctum opening interrupted this budding acquaintance.

'Mr Sneadie will see you,' said the chief clerk. 'As it happens, Major Sheldon is with him.' He ran a critical and disapproving eye over her. 'Wipe your feet,' he ordered tersely.

*   *   *

'Well, Mrs Leach,' Sneadie said, 'my client would, of course, be very pleased to have you testify on his behalf.'

'Hold on, Sneadie!' Luke said sharply. 'What about Leach?'

Kezia's eyes flickered towards him. He looked tired and worried, and not his usual self, though he was a fine-looking fellow, no mistake. Aloud, she said firmly, 'I want to speak up and tell what I know, sir. I want to help you, and your lady. But it ain't just for you. It's for our Rosie, too. I mean to keep her from going the way of me. I'll do anything to prevent it, I swear.'

The lawyer leaned towards his client. 'She is the child's sister. If she stands up and tells the court she asked you to take the child, it knocks the abduction charge on the head!'

That Sneadie was betrayed into the vernacular was a mark of his excitement. Luke knew that he had no choice. He got up and said quietly, 'You are a brave girl, Kezzy, and we shall do our best to see you come to no harm.' He took hold of her reddened hands, the skin chapped by cold, and added, 'They gave me a medal once, but I don't believe I ever deserved it half as much as you deserve one.' To Sneadie's obvious consternation, he stooped and kissed her cheek.

Luke had left Emma at Mrs Somerton's home while he called on the lawyer, and it was there he went now. He found his wife in an unaccustomed restful pose, with her feet up on her aunt's threadbare sofa, before the fire which crackled in the hearth. She had propped her chin on her hand and stared thoughtfully into the dancing flames, her delicate eyebrows puckered. Luke stood by the drawing-room door, and wondered that someone so small and frail in appearance could have the heart of a lion and an extraordinary will-power that far outstripped her fragile frame. That courage would see her through, no matter what happened. 'A quart in a pint pot'—the old saying came to his mind, and he smiled, because it described his Emma very well.

He went across to the sofa and sat on the edge of it and took her free hand. 'Kezia wishes to testify,' he said. Emma looked up, startled and alarmed, and he added quickly, 'She is determined to do it, for Rose's sake. Sneadie thinks it may tip things in our favour.'

Emma sighed. 'Luke, I've been thinking it all over while you were out. I'm beginning to wonder if you weren't right all along. I wanted so much to help girls like Kezzy and Rose. Yet all I seem to have done is to make matters worse. The Home seemed such a good idea!' Frustration entered her voice. 'And it all seemed so easy and—simple. I thought if only I could get the girls away, away from the street corners and doorways, and away from the horrid slums where they lived, to make a new beginning would be so straightforward. But it isn't. It's not possible for anyone just to walk away from the past, is it?' She fixed her blue eyes on his face enquiringly.

'No,' he said quietly, 'it isn't. I know that, Emma.'

'You know so much that I don't,' she said with another sigh. 'I am sorry I have made all this trouble for you. I never thought, you see, that the law would be against me. I thought it must be for me, because I believed what I was doing was right.' She gave a little exclamation of utter exasperation and cried out, 'I've brought trouble to everyone, from you to Kezia, and it's all so unfair!'

Abruptly she pulled her hand from his consoling grip, and scrambled inelegantly from the sofa in a flurry of petticoats. 'It's not only unfair to you, it's unfair to *me*! I have a right to be charged with this so-called crime!'

'What on earth are you talking about?' Luke demanded, feeling the logic of the argument slip away from him. 'Confound it, Emma, whenever I think you start to make sense, you hare off in a totally unexpected direction, making no sense at all.'

The petticoats whirled round in a rustle of silk. 'No, I don't!' she stormed at him. 'You mean, by making sense, whenever I start to agree with you!' Exasperation entered her voice, and she glared at him. 'Why won't you try and understand? By holding you responsible in this case, when you only did as I asked, the law is saying I should be ignored. You alone are able to decide what we do. I haven't got a brain of my own. I am a married woman, and I don't count for anything!'

'Oh, rubbish, Emma!' Luke exploded. 'The law goes by *facts*. The fact is that I suggested removing the child from Bethnal Green while we discussed what to do with her, unbeknown to her legal guardian. Subsequently I failed to return her, first keeping her in a house owned by me in Town, and after that at Hill House, also my property. That I did it because you wanted me to is neither here nor there. I would much prefer you not to make too much of that. It makes me look hen-pecked.'

'You mean,' Emma asked, aghast, 'that you would rather take the whole blame for something than admit you were influenced by a *woman*?'

'A captain is responsible for his ship, Emma!' Luke wished he had not sounded so pompous, but was obliged to stand by his statement.

She told him exactly how pompous, which increased his annoyance, adding, 'I have been completely passed over as though I were no one. I am no one. I ceased to be anyone when I married. Before that, I was at least Miss Wainwright. Now I am only Mrs Sheldon!'

'Well, then,' he said coldly, getting to his feet, 'you are only Mrs Sheldon, and I am sorry if Miss Wainwright is to be preferred!'

'Luke!' she began, colour surging into her cheeks as realisation of what she had implied struck her. But he had already marched out of the room, slamming the door with a thunderous crash which rocked it on its hinges.

News of the impending court action had reached Forbes Street. On Emma's next visit, she found the girls in sober mood. They gathered round her, asking, 'Shall we all have to go, Mrs Sheldon?'

'Go? Why, of course not!' said Emma stoutly. 'This is a private matter. It only concerns Rose Smith, and none of you needs worry.'

That was far from the truth, because whatever happened, the Home must be affected. An unfavourable verdict—Emma closed her eyes and tried to shut out the possibility of such a thing—and resultant bad publicity would have a catastrophic effect. Good causes, like so many other things, become fashionable or not. To help the 'undeserving' poor had never been a fashion, and Emma had worked hard to make the very idea acceptable. A scandal would be the end of everything.

'The girls are all very concerned for you, and for your husband, Mrs Sheldon,' said the matron. 'They have all been so quiet and well-behaved, I've hardly been able to credit it. Why, even difficult girls have turned to and done their chores without a murmur. It's when folk think they may lose a thing that it begins to mean something to them. I haven't heard a word of criticism this whole week. And those girls can grumble, you know, if they've a mind to!'

'I shall not abandon them, whatever happens,' Emma said quietly. 'Even if it means starting out all over again, and just when I thought we were beginning to get somewhere. Oh, it really is too bad!'

'It isn't only for themselves, ma'am. They're fond of you. They know this place means a lot to you.'

'Yes.' Emma walked to the window, which looked out on to Forbes Street, and stared out. 'It does. It means a great deal to me.'

The trial opened to a full courtroom and a buzz of general interest which reached far outside its four walls. As Luke had predicted, the newspapers had discovered the affair, and regaled their scandalised and fascinated readers with all manner of details. Dark allusions were made to 'a sinister traffic in innocent girls', which led worthy matrons to palpitate over the teacups and sponge cakes, declaring how horrid it was, to be sure, before sending the maid out to buy the latest editions.

Ripples had even reached parliament, where a general consensus to ignore the realities of vice in the great cities was severely shaken. On the one hand, the members hoped Sheldon would 'get off', because the fellow was a gentleman, after all, and it didn't do to have gentlemen convicted of abducting young girls. On the other hand, there was a reluctance to admit that a twelve-year-old girl could be at risk. 'We don't want to open that Pandora's box', was the general opinion in the members' dining-room. 'Every reformer in the land will be baying for legislation. Can't be done. The thing's an evil, but a necessary one. This is a very fine claret; we'll have another bottle.'

The indefatigable journalists had even rooted out Luke's military record, and his heroic rescue of a brother officer filled two columns, illustrated. When Luke, furious, ordered Sneadie to put a stop to these revelations, the lawyer counselled discretion. 'One might say it's a good thing, Major. It portrays you as an Englishman of the best sort. Juries and judges are patriotic. Sorry, Major, but I must advise that, in this instance, we let the gentlemen of the Press work for us.'

Court procedure of the day did not permit the accused to speak, other than to declare Guilty or Not Guilty. A plea of Not Guilty having been entered, Luke was thereafter obliged to sit and listen, unable either to refute any accusation or to explain his reason for his actions. He sat in the dock with his arms folded and a slightly belligerent expression on his handsome face, and when Emma attempted to smile encouragingly at him, she received a scowl in response. She noticed, with some distress, that an artist sitting nearby was energetically putting Luke's portrait on paper.

'I wish I could stand up and shout that this is all a nonsense!' she hissed to Sneadie, who turned pale and muttered apprehensively, 'I beg you will do no such thing, ma'am!'

Their barrister, Mr Kennedy, was a portly, middle-aged gentleman with a pink, cherubic face like an elderly baby, and a tendency to wheeze between phrases, which Emma found distracting. She hoped this mannerism would not confuse the jury. Mr Kennedy proved, however, wise in the ways of courtrooms, and was prepared to argue the defence indefatigably, ably supported by Sneadie. The defence admitted that the child, Rose Smith, had been taken away, but insisted that her own sister had requested the Sheldons to take care of her, claiming that she was in great moral danger, which the accused had believed to be true. Throughout, Major Sheldon had acted—wheeze—from the highest—wheeze—motives.

But before this could be argued, the prosecution put its case. Sam had been so successful in working on Micah Smith that Rose's uncle appeared not only both sober and word-perfect, but reasonably clean and shaved, as well. Though understandably nervous on the witness stand, he stuck to his story, declaring himself 'fair distracted' by the loss of his niece and denying vehemently that he had ever envisaged either putting her on the streets or giving her to Old Bessie for a similar purpose.

Was it not the case, enquired Mr Kennedy, that the elder sister of the child, Kezia Leach née Smith, had been set to the oldest profession a few years previously, following a similar arrangement?

'That wasn't my doing!' said Mr Smith virtuously. 'Kezia ran off and took to a wicked life all by herself.' He raised his eyes ceilingwards. 'I pleaded wiv her to see the light and return to the fold. But the devil had stopped her ears.'

'You are a religious man, Mr Smith?' enquired Mr Kennedy.

Micah proceeded to ramble at some length about being brought up by a God-fearing mother, before the judge interrupted and said he felt that had no bearing on the case.

Next upon the witness stand appeared Old Bessie herself, sailing under the flag of Mrs Elizabeth Coggins, widow. Her appearance caused a considerable stir, not only because the journalists present recognised her as a notorious procuress, but because her ample form was clad in an emerald plush gown and she wore a large, lime-green, pleated silk bonnet with a huge curled ostrich plume waving above it, and a mauve cape lined with yellow silk.

The difficulty proved not to persuade Mrs Coggins to give her evidence—about which she might have been expected to be shy—but to stop her talking. Voluble and emphatic, she plunged into an irate tirade, over-riding all attempts to interrupt her.

Yes, she was Elizabeth Coggins, known to some as Bessie Coggins, or Old Bessie. It was a slanderous lie that she had entered into any arrangement with Micah Smith regarding Rose Smith. She had never set eyes on the child, and as for Micah Smith, she had never heard of him.

Under cross-examination, she admitted, glaring ferociously at Mr Kennedy and Sneadie behind him, that she had in the past been several times convicted of keeping a disorderly house. But she had given up the business, and was now a respectable woman, and defied anyone to say anything to the contrary. Moreover, the fact that her establishment—when she had had one—had been called 'disorderly' was a disgraceful slander, for disorderly it most certainly had not been, and it was downright criminal to have termed it so. Why, she had run the best conducted house in London, patronised exclusively by the gentry and some of the highest in the land, said Bessie with meaningful looks at the public; and, what was more, patronised often enough by the accused gentleman over there, Major Sheldon—and many others she could name!

She flung out a plump beringed hand to point at Luke, setting all the journalists scribbling gleefully in their notebooks.

'Mrs Coggins,' said the judge, 'you will refrain from making statements which do not touch upon the present case, and would morever be slanderous.'

'I'm on my oath, your Honour,' declared Bessie, bosom heaving with indignation. 'That gent has many times been in my establishment, and if you want witnesses to what he was a-doing there, you can ask my girls. He wasn't saving of them from sin, anyways, most certain he wasn't!'

The effect of Bessie's evidence upon the jury was hard to tell, but it was a runaway success with the public gallery, where each spectator had slipped the doorkeeper a shilling to be admitted, and wanted his money's-worth.

The defence caused a stir of its own by producing Kezia, who told her story in a clear, firm voice and obviously produced some impression. The prosecution, however, was able to make much of her four separate convictions for behaviour in the street likely to annoy or offend passers-by, and to insinuate that her word should be taken with a pinch of salt.

The cabman gave his evidence with sturdy authority, assuring the court that the gentleman had definitely been unwilling to take the child, but upon cross-examination was obliged to admit that the gentleman had subsequently changed his mind and spoken the words, 'put the child in the cab'.

The judge summed up fairly enough. Had the accused acted at the request of the child's sister, with the best of motives, and reluctantly? Had a deliberate attempt been made to hide the child, by taking her out of London and into the country? These were questions the jury members must ask themselves.

The jury retired. Emma managed to catch Luke's eye, and his stern expression unbent to sketch a brief, wry smile at her. They both knew that if the decision went against them, it would be the end of everything: of Luke's personal reputation, perhaps even of his liberty, and the end of

NO PLACE FOR A LADY

Emma's work at the Home. No one would wish to support her, with a conviction in court against them.

At least they were not kept in suspense for long. The jury returned to their seats, and the foreman gave their decision in resonant tones: Not Guilty.

'Oh, Luke!' cried Emma in relief, jumping to her feet.

Sneadie grasped her arm and dragged her down again. 'Wait, ma'am!'

The judge thanked the jury. He was sure the right decision had been reached. Major Sheldon had acted foolishly and illegally, but from the highest motives and in full belief that he was saving the child from danger. He had no other motive. It would be quite wrong to call the action abduction, as the word was normally understood.

'But,' continued the judge, and Sneadie whispered, 'Here it comes!' 'Defence has successfully shown that Major Sheldon acted without malice but, I feel, under a misapprehension. No doubt he believed the story told to him and to his wife by Kezia Leach, née Smith, to be true. But that story has not been proved. Kezia Leach's way of life and background must make further independent corroborating evidence necessary. There is none. In the absence of substantiating evidence, therefore, I am forced to conclude that no arrangement between Micah Smith and Elizabeth Coggins existed with regard to Rose Smith.'

The result of all this was that the law, in its wisdom, ordered that custody of the child be returned to her family, even though that family was represented by a drunken costermonger, a man whose brutality was such that some fifteen months earlier the same law had declared him unfit to keep a donkey. However, being unfit to have care of an animal did not, it seemed, render him unfit to have the care of a child. The court had no hesitation in returning Rose Smith, aged twelve, to her uncle, Micah Smith, aged forty-two, costermonger, of Bethnal Green.

The judge commended Major and Mrs Sheldon for the excellent work of the Rescue Home, but trusted that the experience they had just suffered would warn them to act more prudently in future, and to stay well within the law.

Emma gasped and whispered, 'Oh, no . . .' and at the back of the courtroom, Kezia threw her shawl over her head and slipped out into the teeming streets of London.

It was a sober little dinner party at Mrs Somerton's which followed. They had indeed 'won', and were personally vindicated, but Rose had been lost, and Emma's future efforts to take girls into the Home would be set about by numerous pitfalls.

After dinner, Mrs Somerton retired, and Luke and Emma sat by the guttering candlelight for a long time in silence. Eventually Luke stood up and went to the fireplace, where he leaned his arm on the mantelshelf and stared moodily into the flames.

Watching his solid, brooding frame, Emma said quietly, 'I have always been so sure that what I wanted to do was right, Now I'm not sure any more. Perhaps you are right, and I should give up the Home.'

Inwardly her heart sank, but she had brought so much trouble on his head that she felt obliged to offer to give up Forbes Street although every fibre of her being cried out against it. Her heart was filled with dread that he would say, 'Yes, you should.' When he said nothing, she asked hesitantly, 'What shall I do?'

Luke seemed to hear her for the first time. He turned and stared at her, his expression almost surprised. 'Do? Why, you carry on, of course.'

Emma's heart leapt with joy. He supported her work at last. 'You really mean that?' she faltered, hardly able to credit it.

'Of course I damn well mean it!' he roared with a violence she had not expected. He left the hearth and strode towards her. 'Confound it, I have been dragged into a criminal court as a defendant on a charge of abduction. My name has been spread across penny broadsheets and my behaviour and that of my wife have been made the subject of public debate! All this, because of the plotting of an uneducated lout like Sam Leach! Do you imagine that I shall now meekly request you to close the Rescue Home, and concede the field to Leach? Do you think I would let that scoundrel exult over me in every public house he patronises with his unsavoury presence, boasting that he forced the closure of the Home? That he outwitted *us*? That he has damn neared ruined me? You are surely not so ignorant of human nature that you think tongues will cease to wag just because a judge declared my motives above reproach? Bessie, if you recall, kindly identified me as an old and valued customer.

Half the people who open their newspapers tomorrow will say, "Oho, but what did he really want with the child?" Are you out of your mind, Emma? I shall permit no such thing as closure of the Home. Of course you will continue at Forbes Street. I insist on it!'

Emma stared at him, hardly knowing whether to laugh or to cry, Yes, he supported her at last—but not for any reason she would have wished. Not because he believed in her work, or wanted to help the girls, or to fight an evil. But because he, Lucius Sheldon, had been personally attacked, had been made the object of scandal and newspaper articles, and had been obliged to sit in court and listen both to Kennedy defend his actions and to the judge declare him imprudent and foolish. His pride had been wounded, and he was not a man meekly to accept such a situation. He wanted revenge, and one means of gaining it was to see the Rescue Home continue.

A painful ache entered Emma's heart. She wanted to tell him how much it would have meant to her to hear him say, 'Yes, Emma, carry on, because I believe you are right.'

He had not said it. Perhaps he would never truly forgive her for being the root cause of all his troubles. The Home had been saved, but at the expense of her marriage, and that newborn understanding with Luke of which she had cherished such hopes lay dead. Emma shook herself and gathered up the fragmented pieces of her self-esteem. Like a broken vase, they had to be glued together again and restored to a whole, and the glue was provided only by her own determination.

She forced away the ache, and said crisply, 'Well, then, as you are agreed, I shall continue with my work.'

CHAPTER TEN

PICKING UP the pieces and going back to Forbes Street seemed at first a monumental task. But there was always some crisis arising at the Home, and Emma soon found that she was as busy as ever. Her greatest fear was that Leach would harm Kezia for daring to disobey him and testify. But, shortly after the trial, she had news which left her hardly knowing what to think.

It had been a particularly trying day—one girl, a newcomer, persistently started fires, not from any desire to burn the house down but in an inarticulate protest against life itself. Much as she wanted to keep Jenny, the safety of the other residents might make it necessary to send the girl away, and Emma, who prided herself that they sent away no one who came to them, found herself in a dilemma. Then, as she left the Home to start on her homeward journey, she was unexpectedly confronted by the shambling form of Leach, who emerged from the tombstones of the Quaker cemetery, and barred her path.

Emma, absorbed in the problem of Jenny, gasped, startled to see him, and then demanded, 'What do you want? Haven't you caused enough harm? What have you done to Kezia? And what has happened to Rose?'

His deepset, cunning eyes narrowed, and he moved his head from side to side in the way he had when he was uncertain. 'I come to ask you that, Miss Meddle!' He flung a grimy hand out towards the Home. 'You got my woman hid in there? Speak up, and if she's there, you just send her out here to me!'

'She is not there,' Emma told him angrily, 'Nor do I know where she is.' She frowned. 'Don't you?'

'No, I don't!' he growled. 'She's never come home, not since that trial. I thought at first she was afraid to show her face, as well she might be, but that she'd turn up in the end. But she hasn't, and what's more, the kid's gone, too!'

'Rose?' cried Emma in alarm. 'But she was returned to Smith, poor child. What do you mean, she's gone?'

'Ay, he got her back, like he was entitled. Not back two days, she wasn't, and she disappears as well. I ain't a fool, Miss Meddle, as you have cause to know. Kezzy's taken the kid and got her hid away somewhere. If you or your precious husband knows anything about it, I'll have the law on you. You got off before, but you won't get off again. Have you got Rose? Speak up now!' He glowered at her threateningly.

'I have neither Kezia nor Rose, nor do I know where they are,' Emma said evenly. 'But I promise you this, Mr Leach. If either of them has come to harm, I hold you responsible for it, and I'll see you pay for your unspeakable behaviour.'

Leach muttered an oath. 'She'll have to come to you, sooner or later. She's nowhere else to go, and she'll come, all right. When she does, you send her straight home to me, do you hear?'

He turned and strode off down the street, his
hands in his pockets and his powerful shoulders
hunched.

'So the wretched girl has run away and taken the
child with her!' Luke said angrily, when informed.
'You can hardly be surprised, Emma. Confound it,
where the devil has she gone? Well, we can only
hope that she will come to us, sooner or later. We
do know that she is out of Leach's hands for the
time being.'

Emma bit her lip. He seemed to think the whole
sorry state of affairs her fault. Perhaps he was right,
and it was. Even so, she thought rebelliously, I
didn't make Leach the brute he is. But it seems as
though everything I try to do goes wrong. Will
nothing ever go right?

The warm spring sunshine beamed into the
breakfast parlour at Hill House, and in the distance, through the window, she could see the
gardener trundling along a barrow full of bedding
plants. Now that Hill House had a mistress,
flowerbeds were appearing in its gardens.

Luke had disappeared behind his newspaper,
and Emma contemplated the outspread news-
sheets morosely. He had set them up like a barrier
between them, and there was a barrier. That Luke
had been taken to court over Rose had brought
it forcibly home to Emma that she could not
pursue her work among the girls without considering him, even if he took no part in it. A man
was responsible for his wife, as he had pointed out.
She enjoyed the protection of his name, but her
actions were in some measure hampered by the

knowledge that any trouble found its way ultimately not to her, but to him. It seemed doubly
unfair, because he had scrupulously fulfilled his
part of their original bargain, though it had cost
him dearly. But she had notably failed to fulfil
hers, in one very important respect: there was no
sign of the son he wanted. Reorganising Hill
House's domestic routine, and having the gardener
plant bulbs and rose bushes, was hardly a substitute
for an heir to it all.

Emma propped her chin on her hands and stared
in frustration at yesterday's beef joint, which
appeared on today's breakfast table as a cold plat-
ter. Since the trial, his manner towards her had
been, to say the least, aloof. He was always polite.
In fact, he was more polite than he had been
before, and that was a bad sign. He was still angry
about the whole episode, and had not yet forgiven
her for having precipitated it. He blamed her for his
public humiliation, and now, in addition, for the
unknown fate which had met Kezia and Rose.

He still came to her bed, it was true, though
perhaps not so often as before, but even there his
manner had changed. It was colder, more indif-
ferent towards her personally. Perhaps it was only
physical need that brought him. Perhaps he had
decided that he had made an altogether bad
bargain and ought to have looked for a wife elsewhere: a different sort of wife, one who could be
relied upon to behave as ladies were meant to
behave, and did not go haring off on decidedly
unladylike schemes that ended by involving him in
unpleasantness.

They had been married almost a year. It had

certainly not been uneventful, yet the one event that might have been expected to show at least a sign of taking place had obstinately failed to materialise. The days when Emma was obliged to retire 'unwell' each month came round with clockwork regularity. Not that Luke had expressed any disappointment to her, or had even spoken again of children, so it was to be supposed that he was not unduly concerned. To be sure, ten months was not a very long time, and some people waited years for a baby. Other women, however, seemed able to conceive at the drop of a hat. There were even girls—Emma had one such unfortunate in the Rescue Home—who had become pregnant after a single foolish 'adventure', and who had been cast out of the parental home as a result. Now it was springtime, and everything reproduced, from budding trees and flowers, to birds in the trees and lambs gambolling in the fields. Increasingly Emma gazed into the mirror and asked herself, 'What is wrong with me?'

Sitting there and contemplating that rustling barrier of a newspaper, she decided that she must take steps to find out, and to consult a specialist. There was one, Aunt Rosamond knew of him, who had built up a formidable reputation for dealing with 'female afflictions', and to him she would go. Secretly, of course, because these were not good days for trying to confide in Luke.

The doctor was a kindly, rotund, middle-aged man with spectacles. He asked her a great many questions which covered her entire life, as far as she could tell, from the cradle, and wrote down a great many notes. Eventually he rose to his feet, folded his spectacles, and began to pace up and down his consulting-room, one hand clasping the edge of his frock coat, while with the other he made conducting movements in the air with his spectacles, as though she had been a choir.

'My dear Mrs Sheldon, you appear to me to be a perfectly healthy young woman, and I see no reason why you should not become a mother. However . . .' He paused and turned a gimlet eye on her. 'You seem to lead an extraordinarily active life. Are you never tired?'

Emma admitted that she was, frequently, very tired, quite ready to drop, but there was so much to do . . .

'I'm sure there is,' he said, interrupting her lengthy explanation of future plans for the Rescue Home, 'but surely there is no need for you to do it all yourself? It is a small vanity to which we are all prone, to think ourselves indispensable. That is seldom the case. I have heard of your work in Forbes Street. Remarkable, ma'am, and a most laudable project. You have my entire support. That your husband was dragged into court in such a way was infamous! I wrote to *The Times* about it. However, perhaps a board of Trustees could manage the work equally well?'

'Oh, no!' cried Emma, shocked, and also hurt, because the Rescue Home was so much her special project, conceived, hatched and reared by her.

To her surprise and discomfiture, the doctor seized immediately on this very point. 'Ah, I understand, believe me! You thought of this, you battled to bring it into existence, and you fight on still to maintain it and make sure it survives. Has it not occurred to you, dear lady, that in many ways this Rescue Home has become your child, and that you have no need of any other?'

Silenced, she could only shake her head, and stare at him with dismay.

'Now, now, my dear,' he said comfortingly. 'It is a sad thing to hear a home truth, but often a salutary one. Allow me to be blunt. You may think none of this a medical matter, but I assure you that my experience has shown me that, especially in cases of childlessness, the way a couple conduct their lives often has great influence. How does Major Sheldon feel about your work?'

'I have my husband's entire support!' declared Emma robustly, and untruthfully. If he supported her, it was for reasons of his own. The best that could be said of his attitude to the real work done in Forbes Street was that he did not actively oppose it.

The doctor seemed impressed by her vehemence. 'Certainly, ma'am, I did not mean to suggest you had not his permission. But, you know, we men are very much like children ourselves, and very easily fancy ourselves neglected.'

'But I do my utmost to see that Hill House is properly run and to take an interest in the estate,' Emma insisted.

'Dear Mrs Sheldon, if your husband's sole concern was to see his house well-run, he would have hired a competent housekeeper. He did not. He married a wife. Put yourself in his situation. Here he is, a healthy fellow in the prime of life, a recently married man with a pretty young wife—and what does she do all day but run hither and thither in good causes, and come home at night tired out. Too tired for much conversation, I fancy, let alone any playful amorous dalliance! Because a couple are married, my dear, there is no reason why they should not continue to treat each other as sweethearts.'

Emma opened her mouth to say, 'But Luke and I were never sweethearts', but closed it again, the damning admission unspoken.

'My suggestion to you, Mrs Sheldon, is that you go home and put on your prettiest gown, that you do not go near Forbes Street for two entire weeks, and that you ask your husband to take you out driving. We are blessed with a spell of particularly fine spring weather. Take advantage of it, that's the prescription this medical man gives you, ma'am.'

You mean, thought Emma gloomily, that Luke and I have to learn how to fall in love. It seemed to her that, of all the many difficult tasks she had undertaken, this one must be the most impossible to achieve.

'Well?' Luke asked, handing Emma down from the pony trap. 'How does this spot suit your artistic talents?'

Emma shook out her petticoats and surveyed the scene. They had stopped by a gurgling stream. Pussy-willow and silver birch lined the banks, primroses nestled in nooks among the roots, and across the stream, through a gap between two elms, she could see sheep and lambs in a field. It was quite idyllic. She did not know if Luke had been surprised at being asked to take her out for a drive into the country. If he had been, he had masked it well, and here they were. Emma had even provided herself with a sketch-book and crayons, as these were compulsory adjuncts to a lady spending a day '*en plein air*'.

While Luke was seeing to the pony, Emma found herself a shady spot which looked, she hoped, suitably romantic, and sat down, her skirts spread out around her, and her new, broad-brimmed hat of Italian straw (which she had purchased surreptitiously just for this expedition) tilted at a provocative angle. That doctor was not going to be able to say she had not tried!

Luke came across and smiled down at her. 'You look as pretty as a picture yourself,' he said, rather soberly, adding more briskly, 'I'm just going for a walk along the bank to see what's to be found. I'll be back in twenty minutes. Draw me a masterpiece.'

'Oh, bother!' muttered Emma despondently, as he disappeared from view round a bend in the stream. This was not what was meant to happen at all. He had not even offered to sit with her. In fact, he had taken himself off with such alacrity that she had to conclude that he had no wish for her company or conversation.

Emma sighed and opened her sketch-book, peering at the sheep and lambs, and attempting to set the scene on paper. But although she worked industriously, she soon had to admit that she had neither the aptitude, nor the patience, for this ladylike accomplishment. Her sheep and lambs looked like a set of wooden dogs, and perspective eluded her completely. So she shut up the book with a snap, and fell to thinking mutinously that the doctor was an idiot, and she a worse one for listening to him. All this sitting about, slapping at midges and communing with nature, was nothing but a waste of time, just as the Italian hat had been a waste of money—and there were so many things to be done in Forbes Street, and also at Hill House. Yet here she sat, staring at a set of silly sheep, while Luke prowled about on his own without even asking if she might like to come with him. Moreover, this effort on her part to introduce a note of passion and romance into a marriage which was steadily becoming more and more one of convenience—this was to last two whole weeks?

I can't keep this going for two whole weeks, thought Emma crossly, attacking a horse-fly with the sketch-book and flattening it against the tree-trunk with a determined wallop. I can't sit about in my best summer gowns and a straw hat, simpering at Luke, and doing nothing—and Aunt Rosamond certainly cannot cope for two whole weeks in Forbes Street without me. I dare say that Jenny will have burnt the whole place to the ground by then, or some disaster will have happened.

But to simper at Luke, he had to be there, which he manifestly was not. The only company she had was the pony. However, at that moment, she heard a footfall. Luke reappeared with his jacket over his arm, and threw himself down under a nearby tree.

'Well, where is this masterpiece which I shall be obliged to have framed at hideous expense and hang in the drawing-room?'

'You won't,' said Emma. 'I've discovered I can't draw sheep.'

'Then you will have to draw me.'

Emma gave him a startled look, since the idea that he might expect her to do that had not occurred to her when she brought along the sketch-book. She put her head on one side and surveyed her undeniably handsome husband, who was reclining against a tree-trunk in his shirtsleeves, patches of perspiration staining the white cambric, and his dark eyes quizzical. 'I could try,' she said doubtfully. Yet, somehow, she did not want to. Not because he was not an undeniably attractive subject, but because he was. The peering and staring and studying involved, the total concentration on the physical form of one human being, all these needed a detachment Emma felt she could not bring to the subject. 'But I am tired,' she said. 'I can't draw you now.'

'So am I,' he said. 'It's confounded warm.' Unexpectedly he got up and came over to her, and throwing himself full-length on the bank, propped his head on her lap and closed his eyes.

She had not been prepared for this. Somewhat at a loss what to do now, Emma took off her straw hat and fanned him with it, and brushed away the occasional insect, while wondering if she could draw him while he slept. The flies buzzed aimlessly around them and a faint splash from the river marked the presence of a trout. Emma studied Luke's face, noting every little line, and suddenly recognised, almost with shock, how much she did love him, and that he meant more to her than anything else—more than Forbes Street and her work, more than anything she had ever previously thought dear to her.

The new knowledge, almost frightening, brought

with it both wonder and despair. She could not understand how she could have been so foolish as to ignore her own heart, and even more foolish to let a relationship, which meant so much, almost slide out of her grip. Perhaps it was already beyond her reach. 'There is nothing so dead as a dead love affair', she had once read somewhere. Had she let her own marriage die like a neglected seedling, withering away unnourished? If she had tried harder at the beginning, if she had shown herself more ready to respond to the overtures he had then been willing to make; if she had thought more of pleasing him, and less of making use of his gift of the Forbes Street house . . .

But all I thought about was my work, Emma mourned. I thought nothing else was necessary. But all I really want is here. Remembering the doctor's advice, she asked herself, What if I did put the administration of the Home into the hands of trustees? I could still oversee it, and I would have more time for Luke and my marriage. She felt a spasm of shame as these words passed through her head because, in truth, Luke and her marriage had occupied her thoughts so little. Forbes Street and nothing else . . . 'Poor Mary Tudor said they would find Calais graven on her heart,' she muttered. 'But when I am dead, if anyone cares to look, they will see Forbes Street written on mine!'

At that moment Luke opened his eyes to see her pensive, solemn face, with untidy tendrils of fair hair framing it, studying his with such a bewildered expression in her blue eyes, and her nose screwed up so comically, that he almost laughed—almost, but not quite.

'Emma?' he said.

Because his neck rested on her knee, she felt the vibration of the vocal chords tingling in her own flesh. Her heart lurched painfully in response. Luke pushed himself upright, so that his face was close to hers, and, without warning, clasped her tightly in his arms and pressed his mouth on to hers in a fiercely demanding embrace that crushed her lips and forced them to part. Trapped against the tree-trunk behind them, Emma threw up her hands and caught at his shoulders. All the frustration and unspoken desire, the yearning for understanding and the inability to explain it in words, all seemed to come together and fuse into one great emotion, which turned into a wild and mutual longing, destroying the old stubborn barriers. Emma's fingers tightened on his shoulders, and she thrust herself towards and against him, instead of drawing back as she usually did. He felt her body yield and sensed the longing within her. His touch grew rougher, his fingers pulling at the little buttons fastening the bodice of her gown, tearing them open to force his hand inside, fumbling at her chemise to close on her naked breast beneath.

There was only one way this encounter could end, and only one way she wanted it to end, but remembering where they were, Emma pushed him away and whispered, almost with a sob, 'No, Luke, we can't, not here . . .'

'Why the devil not?' he demanded huskily. His face was flushed and he was panting, and his dark eyes glittered with a wolfish gleam. 'I want to make love to you, Emma, here and now, right now and right in this place! You're my wife, and there's no blasted reason why we shouldn't!'

'But someone might come along,' she protested pleadingly, and crying in frustration, because she, too, wanted him to take her, there and then, but she could not face the awful possibility that someone might come along the path and discover them.

To her horror, she saw that Luke misunderstood her tears, and was growing angry. 'For pity's sake, Emma, don't turn to stone yet again! There's not a soul for miles about. Look, I've been damn patient. I accepted you were shy, and you had all kinds of odd ideas about men, and were convinced I had spent my bachelor days prowling around the back streets of London seducing young girls. I made allowance for all of that. I've tried not to frighten you, or to hurt you . . .'

'You haven't!' Emma sobbed. 'You've never hurt me!'

'Then what on earth is the matter?' Frustration and disappointment, to say nothing of the considerable discomfort in which his cheated body found itself, its desires both physically aroused and physically unfulfilled, all combined to send him into a towering rage. He shouted at her, as he had never done, and shook her till her head bobbed, and Emma cried all the more, and then, in the middle of it all, their pony threw up his head and whinnied shrilly.

Both froze. 'Oh, Luke,' gasped Emma. 'Someone is coming!' She scrambled away from him and began feverishly to rebutton her bodice and to try to tidy her hair.

Luke swore vigorously and stalked off to collect his jacket, as the dull thud of hoofs on turf filled the air. A sturdy pony appeared, and sitting astride it, with a wicker basket strapped on one side and a set of dismembered fishing tackle in a canvas bag on the other, was a red-faced individual wearing a strange, battered hat bedecked with fishing flies. This he raised, and hailed them cheerily, with a truly British disregard for the fact that he had obviously disturbed this couple at a very bad time, that the lady was dishevelled and red-eyed, and her husband flushed and perspiring.

'Good day to you! Splendid day, isn't it?'

'No,' snarled Luke, alarming the newcomer considerably. 'It is not!'

The fisherman kicked his mount's barrel ribs and hastened out of their way. Emma got up and looked disconsolately towards Luke. He had walked towards their pony and had his back to her, and she saw him stoop and gather up something from the ground. Unexpectedly, he said, 'Emma, I'm very sorry . . .'

Emma's heart leapt up with renewed hope, and she threw out both hands, exclaiming, 'Luke!'

But when he turned towards her, she saw she had misread his apology. He looked flushed but in control of himself, and the former coldness had replaced the passion in his face and in his voice. He held out a mangled handful of straw. 'I am afraid, my dear, that the pony has eaten your hat.'

The following day, Emma returned to Forbes Street and Luke to his stables.

In the crowded, poor streets of London, 'spring fever' had a very different, and an ominous, meaning. The warm sun thawed out the fevers frozen in over the winter, and, deprived of the sealing covering of ice, the open drains once more made their presence felt with a powerful odour. The stench of overflowing latrines and cess-pits found its way into the hovels where families who remembered past outbreaks of the cholera began to ask themselves if this year would see another such, or if they would be spared it. Even without it, babies died, and the old and the feeble, and when it rained, April showers brought forth no spring flowers but overflowing gutters and courtyards swimming in filth. The Thames added its share of noisome odours, but along its banks and on its busy wharves people were accustomed to that, and apart from swearing even more freely than they did otherwise, greeted an increase in the general stink philosophically.

On a mild night, Sam Leach sat in a popular tavern near to a wharf busy in daytime, brooding in a corner over a tankard of porter, and watching the songstress on the rough stage set up at the end of the room, where a procession of 'turns' entertained the customers. The comic song-and-dance man had done his act, and so had the juggler, and the family of acrobatic midgets who balanced on top of one another like an Indian totem-pole, and all had been received with a fair degree of good-natured applause. Someone had earlier thrown a rotten egg at the song-and-dance man, but not, as it had turned out, because he disliked the act, but because the performer owed him sixpense. The perpetrator of the deed had been ignominiously hurled into the street.

Sam listened and watched the singer with more than ordinary interest. She was a strapping woman in a purple taffeta gown, with a great deal of jet-black hair and a voice which made up in volume for what it lacked in musical quality. She was a great favourite amongst the seamen and dockers, and known to all as Spanish Sal. When she had finished, she clambered down off the stage and, nimbly avoiding outstretched hands, came to where Sam sat, to stand before him, one hand planted on her ample hip, and her head cocked on one side.

'Well, Sam, don't you buy a girl a drink these days?'

He grinned. 'Course I will—gin, is it?'

'I won't say no,' said Sal, plumping herself down on a chair. 'Though I occasionally says "No" to other offers!' She folded her arms on the table top and rested her well-endowed bosom on them. 'You still on your own, then, Sammy? Heard your wife had run off and left you.'

The smile left Leach's face, and he growled, 'Good riddance! She was no good to me—no good any more after that meddling female got hold of her and went filling her head with uppity ideas.' More airily, he added, 'How about you, Sal, doing well?'

'Can't complain,' she said, knocking back the fiery alcohol in a single gulp. She stared at the empty glass and observed, 'Done for my voice with this stuff, you know. I had a good voice once. Still, this lot don't care. They isn't musical.'

'You need a fellow to look after you, Sal,' said Mr Leach.

'You, I suppose?' she chuckled. 'I'll think about it, Sam.' A shadow fell across them, and she glanced up. 'Well, here's a friend of yours. I'll be off. I've got to sing again in half an hour. Be seeing you, Sam.'

Sam muttered an oath as Micah Smith's unlovely form replaced Sal's on the opposite chair.

'I been looking for you everywhere, Sam,' said Micah plaintively. 'I was hoping to find you here.'

'Was you?' came the sour reply.

'Buy a man a pint of ale, Sam? Times is awful hard,' pleaded Micah.

'Think they ain't for me, since your Kezia ran off and left me?' Sam asked unsympathetically. 'I've no money to spend on you, Micah.

'Families ought to stand together,' Micah reminded him. 'That's what you said when you came asking me to go and lay complaint against the Major.'

'May be you ain't family no more,' Sam muttered. 'Not since Kezzy went.'

'I ain't responsible for what Kezzy did . . .' Smith whined, 'speaking against me in court like that. I don't know why she did it. But she was always a difficult one. Lend us a few shillings, Sam.'

'I tell you I ain't got 'em!' Sam thrust back his chair and strode out of the tavern.

Outside it was dark, but mild, and the absence of a breeze made the smell of the river less obvious. Sam set off along the wharf, avoiding coils of rope and other obstacles. Here and there the night was pierced by the yellow glow of a lantern hanging from a hook, but the warm weather had caused a mist to rise from the river, so that even these patches of light were obscured by a swirling veil, as if that seething open sewer, the river, bubbled like a witch's cauldron, sending up its poisonous fumes.

Sam paused by one of these lanterns and listened. As he had thought, footsteps followed him along the wharf, stumbling. He stepped into the dark shadows beyond the ring of swaying lanternlight, and waited. After a moment or two a figure staggered out of the gloom and into the light. Sam leapt forward and grasped it by its scraggy neck.

'What do you mean by following me, you old soak?'

'Let go, Sam!' Micah spluttered. 'I don't mean nothing, only I need a few shillings . . .'

Sam swore and pushed him away, and then turned and strode on. Micah sprawled on the ground, toppled less by the force of Sam's shove than by his own unsteadiness, and his outflung hand encountered a length of wood in the darkness. Automatically his scrabbling fingers closed on it. He picked himself up, and still gripping the broken stave, continued to pursue his quarry with the persistence of the drunk and desperate, pleading and cursing alternately.

Suddenly Sam wheeled round. 'I've had enough of you, I have! You and your precious nieces! Your family was never anything but trouble to me, and I'm going to put a stop to it once and for all!'

Micah saw the huge shambling figure advance towards him out of the swirling mist and the night, and with a high-pitched cry of terror, struck out wildly with the wooden stave.

Sam had not realised that the other man was in any way armed, and had made no defence against a blow from a weapon. The stave caught him on the temple, stunning him, and sent him stumbling to one side—and out into a horrifying nothingness, clear off the edge of the wharf into the greasy waters that slapped against the piles below.

Sam was no swimmer, but the waters here were not particularly deep, and had he not been dazed by the blow, he would have had the sense to stand up, which would probably have put his head above water. But, only half-conscious, he began to struggle, and his struggles took him further from the wharf. As he threshed about, the waters closed over his head, and when he tried to thrust himself up to the surface, a long, thin tentacle reached up from below and wrapped itself round his ankle, and held him fast.

It was a rope trailing from a barge, but Sam did not know that. To him, it was as if the devil himself had caught him by the leg. In his panic, he twisted and turned. The water roared in his bursting ears and stars danced before his vision. He swallowed gulps of the filthy river water, and his lungs seemed to be swelling until they must explode. But, after a while, his struggles ceased and he floated motionless. The rope untwined itself like a slippery sea-serpent and slid away into the depths. But it was too late for Sam Leach.

Micah Smith knelt on the edge of the wharf, and peered down into the murky depths. 'Sammy?' he whispered, and then called more loudly, 'Sam?' He knelt there for some minutes, and then it came to him that he was never going to get a reply. His alcohol-sodden brain began to work in an animal reflex, urging him to protect himself. He felt around for the stave and tossed it into the water with a splash.

'Got rid of that!' he muttered. 'Water will wash

off any blood. Good job we didn't leave the tavern together. Ain't no one can say I come this way.' He slipped into the darkness and set off through the night. 'Wasn't my fault,' he told himself, and a tear of self-pity rolled down his unshaven cheek. 'Never is my fault. I just never have no luck.'

CHAPTER ELEVEN

UNAWARE OF the fate that had befallen Leach, her enemy, Emma continued to pursue her own search for Kezia and Rose. At first it seemed she would have no luck whatsoever. Repeated visits to Wapping and to Bethnal Green produced no clues, and she had to admit were unlikely to do so, since these two districts were ones Kezia would be sure to avoid. Over and over again she asked herself, 'What should I do if I were Kezzy?' The simple answer was that she did not know, because she was not Kezzy and her knowledge of Kezzy's world was incomplete. But there were those who knew it better—the girls who at present lived in the Rescue Home. It was to them that Emma decided to appeal.

There were six in residence at the time, including Jenny, of whom Emma entertained optimistic hopes, as she had not lit a fire anywhere for a week. She convened her 'family' in the parlour in Forbes Street, and explained, as briefly as possible, the circumstances in which Kezia had vanished, and appealed for any ideas as to where she might be.

Shuffled feet and furtive glances met her initial request. This was followed by a general opinion, expressed as 'Got herself another fellow, most like'. Emma was beginning to despair, when Jenny, who had been sitting in a corner, twisting a finger in one of her ringlets and staring moodily at the empy fireplace, unexpectedly offered, 'Ask the relatives, why don't you?'

'I can't ask Leach,' said Emma. 'Anyway, he doesn't know. The only relative is the awful uncle.'

'Ask him, then,' said Jenny simply.

'Thank you, Jenny, but I'm sure he doesn't know either, or he would have told Leach.'

'Family always knows something,' Jenny's eyes switched from the fireplace to Emma's face. 'You haven't asked the right questions, Mrs Sheldon.'

'Micah Smith . . .' said Emma thoughtfully.

Just finding Smith was not going to be easy, and tackling him even less so. Above all, Luke had not to find out what she was about, as his feelings towards Mr Smith were less than charitable.

Emma returned to Bethnal Green, but this time enquired for Micah, not Kezia, Smith. At first she drew a blank. Smith had quitted his lodgings, an unremarkable fact in a constantly shifting population which aimed to keep one step ahead of the landlord. Natural reticence on the part of his former neighbours, together with the fact that Smith was such a common name, made it difficult to discover where he had gone. Remembering that Micah's occupation had been given as coster-monger, Emma decided to concentrate her enquiries on this fraternity.

She discovered immediately that the coster-mongers formed a closely-knit unit within the larger community. A large number of them were of Irish descent, and in many of their homes—— wretched, bare places—still room was found for some crudely coloured religious picture or plaster statuette. This gave her the idea of seeking out the nearest Catholic priest.

He proved an elderly man, himself living in considerable poverty, who had laboured many years in an unrewarding parish.

'They bring their infants for baptism, but likely as not I don't see them again till I bury them. They've a great fondness for a funeral. I've known many a man die and leave his family in great distress and want, yet they'll spend the last of their money to put up a fine monument over his grave. I've knowledge of several Smiths. But, from what you tell me, I fancy the man you seek is a rough, ignorant fellow, probably of tinker origin, and sadly addicted to the drink. I've not set eyes on him these five years or more, but I've not buried him, so I know he's alive. As I was telling you, Micah Smith might be the greatest rogue, but his family would bury him decently. Public houses and stableyards would be the most likely places to find him—but don't go alone, dear lady, I beg you. It wouldn't be wise.'

He did not know Mrs Sheldon. She had already drawn a blank in public houses and taverns, so she set off around every mews, horse-dealer and even knacker's yard she could locate. The weather remained very warm. She found her quest not only difficult because local people disliked answering questions, but highly unpleasant because of the nauseous odours and the piles of rotting garbage in the streets and yards, all made worse by the heat. Between visits, Emma sat in the cab with her handkerchief clamped to her nose, and had frequent resort to the sal volatile. She had almost

given up, when she arrived one afternoon at a small
yard, stabling perhaps half a dozen costermongers'
donkeys. Several rough-looking fellows lounged
about, dressed in the manner young men of their
kind affected, and which she had first seen in
Leach. There was much evidence of red necker-
chiefs, brass buttons and watch-chains, and less of
soap and water. They all eyed her insolently, and
all denied knowing any Micah Smith.

Emma sighed. Her head ached, and she per-
spired freely. Her one desire was to get home to
Hill House, and to wash. It seemed not a bit of good
looking for Smith, and she began to fear she would
never find Kezia or Rose. Outside the yard, in the
street, stood a pump. Wearily, Emma asked the
cabman who waited for her to draw her a cup of
water. It was the man who had first taken her to
Bethnal Green and subsequently testified at Luke's
trial, and now she sought him out regularly to take
her on her missions.

The water had a brackish taste, but refreshed
her. As she turned away from the pump towards
the cab, the cabbie unexpectedly exclaimed, 'Why,
here he comes, ma'am. I recognise the fellow,
though he looks a sight rougher now than when he
was in court!'

Emma looked up and found herself face to face
with the unprepossessing, shabby figure of Micah
Smith, who was approaching the entry to the yard,
with his hands in his pockets and an unlit clay pipe
stuck in his mouth.

'Mr Smith!' exclaimed Emma. 'I have been looking for you everywhere!'

Micah gaped at her, and the clay pipe fell out of

his mouth and shattered on the ground. For a moment he appeared about to turn and run, so she urged him, 'Please wait! I only want to talk!'

He paused, shuffled his feet and glanced longingly towards the interior of the yard. 'I haven't done nothing!' he said truculently.

'Mr Smith,' Emma said, 'Sam Leach tells me that Kezia and Rose are missing. I am very concerned for their safety. If you have any idea where they are . . .'

'I ain't!' Smith squawked. At the mention of Sam Leach, the colour had faded from his cheeks, which were a pasty grey beneath the grime and whiskers. 'How should I know? Gone—that's all!'

'But you must have some idea where,' Emma persisted. She cast a speculative eye over him. 'If you are afraid of Leach . . .'

'Who says I was afraid of Sam?' Micah demanded hoarsely. 'It's a lie! He was like a brother to me, was Sam. Like me own flesh and blood. Married to our Kezzy, too. Who says I was afeared of Sam?'

Emma frowned, puzzled by his use of the past tense. 'Has Leach gone away?'

'Gone?' Micah stared at her owlishly. 'Oh, gone, right enough. Gone on through them Pearly Gates. Or down to the other place, how should I know? I don't know nothing!' He thrust out his stubby chin and glared at her with red-rimmed eyes.

'You mean he is dead?' she demanded incredulously.

'Ay, dead and gone, poor Sammy!' Micah sniffed lugubriously. Then his demeanour changed, and he added fiercely, 'I didn't have nothing to do wiv it!

He was drunk and fell in the river. Drownded. Accident. I wasn't there! I heard about it afterwards. I had no part in it. Don't you go saying I did!'

Emma's dealings with the girls in the Home had led her to recognise certain tricks of behaviour common to them all. If guilty of some misdemeanour, they invariably chose attack as defence. Usually they declared in hostile tones, 'I didn't do it!' before anyone had even asked. Listening to Smith's energetic denials and watching his furtive and cunning manner, she knew instinctively that somehow or other there had been foul play, and that Smith was involved. A prickle of apprehension ran up her spine. But the man was clearly so frightened that she began to think that perhaps he might be willing to strike a bargain, in order to get her to go away and not to ask more questions about Leach.

'I'm sure you're anxious to have Rose back,' she began carefully.

'No, I ain't,' said Micah sourly. 'I never want to set eyes on her, nor on Kezia. What good are they to me? A poor man like me can't feed no growing kid like Rosie . . . Can't feed meself. Bessie won't take her, not now, not wiv all the fuss.'

'So, if she were found,' persisted Emma, 'you would not mind returning her to us?'

'You can 'ave her, if you want,' said the loving guardian. 'It was all Sam's idea. Daft. Asking for the kid back. I never wanted her.'

'If I wrote an agreement . . .' Emma hunted feverishly in her reticule, and Micah's eyes brightened as he scented the possibility of money. She could only find an old letter, but the reverse was blank, so she wrote on it in pencil quickly: '*I, Micah Smith, agree that Major and Mrs Sheldon shall have care of my niece Rose Smith, and I make no further claim on her, or on them.*' She read this aloud to Micah. 'Do you understand? Will you sign this, and the cabman here will be a witness, and perhaps the publican in the tavern over there.'

'Can't write,' said Micah quickly.

'You can make your mark. Of course you shall have half a guinea for your trouble.'

'Got to buy a moke,' said Micah, squinting at her.

'A what?' asked Emma, bewildered.

'A donkey, missus,' said the cabman, translating. 'Don't you give him no more than a guinea, ma'am. 'Tis all bottles of gin to him, as that purple nose there would tell anyone.'

'Who asked you?' demanded Mr Smith in a surly voice. 'All right, I makes me mark, in front of witnesses, for a guinea. Cash down, mind!'

'And he did!' declared Emma triumphantly, laying the paper before Luke. She watched him read it through, and asked more anxiously, 'It is legal, isn't it?'

'I'll have Sneadie study it. I don't see why it shouldn't be. Smith understood what he was being asked.' Luke's gaze shifted abruptly to hold hers. 'You had no business going there alone, Emma.'

'I got what I wanted,' she returned defiantly.

'Up to a point.' He began to sound both irritated and obstinate in a way she recognised only too well.

'You haven't found either Kezia or Rose. This is not to happen again, Emma. I absolutely forbid it. Next time, come to me.'

'Yes, I promise,' she said meekly. She no longer felt like arguing. Her head still throbbed abominably and the room seemed unbearably stuffy, although the windows were open. She could not seem to get the smell of Bethnal Green out of her nostrils. Probably it had permeated her clothes. She needed to have a bath, and to change. Luke was still talking, but though she could hear his voice, she could not, for some strange reason, make out what he said. She felt very sick.

Luke suddenly saw how pale she had become and the glazed look in her eyes. He jumped to his feet, and caught her in his arms as she sagged at the knees.

'I'm all right,' she muttered. 'Only it was very hot there, and smelled so bad. I was very warm . . .'

'Emma . . .' he said urgently, and when she did not seem to hear him, he shouted her name into her ear. 'Emma! For God's sake, did you drink any water there?'

She heard the word 'water', as through a fog, and muttered, 'Pump . . .' before passing out completely.

Luke swept her up into his arms and carried her upstairs, shouting to the butler in the hall, 'Tell Riley to ride for the doctor, and he is to come at once!'

By the time the doctor arrived, Emma was delirious. Luke stood by his wife's bed, and when the medical man straightened up, demanded, 'Well?' in a strained voice.

'She has been visiting the poor, you say?' the doctor asked. 'In Town? Inadvisable, in such warm weather.'

'Yes, yes, confound it!' Luke wiped a hand over his own perspiring brow. 'I think she may have drunk some water from a street pump.'

He glimpsed the expression on the doctor's face, before professional impassivity masked it. 'Opinion is not agreed concerning the dangers of impure water. I myself believe it to carry contagion. Others disagree,' the doctor said.

Quietly, Luke asked, 'Is it, then, the cholera? I have seen it—in India. It always seemed to be connected with fouled drinking water.' His memory threw up an image of the ghastly, shrivelled bodies of the cholera dead, twitching on the funeral pyres, as wasted muscles contracted in the heat of the flames. 'Not Emma!' whispered a voice inside him. 'Not such a death!'

'Well, then, if you have seen it,' the doctor said resignedly, 'you are as well aware as I am of the form it takes. I visited several victims during the epidemic of 'thirty-seven here. Since then we have been spared an epidemic, and I have not heard of any cholera cases this year. It's possible Mrs Sheldon has contracted some other low fever that is common in the slums.' He cleared his throat. 'We shall proceed, however, as for the cholera. We have no time to wait and see. Brandy and water, administered as often as possible, often soothes the patient. Hot mustard poultices should be applied to the stomach, and cloths soaked in hot vinegar to the limbs. The circulation of the blood must be encouraged. I will make up some pills: cayenne pepper, calomel and camphor make an efficacious medicine. Give them with the brandy. If it is a common fever, we shall see an improvement.'

'And if it is the cholera?' Luke asked harshly.

'Then I fear Mrs Sheldon may be dead in a few hours,' the doctor said bluntly.

While the drama unfolded itself, the two people at the heart of things, Kezia and Rose, were far away where neither Leach nor Emma had thought to look for them. The sun shone down on the long, dusty high road. Since early morning, little had travelled along it but a carrier's cart or two, and the only moving figures to be seen were those of the two girls who trudged along, side by side, carrying bundles wrapped in rags.

'My feet are getting awful sore, Kezzy,' Rose said plaintively. 'Can't we sit down for a bit? By those trees, up yonder. It's nice there, and shady. There might be a river or a pond or something. I'm thirsty.'

She might have added that she was hungry, too, but did not, because she was a child of the poor, and knew that hunger was the one thing it was no use complaining about. Kezia glanced up at the sky and saw the sun was rising to its zenith.

'All right,' she conceded. 'There's a wood down there, look!' She pointed across a field. 'We'll go over and sit down for a while.'

They scrambled over a stile, and made their way to the edge of the wood and sat down under a venerable oak. Kezia unwrapped her bundle and produced a dry-looking lump of bread and a congealed mess of cold pease-pudding. She divided this unappetising fare with Rose, warning, 'You make that last, now, for I haven't any more. If we pass a farm or such, we'll beg a cup of milk, or offer to scrub some floors in return for a bit of dinner.'

'I wish I knew where we were going, Kezzy,' Rose said, devouring the pease-pudding with gusto.

'I told you. Tomorrow I want to be in the next town along this road, on account I heard it will be market day there. There's always work to be had washing dishes in eating-houses and taverns on a market day.'

Rose lay down on the grass and shaded her eyes with her hand as she peered up through the leafy branches above them. 'Reckon neither Sam nor Micah will ever find us, will they, Kezzy?'

'We're more than a hundred miles from London,' her sister said with some pride. 'I saw it written on a stone, a little way back. Reckon we done very well, you and me, Rosie. Why, I never thought I'd travel so far in my life. It's like a different world altogether out here. Even the people is different. I don't think I ever want to go back to London again.'

'I'm powerful tired, though,' Rose mumbled drowsily. 'And we can't go on walking for ever, Kezzy. We'll walk clean off the end of England and fetch up in the sea.'

'You get yourself forty winks,' said Kezia severely, 'and don't you worry about such things.' But Rose had fallen asleep already, with the ease of the very young. Kezia bent over her and sighed.

After the trial it had been impossible for her to return to Wapping and the anger of Leach. Sam's

fury would know no bounds, and he was quite
capable of killing her. So Kezia had hidden round
and about the streets and alleys, sleeping under
arches and in doorways, and all the time waiting for
Rose to be returned to her squalid home with their
uncle in Bethnal Green. When Rose re-appeared,
Kezia had waited her chance, and Micah once out
of the way, had appeared before the astonished
child, ordering, 'Come quick, we're running away!'

Run away they had, though to where, Kezia had
no idea, just so long as it was a long way from
London. At first it had been hard, sleeping rough
in the cold weather. But now that it had turned
warmer, sleeping out was less of a hardship, though
the walking was a slower business. Most of all they
feared rain, because they soon became soaked and
had no way of drying their clothing. They had taken
casual labour wherever it was offered, and begged
when all else failed. By hook or by crook, Kezia
had kept herself and Rose fed, if very badly. They
were also getting adept at finding shelter in outlying
barns, though that meant getting out at dawn
before the farmhands arrived.

But they could not go on for ever like this, as
Rose had pointed out. Sooner or later they had to
find a place to stay. Secretly, Kezia was beginning
to get desperate. But so far she had managed
to hide her despair from Rose, and keep up an
optimistic mien in front of the child.

Rose looked set to sleep for the whole afternoon,
but they could not allow themselves that luxury. An
hour should do it, thought Kezia. In an hour, we'll
both be rested, and up and on our way. She pushed
back her long brown hair, no longer twisted into

complicated ringlets but left in its natural curl. The sun and wind had tanned her skin and brought colour to her cheeks. Perhaps even Leach would have been hard-pushed to know her. Kezia closed her own eyes and dozed off, the warm sun playing on her face.

She awoke suddenly, aware that someone was nearby and that they were observed. Instinctively she flung an arm protectively over the sleeping Rose, and stared hard into the overgrown coppice behind them. At first she could see nothing, and yet she was sure eyes were watching. Kezia felt the hairs prickle on her neck, and she called out angrily, 'Just you come out of there, whoever you are, instead of frightening folk half to death!'

Silence followed, and then a bird flew out of the branches with a frightened flutter of wings. There was a faint snap of a twig, and a man emerged from the undergrowth, appearing suddenly, like a woodland animal. He was quite young, and very dark complexioned, with untidy long black hair. He was in his shirt-sleeves, and wore soft top-boots and the sort of moleskin trousers and scuffed velvet waistcoat popular among country labourers. Yet he had not the look of a labourer, unless he were a groom. Then Kezia saw that a brace of rabbits dangled lifeless from his hand and heaved a sigh of relief. She had been afraid he might be a gamekeeper, who were bad-tempered individuals, apt to haul trespassers before the landowner. But instead it was a poacher, making the rounds of the snares he had set earlier, and more anxious to avoid a gamekeeper than she was.

'I thought you was the fellow in charge, as goes

round with a gun under his arm,' she said crossly. 'Give me a fright, you did!'

He grinned at her, white teeth flashing in his dark face, and pointed away to the right. 'He's away over there. I passed him early, close enough to smell the tobacco in his pipe, but he never saw me.' He jerked his head towards the sleeping Rose. 'Are you travelling?'

'In a way,' Kezia answered cautiously. 'We're on our way to the next town.'

'I didn't mean that,' he said impatiently. 'I meant, are you travellers, like us?'

Now she understood him. He was a gypsy. From time to time she and Rose had glimpsed this wandering tribe camped by a roadside, or slowly making their way along the road in painted caravans. They had avoided meeting them face to face because Rose was afraid of them. Now their voices awoke Rose, who sat up, and seeing the stranger, gave a cry of fright. Kezia put her arm round her quickly and whispered, 'It's all right.'

'No need to be afeared of me,' he said. 'Davy, my name is. What do they call you?' When she told him, he squinted at her appraisingly, and said, 'Kezia, that's a Romany name. Is the little one hungry?'

'Yes,' said Rose, before Kezzy could answer, and he chuckled.

'Then you'd best come with me.' He turned and set off, skirting the edge of the coppice, moving lightly and easily, ready to blend in an instant into the trees. Kezia and Rose followed, and after a while they descended into a sheltered hollow by a stream. A gaily-painted caravan was drawn up

under the trees, and a piebald pony grazed nearby.
Smoke curled into the air, and as they came nearer,
Kezia saw an old woman sitting hunched over a
fire, puffing on a clay pipe and stirring some kind
of stew, while two very small children played on
the grass. There was no sign of anyone else. As
they approached, one of the children ran to meet
them, and Davy picked him up and set him on his
shoulder.

The old woman glanced up. 'It's my mother,' he
said. He went over to the old lady, and they exchanged some words in a language Kezia could not
understand. She grasped Rose's hand, and glanced
about them nervously.

'My mother wants to know if you have another
name,' Davy asked suddenly.

'Smith,' Kezia told him unwillingly.

'It's a travelling name, is Smith,' said the old
woman, fixing her button-bright eyes on Kezia, and
addressing her directly for the first time. 'You've
travellers' blood in your veins, Kezia Smith. It's
brought you back to the open road in time of
trouble. Sit down.'

Kezia sat down and glanced curiously at the two
children.

'They're mine,' Davy said, reading the question
in her mind. 'My wife died six months back. She fell
sick, and I went to fetch the doctor out of town. He
wasn't too keen to come to travelling folk, and told
me to take her to the workhouse infirmary!' He
gave a snort of derision. 'I showed him the colour of
my money then, and he decided to come after all,
but couldn't do anything for her. Didn't think it
worth his while, maybe.'

The old woman was ladling the stew into pewter bowls. Kezia had not seen dishes like them before, and even she realised that they must be very old. Though probably neither she nor the gypsies realised quite how old, or how valuable, and what a small fortune an antiquary would have given for them. The stew was very good, and when they had eaten, Rose took the dishes down to the stream to scrub them out. Kezia sat opposite Davy and waited. She had never met a man yet who didn't want the usual thing in return for any hospitality. She wondered in what form the proposition would come from her host. As it happened, it came in a guise she had not anticipated.

Davy leaned back against the wheel of the caravan, the sun shining on his long black hair. The spokes of the wheel were painted scarlet, with a neat yellow line running round the rim. He crooked one leg up in front of him, resting his arm on it, and stretched the other leg out along the turf.

'Living is easy in the summer,' he said, watching her face. 'What will you do in the winter, Kezia Smith?'

'Make out somehow,' she replied sturdily.

He shook his head. 'Not on your own, you won't. Finish in a ditch or in the workhouse. Of the two, the ditch is the better, but not what you intend, I suppose.' He treated her to another appraising look, yet when she tried to return it and stare at him, she found it difficult to catch his eyes. He would only smile, and look away, almost as if he were embarrassed. It was like trying to watch a wild animal which is shy of observation. Suddenly she was no longer afraid of him.

'You can travel along with us, if you want,' he said.

'Oh, yes?' said Kezia suspiciously, but waited, because she sensed there was more to come.

He gestured with his hand towards the old woman, who was busy a little way off, gathering up sticks. 'My mother is old, and suffers from rheumatics. I've no woman now and need one. My children need a mother.'

'I've had one husband,' said Kezia bitterly, 'and run off from him, if you want to know.'

'My mother says you will not see him any more.'

Kezia was startled by the assurance with which Davy spoke, and a stab of superstitious fear touched her heart. 'How does she know?'

'She knows. If she says it, she is right. He is dead, your man.'

Kezia digested this. 'Well, he wasn't any good, anyway, and I don't know that I want another —even if your mother is right.'

'I'm not a drinking man,' he said unexpectedly. He got up, and walked towards the caravan. 'Come and look, why don't you?'

Kezia scrambled to her feet and followed him. He opened the painted door at the back of the caravan, and stood back so that she could climb up the steps. She peered into the interior, and could not prevent herself gasping aloud, 'Why, it's beautiful. I never saw the like!'

So it was. Every inch shone, the brass was polished, decorative plates were fixed to the walls and every piece of linen was trimmed with crocheted lace.

'Well?' he asked.

Kezia turned round and stood at the top of the steps, considering him. 'What about Rose?'

'She can come along, too. Pretty kid like that will sell plenty of clothespegs round the doors.'

'It isn't what I want for Rose,' Kezia said firmly. 'I want Rose to have a proper home, in a proper house, with respectable folk. I want that understood!'

Davy looked disgusted. 'It won't be better than that.' He pointed into the interior of the caravan.

'Never mind. It's what I mean Rose to have. I made a sort of promise, to myself.' She turned back to the neat little caravan. 'But I'd like this fine, for me.'

CHAPTER TWELVE

IT WAS not the cholera, although an anxious twenty-four hours passed before they could be certain. Even so, Emma was very ill, tossing restlessly on the pillows and muttering in delirium. The whole house seemed to have fallen silent and to be waiting. The servants talked in whispers. The doctor came and went, looking grave, shrugged his shoulders and said resignedly that time would tell. But time had lost its meaning for Luke, for whom seemingly endless days passed into sleepless nights. In the kitchen, where the clatter of the very plates seemed muted, Cook shook her head over food sent up to the dining-room, to be returned, day after day, hardly touched.

Mrs Somerton had come to stay at Hill House and take care of the nursing. 'It is not a bit of good hiring professional nurses. One can never be sure of them, and so many seem unfortunately addicted to the gin-bottle,' she observed.

She did no more than state a well-known fact. The risks of nursing fever patients, especially, were so high that few undertook it who were able to get employment elsewhere. So little was still understood about the way contagion spread that it was not unknown for an entire household to decamp, when one of its members went down with 'putrid fever', and to leave the house in sole possession of the sufferer and whoever might be persuaded, or be devoted enough, to stay behind and nurse the patient.

'I am much obliged to you,' said Luke quietly.

Mrs Somerton eyed his untidy, burly figure slumped in a wing chair, and clicked her tongue reproachfully. 'Come, come, Major. Emma is my niece. Goodness me, Henry, my dear late husband, christened her. He was very much the new young curate then, you know, and somewhat ill-at-ease with babies. He had a recurring nightmare, he later confessed to me, that he might drop an infant in the font and inadvertently drown it! But Emma behaved perfectly, as I remember very well. She was a very healthy baby, and hardly had anything wrong as a child, so I know for a fact she has an excellent, sound constitution, and I'm sure she will pull through this unfortunate bout of fever. So cheer up, Major, and don't look so despondent. You must keep up your spirits, dear man!'

Luke shifted slightly in his chair, and Samson, lying with his nose on his paws and his gaze fixed on his master, rolled his eyes to follow the movement. 'It is my fault,' Luke said in the quiet, obstinate way which Emma called 'particularly difficult'.

'How so?' asked Mrs Somerton in practical tones, putting down the ball of wool she had been busily winding.

'Because, confound it, I let her go running round those places, associating with every kind of low person. Of course she fell sick! I should have put a stop to it, once and for all!' His voice rose irritably, and he got up with a sudden jerk as if impelled by some sort of emotional spring, and began to pace restlessly about the room.

'My dear Major,' said Mrs Somerton, a little hesitantly, 'it has never been, in my experience, easy to stop Emma doing anything, once she had set her mind on it.'

'I could have stopped her, had I put *my* mind to it,' he said fiercely. 'I should have done so. I didn't.'

Mrs Somerton sighed. 'I'll go up to the sick-room and take a look at her. It's time for her medicine.'

'I'll go,' he said quickly. 'But if by medicine you mean those pills the medical man left, I believe they're worse than useless, like the rest of his advice.'

Oh dear, thought Mrs Somerton, I fear the pills will go the way of the mustard poultice.

The application of hot mustard poultices to her stomach had caused Emma such distress that Luke, chancing to come into the sick-room in the middle of such treatment and seeing his wife writhing in agony, had flown into a rage and hurled the entire poultice, together with the ingredients and implements used to make it, out of the window, and refused to allow the treatment to continue.

'Men are apt to lose their heads around sickness,' observed Mrs Somerton, alone. She retrieved her ball of wool and cast her eyes to the ceiling, and the floor above, and clicked her tongue again.

Luke pushed open the door of Emma's room and gave a muttered exclamation of annoyance, because once again someone had closed up all the windows and the room was like a Turkish bath. He threw open the nearest one and let in the clean, sweet air before going across to the bed. He thought at first, as he stooped over her, that she was asleep, but she seemed aware of someone's presence, and fidgeted on the crumpled pillows, mumbling. Luke smoothed the tangled fair hair from her damp, hot forehead, and then sat down on the edge of the bed, and took hold of her hand lying on the coverlet. He sat looking down at it, as it lay in his own palm. Her skin had taken on an alabaster appearance, the veins easily seen as blue threads running under the transparent surface, and the whole hand seemed weightless and as tiny as a child's. He experienced an irrational fear that she might simply fade, until she vanished.

'Emma,' he called softly.

She did not respond, and he felt the same helplessness he had felt all those years ago, sitting by Emerson and watching the life ebb away. Yet that had been different, because he had wanted the boy to die, and to see that pain stilled. His helplessness had then sprung from his inability either to comfort or to hasten the desired end. Sitting by Emma, he wanted her to live, as he had never wanted anyone or any creature to cling to life. He had never prayed for anyone to be spared. Not even for his mother, because he had been too young, and he remembered her passing only as the feeling of grief and anger that had filled the house and centred upon his father. For the first time, now, he had some conception of how his father might have felt.

When his father died, he had not grieved particularly for the old man because that would have been hypocritical. His father had never had time for him, not even for his dead mother's sake. Luke, on his side, had never really felt he knew the old Peninsular veteran. Other relatives he remembered vaguely from his childhood as being old, cantankerous, hard of hearing and antagonistic towards small boys. He had not liked them then, and saw no reason why he should pretend to a liking now that they were dust.

Yesterday, for the first time ever, he had wanted to make some private intercession, a plea to ward off the grim reaper. He had gone down to the church and sat in a pew at the back, all alone in the empty building, and wanted to pray for Emma to be spared. Except that he did not know how to do it. So he sat for a while, reading the marble tablets on the walls, two-thirds of them to members of his own family, and watching a sparrow, which had somehow flown in and become trapped, flit about the huge medieval wooden beams of the nave. After a while it occurred to him that the sparrow was a little like the human soul, trapped for a while in the body, and he entered into a sort of one-sided argument with the deity in his head, trying to explain how he felt. It sorted things out in his mind a little, so perhaps the conversation had not been so one-sided after all. When he went out, he propped open the door carefully, so that the sparrow could fly out to freedom, if it had any sense.

From the church, he had walked down to the family mausoleum. It was a personal penance, because he hated the place and knew that he had to force himself to go and inspect it. The mortar was crumbling round the brickwork, and he would have to get that seen to before the next winter frosts. Then he thought: Let the damn place fall down! They could bury him in a corner of the paddock, along with the two or three aged hunters which already occupied the spot, nourishing the grass on which they had once grazed. That it might be Emma's turn to escape, like the sparrow, out of the prison of the body, he refused to accept. Emma was a fighter, and would fight the fever as she had done everything else: Leach, authority, polite convention and Luke himself.

He had turned away, feeling better. He tramped across the fields back to Hill House. Passing the paddock, he paused to watch Sultan grazing a little way off, swishing his tail and occasionally swinging round his handsome, wicked head and snapping at the biting flies. Emma had wanted him to get rid of the horse, and he would. He had refused before, because it had seemed like giving in. But now he knew it wasn't giving in, it was doing something to please her. You have to give, in order to receive; to surrender, if you wanted to win. It had taken him a long time to learn that. But he was beginning to learn it now, slowly and rather painfully. He hoped he was not learning it too late.

In the sick-room, Luke gave himself a little shake and realised guiltily that he had almost dozed off, sitting with his back propped against the bedpost —it was an old-fashioned four-poster—and holding on to Emma's hand. She looked peaceful now, lying still, and with her fair hair spread out across the pillow, like tangled skeins of amber and buttercup yellow silk. As he watched, she opened her eyes and muttered, 'Luke?'

His fingers tightened on her hand and his heart lurched, because it was the first time in days that she had recognised anyone. He leaned forward and asked, 'Do you need anything?'

But the lucidity was illusory. She muttered 'Luke' again, and he realised she had not recognised him, but that her fevered mind dwelt on him for some reason. She said, quite clearly, 'I'm very sorry.'

'About what?' he prompted.

'Because there isn't any baby. The doctor said there wasn't any reason . . . but I haven't . . .'

Luke expelled his breath in a long hiss. When she seemed quieter, he released her hand and went downstairs.

Mrs Somerton looked up as he came into the room, and jumped up in alarm at the expression on his face, dropping her knitting. 'Is she worse?'

'No,' he said in a clipped voice. 'Mrs Somerton, ma'am, perhaps you would be so good as to explain to me why it is that no one ever sees fit to tell me anything.'

'About what, exactly?' asked Mrs Somerton cautiously.

'Emma is muttering about babies and doctors. I am sure, ma'am, that you know what it is all about. I am equally sure I do not.'

'Oh, yes,' said Emma's aunt nervously. 'I did suggest at the time that she should consult you about that, but she was very set against doing so. I think she was a little shy of mentioning it, which is quite to be expected, you know.'

'I don't know!' Luke exploded, increasingly baffled and thwarted. 'What did she do?'

But now Mrs Somerton was overtaken by a fit of coyness. 'I have never had the fortune to be a mother myself. But since Emma lost her parents when she was quite young, I had the consolation of bringing her up.'

Luke groaned and began to think that perhaps he and Mrs Somerton did not share a common language. He felt as though he was trying to communicate with a hill tribesman of alien tongue and culture. But Mrs Somerton was arriving, at what she considered a delicate subject, by her own roundabout means.

'I'm sure dear Emma is very fond of little children, and naturally she understands how important it is to you to have an heir. So many generations . . .' Mrs Somerton gestured vaguely towards the family portraits. 'The specialist was a highly-recommended man, and he assured Emma that she was, um, perfectly healthy in that respect, you understand—but there you are, these things lie in the lap of the gods, as it were.' Mrs Somerton fell silent, rather pink in the face, and obviously under the impression that she had spoken with alarming frankness to a gentleman on a taboo subject.

'Am I to understand from all this,' Luke said, controlling his voice and temper with some difficulty, 'that Emma consulted some kind of medical expert because she feared she might remain childless and I might be offended in some way?'

'Well, not offended, exactly,' said Mrs Somerton precisely. 'Disappointed, of course. But naturally, she did not wish to trouble you about it.'

'Not trouble *me*?' Luke stared at her with disbelief, then, with his voice mounting in vehemence and volume until it rang about the room, demanded, 'Am I not, then, concerned? Do I have no role to play in the affair? Am I not required to father this child, or has some means been discovered by which my wife can oblige without me?'

'Oh dear,' gasped Mrs Somerton.

He fell into a scowling silence, then muttered, 'Well, perhaps I am not the easiest person to talk to.' He swung round on his heel and strode over to the window, where he stood glowering though the panes. After a moment, he said brusquely, 'I'm going down to the stables.'

Mrs Somerton, who had found both his presence and the conversation unsettling, looked her relief.

Riley was prowling round the tack-room, peering at bits and buckles, leather and stirrup-irons, trying to find some failure on Tom's part to do a proper job. A shadow fell across him, and he looked over his shoulder to see the large, solid form of his employer blocking the entrance.

'Is it yourself?' asked Riley placidly. 'You'll be a ruined man if that boy goes on using twice the saddle-soap as is needed. You'll be telling him.'

'I don't give a damn if he baths with it,' Luke said. 'Riley, I'm sending the sorrel to the sale-ring.'

The groom was sufficiently taken aback as to gape at him, before replying, 'I'll not be sorry to see the last of the animal.'

'I dare say. I'm not selling to oblige you, but Mrs Sheldon, who has long wanted me to get rid of the horse. I want him sent to be sold without delay, so that the animal is gone by the time Mrs Sheldon recovers her health . . .' He broke off, and began to fiddle with a set of harness hanging on the wall.

To be sure, thought Riley, observing him sympathetically, the man is taking it all terrible hard. Isn't it clear, for anyone to see, that he thinks the sun rises and sets with that woman's smile? Women get a man in a terrible confusion.

He sidled up to the brooding form of his master. 'If it's quickly you want the animal gone, Major, there's maybe a quicker way than waiting for the next auction sales. There's the horse-fair, three days from now, and only five miles away. Of course you get a terrible lot of rogues and gypsies there, but plenty of honest dealing done as well. I'll take the animal over there, if you want.'

Luke considered. 'Very well. I'll come with you.'

The noise, the bustle and the disorder of the horse-fair would be hard to equal, and it spilled over the streets of the small market town where it was held, re-creating a medieval confusion and riotousness. As Riley had prophesied, it attracted a wide diversity of people, some come to view the horseflesh, or to sell, some to cater for the many needs of the crowds, and a few to enrich themselves by picking pockets and pilfering. From time to time a wild whoop would herald a scattering of the throng, and a horse would be 'trotted out', the groom running alongside, to display its paces and demonstrate that its action was sound and showed no sign of 'dishing'. Red-faced suspicious men in hard hats and gaiters peered in horses' mouths and picked up their hoofs, and scornfully dismissed animals designated as 'broken-kneed'. There was a popular belief that a horse which had been 'down' in the shafts would fall again. Cab-horses, frequently badly harnessed, roughly driven and cruelly over-worked, were particularly prone to 'broken knees', and changed hands for a song.

Luke left Riley in charge of the sorrel and set out towards the town's most reputable hostelry, to see if he could find any old acquaintances there. As he pushed his way through the jostling throng, he spied a young woman ahead of him carrying a basket of lace and trinkets such as gypsy women peddled among the crowds wherever they gathered. Luke narrowed his eyes and tried to hasten his step to get a closer look at her, but the flow of the crowd was against him. In increasing frustration, he pushed, swore, apologised and side-stepped, all in vain. Slowly but surely she was drawing further ahead and he was losing sight of her. From time to time he just glimpsed her ker-chief, but by the time he reached a meeting of the roads at an ancient market cross, she seemed to have disappeared.

Luke swore softly and wondered if he had im-agined it. The noisy passage of a pair of heavy dray-horses forced him to retreat. He walked on slowly, seeking her, but without luck, and eventu-ally gave up, more than half convinced that he had been mistaken, and turned back. Then he saw her disappearing down a narrow alley.

'Kezzy!' he roared. He broke into a run and raced after her, catching her by the elbow. She gave a cry and looked up, startled. He opened his mouth to speak, but at that moment felt a sharp point digging into his ribs through the linen of his shirt, and a man's voice by his ear said politely, but cold with menace:

'Take your hand from her, *Gorgio*, or your next breath will be your last!'.

Luke released Kezia and froze, waiting.

She gasped, 'It's all right, Davy! It's only the Major, Major Sheldon! It's Miss Emma's man, as I told you of.'

If anything, the point of the knife dug deeper into Luke's skin. 'And what does the gentleman want?'

'To talk to Kezia and to know where Rose is, for my wife's sake, not for mine!' Luke said over his shoulder. 'Kezzy, do you think your friend might like to put away that knife?'

The sharp point digging painfully into his flesh was removed. Luke turned slowly, and saw a gypsy standing a little behind and to one side of him, watching with hostile, suspicious eyes. 'Who is this?' he asked Kezia in a low voice.

'My man,' she said proudly. 'Davy Lee. He don't mean no harm, Major. He thought you meant me a mischief, that's all. Rose is fine and well, sir, and travelling along with us.'

'Listen, Kezzy!' Luke said urgently. He glanced at the gypsy. 'You, too, Lee! It's important that I talk to you. A great many things have happened since you ran away. Look, it's mid-day, so can't we all go and eat somewhere? That tavern across the way looks reasonable enough.'

Kezia and the gypsy exchanged glances, and he moved away a little, avoiding Luke's eye. 'Davy will come and talk, Major,' Kezia explained in a low voice, 'but not eat with you. Leastways, not in that tavern. It's no offence to you. It's that travelling folk are particular about where they eat, and powerful fussy over dishes and cups and the like.

They like everything clean, and want to know who has handled the pots before. If a dog were to eat off a plate, say, they would break that dish straight off, to stop anyone eating off it later, no matter if it were washed fifty times over.'

'I understand,' Luke said slowly, eyeing Davy with new interest. 'Unclean. Tell Lee that I have lived in India. I've heard it said the Romany people originate from there, and, from what you say, I think the legend must be true. Tell Lee I understand, and I respect his feelings in the matter. But can we at least go somewhere and sit and talk? Will Lee drink a pint of ale, if it's drawn off the wood?'

'He might,' Kezia said cautiously. Davy said nothing, and seemed prepared to let Kezia talk for him.

They set off through the streets, an unlikely trio, thought Luke wryly, and at a corner they met with Riley, holding the sorrel and looking very put out.

'There you are, Major! I looked high and low for you. I could have sold this divil of an animal three times over, if the brute didn't kick out like he was possessed and try and maim anyone who wanted to look over him!'

For the first time since he had put away the knife, the gypsy spoke. 'That's a fine animal.' He moved forward, past Luke, and went up to the sorrel.

'Have a care!' Luke warned him sharply. 'The horse is vicious.'

Again Davy gave him that odd, shy look. He walked along the horse, running his hand the length of the animal's spine, and composedly picked up each of the four hoofs to examine them. Sultan snorted and tossed his head, but made no attempt to kick out. Davy, having made a round of the horse in dead silence, reappeared at Sultan's head and put one hand on the horse's withers.

'And what would your honour want for a horse like this?'

'You've a way with horses, Lee,' Luke observed. 'Think you can ride him?'

In answer, Davy vaulted easily into the saddle and disappeared down the street with a clatter of hoofs.

'I'll be hoping he comes back again!' observed Riley heavily.

'Course he will!' stormed Kezia at him. 'He's won a lot of races, has Davy. Travelling people hold their own horse-races.'

'All right, Kezia,' Luke said briskly. 'Before Lee gets back, let me have the truth! Leach is dead, that I can tell you—and your uncle has agreed to let Rose come back to us. Where is she, and what about you?'

Kezia looked relieved. 'I ain't surprised about Sam. Davy's mother said he was gone, and she's got the second sight and knows things. I'm glad you'll take Rosie back with you, for it's what I want for her, though Davy won't think it such a good idea and might make trouble. He don't think too much of folk living in houses. But as for me, I stay with Davy. He's a good man, and has looked after Rose and me just fine, so tell Miss Emma not to worry.'

A further clatter of hoofs heralded the reappearance of the gypsy, who slid from Sultan's back. 'Will your honour sell? I'll pay a fair price.'

'I want a shilling,' Luke said. 'And the girl, Rose.'

Davy's eyes sharpened and flickered towards Kezia. He contemplated the horse for a few moments, then asked, 'Will your honour give me a bill of sale, made out properly?'

'I'll write the bill of sale when you give me the shilling. You get the horse, and the paper, when you hand over Rose,' Luke told him.

It was evening when Luke got back to Hill House and was met in the hall by an agitated Mrs Somerton. She grasped his arm, exclaiming, 'Oh, there you are at last! I did begin quite to despair that you would come tonight! Dear Emma is awake, and asking for you. The fever is broken and she is quite clear, though very weak.'

Throwing an excuse over his shoulder, Luke left her in mid-speech and bounded up the stair-treads two at a time. Emma was propped on a pile of pillows. She looked pale and thin, but the glitter of fever had left her eyes, and when he stooped to kiss her forehead, her skin felt cool and naturally damp.

'I'm glad you have come back,' she said. 'They said you went to sell Sultan.' Her voice was almost inaudible, so that he had to bend his head to catch the words.

'I've been to the horse-fair, and I've brought you a fairing back,' he said. 'Just wait a little, and I'll fetch it.' He went out of the room and returned, propelling Rose in front of him. 'There, see what I found!'

'Rose?' Her voice echoed incredulity, and she struggled on the pillows to push herself upright.

'Oh, Mrs Sheldon!' cried Rose, running to kneel

by the bed and clasp Emma's thin hand. 'I am that glad to be home!'

Emma's gaze rose to meet Luke's, standing behind Rose. 'I think I have come back, too,' she said. 'I was away a long time, wasn't I?

'A long time,' he said soberly. He moved Rose to one side, and sat down on the edge of the bed. 'Welcome home, Emma.' He stretched out his hand and touched her pale cheek. 'Promise me you will not go so far away again,' he whispered.

CHAPTER THIRTEEN

EMMA'S JOY at Rose's safe return was tempered with alarm at the news brought her of Kezia.

'Travelling the roads and living in a caravan with a gypsy? I can hardly think it's any better than being with Leach!'

'It's the girl's free choice, Emma,' Luke reminded her.

Emma sighed. 'Yes, I suppose so. But we don't know what kind of a man he is.'

'I made enquiries about Lee. He seems to enjoy a good reputation and hasn't been known to get into any trouble. To my mind, he is a great improvement on Leach. I rather liked the fellow, though I fancy he didn't care very much for me! But I really believe she is happy with him. At any rate she seems quite proud of him, and I suspect he is rather proud of her, in his own quiet way. Quiet doesn't mean harmless—I've not the slightest doubt he would have killed me if I had done her any injury. There is an odd sort of dignity and independence about the fellow which commands respect. He's elusive, a little like a wild animal, secure on its own ground but uncertain on any other. That makes him wary of anyone who is not of his own people. He let Kezzy do all the talking to me, except when it came to dealing over the horse. Then he showed himself shrewd enough. He insisted on a bill of sale. I dare say he had no wish to be transported for horse-

stealing. But when I'd written it out, he passed it to
Kezia so that she could read it for him. He did so
quite openly. He wasn't ashamed to let me see that
he couldn't read; rather, I think he was proud that
Kezzy could. It seems to me that a relationship
founded on a mutual respect like that is a good
relationship. I'm quite happy to leave Kezia in his
care.'

Luke fell silent, remembering his last view of
Kezia. It had been a dignified, beautiful and moving sight. The gypsy had led away the great red
horse, docile beneath his hand, and Kezia walked
along on Davy's other side, her hair tied up in a
scarlet kerchief. Man, woman and horse all moved
together in a natural unity. Had he been an artist,
he would have tried to put the scene on canvas. As
it was, something like a pain had briefly touched
Luke's heart as he envied Davy and Kezia the
unspoken understanding and harmony of mind
which existed between them, and which Luke knew
was so lacking between himself and Emma.

He said, 'I am sure Lee looks upon her as his
wife. There may even have been some sort of gypsy
ceremony. Nor is he a poor man. Kezzy had gold
earrings, and Riley enquired among the horse-
dealers. Lee always pays up promptly—and in
sovereigns.'

He was beating about the bush. He wanted to say
that he had sensed a genuine affection between
Kezia and Davy, which was almost certainly strong
enough to qualify as love. But he did not know if he
could explain it adequately to Emma . . . or how
she would react to the idea.

He patted her hand. 'So cheer up, it might not be

what you wanted for Kezia—but I'm sure it's what she wants for herself.'

She glanced at him. He looked awkward and rather embarrassed. He got up from the end of her convalescent sofa, where he had been sitting, and began to wander about the room, avoiding her eye. Watching his handsome, prowling figure, Emma thought sadly that what she wanted for herself was Luke—but she had not the slightest notion how to tell him so.

She continued to make a steady recovery, slowly regaining her strength, and soon felt impatient to be back in the thick of things. But whereas there had once been a time when she would have gone back to Forbes Street without a moment's hesitation, as soon as she was fit enough, now she knew that she could not do it without discussing it with Luke first. The whole vexed question of Forbes Street, and her work, had to be straightened out, once and for all. It would not be easy. He had never liked discussing the subject, and he had made not a single reference to the Rescue Home since she had left her sick-bed. But the subject hovered in the air, and one of them had to grasp it and bring it sharply down to earth and into view.

There was another matter, too, that lingered undiscussed, though both must be conscious of it. It was the absence of any attempt on Luke's part to resume their physical relationship. Even when there had been a certain coolness between them, during and after the trial, he had still come to her—although not so often, perhaps. Now he passed by her door. Short of asking him outright why he had not done so, there was little she could do. At first she had assumed that it was her convalescent state of health that kept Luke from her bed. But as time went by, and she was obviously so much better and quite active again, she knew with growing certainty that it was something else. He watched her sometimes, when he thought she was not looking, with such a sober expression in his dark eyes that it almost frightened her. In some ways her illness had brought them closer: in others they remained as far apart as ever.

Summer was already past its height, and the very first signs of autumn were in the air. Blackberries were ripe on the bushes, and local children scoured the fields and hedgerows, picking great basketfuls so that their mothers could make jam, pies and puddings. Emma tied on her bonnet and pinned up her petticoat on one such fine, warm evening, and asked Luke if he would mind if she came with him on his evening stroll.

He looked mildly surprised, but then said, 'By all means.' On their way out of the house, he paused to collect a walking-stick from the collection housed in a stand by the front door. 'All of them my father's,' he said. 'Kept here fifty years, probably. One or two might even be my grandfather's.' He pulled out a stout hickory, and they set out, following a path that crossed the grounds of Hill House and ran through the surrounding fields which belonged to the estate.

Emma linked her arm through his, and they strolled along, Luke swishing the stick at nettles and using it to hook trailing bramble-stems out of the way of her skirts. They probably presented any chance onlooker with the perfect picture of domestic felicity. A false picture, thought Emma. She had intended to take the opportunity to tackle, once and for all, the question of Forbes Street, but still did not know how to broach the vexed subject. Perhaps Luke sensed her indecision, because he was unusually talkative himself, but kept the conversation firmly on his plans for the estate, chiefly on what he intended to do next year. Emma could not help but ask herself, For whom does he do all this? Just to please himself? She watched the hickory stick fell another head of nettles, remembering that it might have accompanied old General Sheldon on his evening stroll, or even his father before that. When the time came that Luke put away the walking-stick for the last time, would there be a younger hand to stretch out and take it up? Certainly not as things were at the moment.

Eventually they sat down on the dry, springy turf at the top of a long slope. Below them, at the foot of it, lay an overgrown spinney, which Luke meant to clear. It was ringed by the ubiquitous trailing, tangled brambles, and two figures could be seen making their way slowly along the line of bushes. They were those of Rose and Tom, industriously picking fruit for Tom's mother, who was a 'dab hand' at jelly. Rather, Tom was doing all the work, clambering about as ably directed by Rose, who sent her devoted admirer into the thickest bramble patches, regardless of how scratched and cut he got.

Rose is already thirteen, thought Emma. Before we know it, she will be sixteen or seventeen, and wanting to marry Tom, I suppose.

Perhaps the sight had inspired Luke to something of the same thought, because he observed, 'I dare say, next year, I shall have to promote Tom to under-groom. We can't go on calling him stable boy for ever.'

'How will Riley take that?' she asked.

'With a lot of grumbling, like everything else.' Luke picked up the hickory stick and prodded at a dandelion in the turf by his foot. 'You will be wanting to go back to Forbes Street, I suppose.'

She had not expected it, but there it was at last. Luke had grasped the thorny question, and it was out in the open. He was not looking at her as he spoke, but concentrating ferociously on digging out the dandelion.

'You don't wish it,' she said quietly, and with a touch of resignation in her voice, because she knew that if he asked the sacrifice of her, she had to make it.

'I've never prevented you. This running round the slums is to stop, however. There's no need for it. There are more than enough candidates for the Home being referred from the magistrates' courts.' He sounded as prickly as the brambles.

Emma watched the distant figure of Tom stumble backwards out of the bramble patch and tip his treasure-trove of berries into Rose's outheld apron. Their young voices, still childish, and yet with the maturer resonances of young adulthood already audible in them, floated up the hillside towards the watchers.

'Aunt Rosamond says she and the matron are coping very well, and I'm not to worry. I'm not worried. I know they can manage. But yes, I do want to go back.' Luke nodded silently. 'Do you mind very much?' she asked with some hesitation, peeping from beneath her bonnet-brim at his averted face.

'No.' He glanced at her, and saw the dubious reaction his denial got. 'No, really,' he repeated more forcefully. 'I've had a lot of time to think things over, Emma. You were right, and I was wrong. The Rescue Home is a necessity. The work there must go on.'

'You have no idea,' Emma said slowly, and with a slight tremor in her voice, 'how much I have wanted you to say that.'

Luke abandoned his attempt to disembowel the dandelion, and threw down the stick. 'Emma, we have not been as frank with one another as we could have been. That has been very largely my fault. I'm an awkward fellow, and obstinate, I know. Also, there's a world of difference between my allowing you to carry on at Forbes Street and my actually supporting you. I can hardly have expected you to confide in me when I never showed any sign of true interest.' He paused and rested his arms on his knees, squinting into the hazy distance. 'That's why, I suppose, you felt you couldn't talk to me about other things . . .' With a slight change of tone, he added, 'Mrs Somerton told me you went to see a specialist.'

'Oh,' Emma said.

'She didn't betray your confidence. I asked her, because when you were sick, you rambled quite a bit.'

'You mean I rambled on about babies?' she asked uncomfortably. He nodded, and she said a little forlornly, 'I did want to give you your son, you know. You told me that was what you wanted.'

'Oh God, Emma!' he burst out suddenly in a tormented voice. 'I *love* you! I don't care about anything else! When you were so ill, I thought for a while that I might lose you. I couldn't think what to do. I wandered about all over the place like a lunatic, and I don't think I knew from morning till dusk what I was doing. I just couldn't imagine going on, if you weren't there with me. None of the things I had thought mattered, mattered a jot. The house could have fallen down, and the land gone to rack and ruin. I didn't care.' He broke off abruptly and bowed his head, staring fixedly at his interlaced fingers. 'I thought of all the things I hadn't said to you,' he went on quietly, 'and that I could have said. People sometimes say we live to regret things we've said. But living to regret the things we've never had the courage to say is far, far worse.'

Emma leaned forward and put her arms round his neck. 'Don't, Luke,' she whispered softly.

He leaned his head against her breast, and muttered, 'I'm pretty good at shouting at people, but when it comes to explaining what I feel, I can't string two sentences together.'

'You don't need to, I know what you mean.' Emma paused before making her own confession. 'I felt that way, too. Before I was ill, and after I went to the specialist. Do you remember, down by the river-bank? I never knew, till that afternoon, how much I loved you, how much you meant to me. And I thought I'd let you go, lost you. The matron once said, when I went to the Home during the trial and found all the girls so worried, that we don't

appreciate things till we think we might lose them. I
love you so much, Luke, that it hurts. I wanted to
tell you, but there—there always seemed to be
some obstacle.'

'I'm an insensitive brute,' he growled miserably.

'You most certainly are not!' Emma denied
fiercely, tightening her arms round his neck. 'You
are the kindest, most honourable and best man I
ever knew, or could know.' She conquered an
impulse to sniffle, but could not hide the catch in
her throat. 'You just don't want people to guess it!
You go round, huffing and puffing like the big, bad
wolf, and it doesn't deceive a soul. Not anyone who
really knows you, anyway. Ask Ned Bryant, or
Riley.'

'I'm asking you . . .' he said, looking up at her.

'What?' The delicate eyebrows puckered, and
the blue eyes took on that faint air of puzzlement
which always made him want to laugh.

A smile touched his face. 'The old, old question,
the one a man usually asks a woman—if she takes
his fancy at all, that is.'

Her heart gave a little lurch. 'Oh? I take your
fancy, Major Sheldon, do I?' Emma asked, a little
shakily.

'You do, ma'am. Well, you always did. Though
when I first met you—other than incognito at
Bessie's, I mean—you reminded me a little of a
mongoose, small, determined and always ready
for a scrap. Endearing little beasts, though. I
had a pet one for a while in India. It attacked
everything.'

'Lord bless us, Major Sheldon—you've a singu-
lar style of gallantry!' she exclaimed. But she had to

laugh, and crooked her arm under his head, twisting her fingers caressingly in his black curls.

'Gallantry is an empty thing. If I'd ever been gallant to you, you would quite rightly have boxed my ears. No, I most definitely took a fancy to you. I never went about proposing marriage to women all over the place, you know. Only to you.'

'It was a very sensible proposal of marriage,' she reminded him.

'It was the only sort that would have stood an earthly chance of being accepted.'

'Yes, I suppose it was.' Emma paused. 'I had my head so full of what I wanted to do. I'm ashamed now, because really I think I was more interested in Forbes Street, and getting the house, than anything to do with marriage. I never meant to hurt your feelings, but I suppose I must have done, being so obsessed with the work and having so little time for you. I was thoroughly selfish—and thoroughly punished for being so. I would like, if it's possible, to start all over again. Do you suppose we can?' She hesitated, waiting for his reply.

'I think we already have,' he said quietly.

She smiled at him, a little shyly. 'Luke? Propose to me again, now? Only not like last time.'

'Not like last time? How's this: Would you like to come to bed with me, Emma? And don't squawk and say, Not here, because Tom and Rosie are chaperoning us down there. I mean, back at the house. I dare say that isn't quite what you had in mind, but it's what it's damn well all about.' His dark eyes met her blue eyes. 'Well, Emma?'

'I've been better a long time,' Emma said gently.

'You could have come, before now. Did you think I didn't want you?'

'I—wasn't sure. I always wanted you. But it was a selfish sort of wanting. It was when I stopped only wanting, and started loving, then coming to your bed and—and just taking you was no longer enough. What I really wanted was for you to love me, Emma. That sounds even more selfish and demanding than before; perhaps it is. It's devilish difficult to talk about it, without sounding maudlin. But, you see, I never had anyone to love, or to love me. Love never seemed to have any part in my life. I felt there was a sort of gap there, but I didn't know what to do about it. I wasn't even sure how one went about loving someone—and I certainly didn't know how to make anyone love me. I suppose I was just jealous of Forbes Street, and sulked about it like a spoiled child.' He pulled a wry face at her. 'You would think, wouldn't you, that at my age I would have made a better fist of it. I don't know if it was ignorance or stupidity, or a combination of both.'

Emma looked at the hickory walking-stick lying a little way from them on the turf, and thought: If I had old General Sheldon here, I truly believe I'd hit him with that. How could he let a child grow up like that? So deprived of loving that he reached manhood not even understanding what it was, or how to set about either winning love or giving it.

Almost apologetically, Luke said to her, 'I couldn't have explained this to you before. I would have felt such a blasted idiot. But now—now it's different . . . or I think it is.'

'Yes, now it's different . . .' Emma said. 'And

it's going to stay different, because now I love you, and you love me, and what we don't know, we'll learn together.'

The setting sun stretched rosy fingers into the quiet bedroom and touched every object with fire, so that dull burgundy glowed ruby-red, pale shades of yellow revealed depths of orange, and brass became gold. The sun's rays played with Emma's fair hair and set copper hues nestling in the depths. Luke, running his fingers through the silken strands, said soberly, 'You are very beautiful.'

He leaned towards her to kiss her, pushing her gently back on to the feather pillows, which sank beneath their combined weight. Emma ran her hands over his powerful shoulders. The setting sun was playing another of its tricks, making his swarthy complexion almost the equal of Davy Lee's. The skin was smooth and slightly moist, so that it adhered to her exploring fingertips. She was almost frighteningly aware of the physical attraction he held for her, of the essential maleness of that muscular body and the latent power in the hands which touched her so gently. Beneath their persuasive and demanding caress, she felt her own body come to life. It tingled as if the blood flowed more quickly and freely, and every sensation seemed redoubled, as if he had reawoken within her all those old, primitive instincts that centuries of civilisation had striven to blur and hide, and yet which lurk untamed deep within us, waiting for the moment which belongs to them. There was a truly animal tension in his nearness, in the air about them. Yet she was not afraid, only happy. As he moved closer, she sensed the thrill run through her which was not fear, but anticipation, the old knowledge, old as time. Her body moved in harmony with his, the easier to receive him, so that when that longed-for moment of union came, the little sob which broke from her parted lips was one of fulfilment and joy, the bonding of more than flesh, a fusion of mind, and heart and spirit.

The sun went down and the room grew dark, as Emma lay in Luke's arms, and the old house in its ivy garments seemed to rest content at last, as the love which had been so long absent re-entered its ancient walls and took up residence there once more.

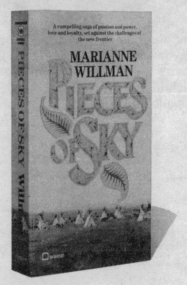